GODS' Fool

Derek E Pearson

First published 2017
Published by GB Publishing.org

Copyright © 2017 Derek E Pearson
All rights reserved
ISBN: 978-1-912031-72-6 (paperback)
978-1-912031-71-9 (eBook)
978-1-912031-70-2 (Kindle)

No part of this publication may be reproduced, stored in a retrieval system or transmitted in any form or by any means without the prior written permission of the publisher. Enquiries concerning reproduction outside of the scope of the above should be sent to the copyright holder.
You must not circulate this book in any other binding or cover and you must impose the same conditions on any acquirer.
Names, characters, businesses, places, events and incidents whether in a future context or otherwise are entirely the products of the author's imagination and/or used in a fictitious manner with no intent to cause any defamation or disrespect or any other harm to any actual persons or party whether living, dead or yet to come into being.
A catalogue record of the printed book is available from the British Library

Cover Design © 2017 Tillier Designs
Cover Illustration by Derek E Pearson

GB Publishing.org
www.gbpublishing.co.uk

To Sue, who suffers the birth pangs with me, and for Sarah Bradbury and Andrea Johnson, special friends who enjoy the fruits of my labour.

Acknowledgement
To the good people of GB Publishing.org, especially George, Bee and Wills, who work constantly to make these offerings look great and read well.

CONTENT

Beginning: Texas	1
Chapters	3
End: Scytaer Faehl	209
Author's note	213
Other GBP Science-Fiction	215

Beginning: Texas

The next call had come soon enough. Too soon. And, as always, he had answered. He had no choice. In some ancient standing places, time has worn thin, thin enough for messages to leak through from other centuries and distant realms. People skilled in certain atavistic crafts can hear them and respond. The preacher called Spindrift swung down from his saddle and regarded the empty space before him with narrowed eyes. The Texan air shimmered in the singing heat. He knew that indigenous Americans had once danced around this spot and communicated with their ancestors. The ancestors had listened; some of them had replied. The echoes of those long-lost messages whispered at the very limit of his hearing. The dead were safe enough. It was the living he feared for.

An enemy so ancient it pre-dated even the dinosaurs by thousands of millennia had finally been defeated in the friendship state. Dozens of men and women had died before it could be vanquished, but its curse had been cleaned away by fire. Texas was safe for a while but the rest of the world was still under threat.

And the call had come once more.

His horse nickered quietly. He answered. 'I know old friend. I know. Which of us is the bigger fool? We must protect the Eden born whenever they're threatened, but all the while they keep themselves busy trying to kill each other. What's going on over there in Europe is a criminal waste of young lives. Criminal waste. Stupid.'

He regarded his powerful bay horse obliquely and grimaced. 'You'll have to think about your shape. You're too big a target like that.'

The horse neighed again.

'Yes, yes, you are beautiful. But a blast of shrapnel would rip you to shreds and then where would you be?'

The horse gazed at him.

'It's your choice old friend. Your choice. Come on, its time, let's go.'

The man in the long black coat and a preacher's collar stepped forward with his mount. The landscape seemed to twist and fold around them – and they were gone. A small, sand coloured lizard scampered over the ground where they had just been standing, and a spinning breath of wind spiralled dust around the closed portal. Nothing else moved.

In France, a half mile back from Flanders' front-line trenches, a tall lean man in the uniform of a captain in the American 11th regiment looked around him. On his collar the man called Spindrift was wearing the insignia of a padre. He looked down at the large, glossily black dog now at his side.

'Still beautiful,' he said. The dog growled low in its throat.

The date was mid-September 1917.

~1~

It had been raining all summer and the algae coated mud looked bright green and acted like glue. I didn't like the mud much. It sucked at my boots. When it was dry, the raw soil floated around like a choking veil of fine dust that tasted foul and dried my throat, but when it was wet it tugged at my boots like hungry hands trying to pull me down amongst the dead men. And there were lots of dead men. I could smell them.

I checked my watch. Nearly time. My guts churned. What were we doing there? We were engineers, not soldiers. We had been brought to France to assist with the little narrow gauge railways the British used to ferry men and supplies backwards and forwards to the front. Most of our officers had been sent away for extra training and that left just five of us in charge of three regiments. To bring some order to our ranks we had been loaned some British guys. They were experienced officers who barked orders at us during practice and shared their smokes when we stood down. They called us 'good blokes', 'fine chaps' and 'righteous fighting men'. The sergeants were less than polite to our guys while they drilled, but they were full of good cheer when their stripes came off. They were trying to make us feel better. It wasn't working. We had arrived at Flanders Fields riding a wave of song, and believed we would help the British and the French sweep the Boche back to the Rhine in a matter of weeks. The Yanks are coming, we shouted from the rails of our transport ships. The Yanks are coming and we won't come back 'til it's over, over there. We'll be home for Christmas, just you wait and see. Funny.

I guess I got on better with Clyde Bellwether than any of the other Brit officers. He talked with me rather than at me. Explained things. Asked my opinion. He was a captain like me, but unlike me he'd earned his pips in the field, starting with that mess over in Gallipoli. He didn't talk about it but the other Brits knew what he'd done. They treated him like a hero.

The previous night we had shared a few fingers of good ol' Kentucky bourbon in the dugout. My treat. He had sipped at his glass gingerly.

'Colin,' he said. 'Be careful with this stuff. When you're in the shit everyone smells the same, and looks the same. Not all the Boche wear a spike on their hats. Best keeps your wits about you, son. Thanks for this, but I'd rather have a good pint of brew behind the lines when we get back than be an addle-pate the night before an action. Not even with this fine Kentucky spirit. Tomorrow the Boche will be prepared to die defending his pitch, and our job is to do our damndest to make sure he gets his wish. I got this far with a clear head and a sharp eye. I ain't shot one of my own boys yet, and I don't plan to start tomorrow with a bear's head and a sore eye. Might affect my aim.'

'It's called sippin' whisky for a reason, Clyde. We won't overdo it. I sure would welcome a cold beer myself but this is all we got. Bottom's up.'

'Cold beer? Who drinks *cold* beer? You Yanks got some strange ideas.'

We drank barely enough to wet a baby's whistle then corked the bottle. It didn't help. I had hardly slept a wink and it was already morning. My crowd was the 11th Regiment of engineers. Including the 12th and 14th there were about five hundred of us. It was seven in the morning and we were about to go over the top. There was no artillery bombardment and the clouds overhead were nearly as dark as my mood. I tried to take a deep breath but my chest felt leaden.

'Good luck, Colin.'

'Good luck, Clyde. Eyes sharp? Head clear?'

'Clear as virgin's water, mate. Sharp as a pencil.'

Then he blew his whistle and I blew mine. The sound was echoed over and over down the line. It was December fourth, nineteen seventeen and we didn't know it but we were about to make history. I was told later that we were the first troops with the American Expeditionary Force to go face to face with the Boche since we'd declared war on them back in April. And apart from basic training we didn't know squat about trench warfare. We were best at fixing railroad tracks and keeping little trains chugging away. I drew my pistol and climbed the ladder, expecting to be shot straight back down by one of the damn snipers.

Two weeks before on November twentieth, British forces had cracked through the Hindenburg Line at Cambrai and taken miles of territory plus thousands of prisoners. Scuttlebutt back then said we really would be home by Christmas – and the reason? Tanks. Twenty-eight tonners, Mark IV Landships. Hundreds of the heavy, motorised forts crunched forward at nearly four miles an hour, rolling over the German lines like they were no more than wet tissue paper. They took over eight thousand prisoners on the first *day*! It must have been a terrifying sight from the German lines when those monsters came growling out of the morning mist like visions from Hell and started blasting away with heavy machine guns and eight-inch cannon.

Three belts of the notoriously vicious German wire had been crossed like so many beds of nettles and when the tanks reached the German trenches they just slewed to the left and opened-up directly onto the cowering troops. The Boche could do nothing but surrender or die. They came out of their dugouts and found themselves the wrong end of a gun barrel. And all around them they saw tanks, and yet more tanks.

The big guys didn't have it all their own way. I heard tell about one Boche sonofabitch who kept his gun crew by his cannon and aimed at the Mark IVs along the barrel. He boiled a few crews alive in their steel boxes before they finally got him. That man must have had cojones the size of my head, I swear, but they got the heroic son-of-the-Fatherland in the end. The tank that got him was called Matilda and like the rest of them had the ace of spades and its name painted on its side.

Then it all went wrong. The tanks could travel fifteen miles before they had to refuel and that seemed plenty to be getting on with. There and back again easy. Then one of them broke the back of the main bridge over the St. Quentin Canal. It was the very bridge the cavalry planned to use to establish a new front, and everything behind got bogged down. I honestly believe the soldiers' scuttlebutt was right, that those tanks had been too successful. They moved too fast and the rest of the army couldn't keep up. The Germans had the time they needed to bring their big guns to bear and God alone knows how many troops were pulled in for support. The Brits began losing men, and what had started out as a walk in the park turned into a bloodbath. And that's where we came in.

We were being sent out as part of a support group to help bring the boys home while the Boche regained every inch of land they'd lost. It was our turn to be slaughtered and taken prisoner.

We moved forward. The land was pock-marked with shell craters and we kept our heads down while we ran from one crater to another. They stank with that brew of gas and decay that seemed peculiar to the Western Front. Some of the craters were occupied. Vague shapes of men were in there, dead men with their outlines softened under layers of green algae, floating in filthy, stagnant water. Lying there they looked deader to me than a man in a coffin, but something in my bowels loosened when one of our men accidently slid into crater's water and the ripples of his waves made the resident corpse move its arms about, as if it was reaching out for mercy. I thought the poor goddamned bastard was going to sit up. That place could play merry games with a man's imagination. Merry games before Merry Christmas.

We saw a tank tilted over on its side in a trench. It had 'Welcome to Hell, Heinie' painted on its side in white under the ace of spades. The air was cool but we could already smell the crew. I didn't want to look inside but Clyde squinted through a hatch and jerked back a little. He slammed his hand against its hull. It made a sound like a flat gong. A small cloud of complaining flies rose out of the hatch then settled back down to feed and lay their eggs.

Clyde walked back to my side, his face grim. 'Hand grenade in an enclosed space. At least it would have been quick.'

'How? I mean, how would they throw the grenade? How would they get past the guns?'

'The crew got unlucky I suppose, poor bastards. Must've slid down into the crater and Heinie took his chance and got straight in there. Must've been one of the first crews out to catch it here, this far back.' He looked up, lifted his arm, and indicated the enemy side of No Man's land. 'Here they come.' He raised his voice a little. 'Okay boys, don't get trigger happy. Those men are ours. Let them come and we'll see them home to a nice warm bed and a good hot meal.'

His weak joke received a grumbled response. I distinctly heard one of the Brits mutter, 'Chance 'ud be fine thing.'

We Americans were too scared to be joshing on the battlefield. Maybe that would come later.

Someone else said, 'We'd cook 'em some bacon and eggs on the hot plate. If we had some bacon and eggs.'

Another voice, 'If we 'ad a flippin' hot plate.'

'I'd kill for a plateful of bacon and eggs and a nice fried slice.'

'Add a kidney or two and a few bangers for me. Just like home.'

'Kidney and flippin' bangers? Blimey, where's 'ome? Buckin'ham flippin' Palace?'

'Of course, I'm just over on a troop inspection and got caught in the rush. Toodle-pip old lads, best waddle back home to mama.'

'All right, lads, knock it on the head. Work to do.'

I thought I'd heard someone's belly rumble loudly with hunger, but I was wrong. The Brits described German artillery shells as 'whizz bangs'. I guess that was a good description of what happened next. The ground shook around us and the air was filled with a deep fluttering noise. Giant geysers of mud and water were flung towards the sky. I never even heard the one that got me. I just felt myself grabbed by a big fist and lifted helplessly into the air. Then the wind was punched out of me and for a moment I felt as if I was a baseball struck clean out of the park by a giant bat. But this was no home-run as I was flung towards darkness and fell in, head first.

~2~

Light sucked my eyelids open and after a few moments I realised I was still alive. I had to be, I was sure death couldn't hurt that much. I was in a bed under canvas when I'd expected to be in a field under a mountain of clay. Even so it felt hard to breathe and the canvas seemed to be pressing down on me. I panicked a little. I couldn't see the sky and for some reason I couldn't turn my head to find it. Do you look at the sky much? I did, whenever I could. Especially out there in the trenches. When the landscape or the people around me became too dreadful to contemplate for another minute the sky offered me somewhere big and clean where I could rest my eyes awhile. I remember seeing the single black shape of a bird in the winter sky out there in No Man's land and I'd wondered if there was anything else that had ever looked so lonely. So, desolate. I wished I could see that bird from my bed.

The sky was my companion. It offered the promise of redemption in its silver rimmed clouds, even on the darkest day. I thought of the sky as being like a man's immortal soul. It was a lesson written in the clouds, which, like a man's soul, are never truly white – except for our Lord Jesus Christ of course – and never truly black. Instead I believed our souls are coloured by an infinite palette of greys and silvers. Some a little lighter and some a little darker, but all grey nonetheless. Experience of evil would change that theory. Some souls are black as pitch. Blacker.

I remember the sky that day the artillery shells fell and hammered me down onto that hospital cot under canvas. It was like a pall of ash and grey silk across the barely risen sun, pricked with the tiny shadow of that single bird. But it was still beautiful to me then. When I see a sky like that, even now, I get a sense of deep foreboding that has nothing to do with whizz bangs or the Battle of Cambrai. No, not really. It has more to do with what followed, events that started from the day I awoke in that hospital cot under a canvas ceiling.

The war was bad enough though. A lot of fine men had been ripped to rags and tatters by it, more than you could count. The war. I'd heard it described as a great cloud of hate squatting across the pounded landscape of Flanders. A continent of woe.

Guys have told me they remember the battlefield's landscape as being 'shattered' or 'blasted', but I believe they weren't seeing what was there.

They were remembering how it was when the whizz bangs fell. I recall young men on furlough, relaxing behind the lines and foolishly deep in their cups. And they would compete to try to best describe what a barrage was like by pounding on their tables after howling like Irish banshees at a dead man's window. Every time they struck the table they bellowed BOOM! Some of the quieter guys would jump and complain about the noise. Others might weep and hide away in the corners of the room, or maybe sit there silently twitching. After a while those broken men merged in with the rest of us, became part of the company, and no-one noticed them anymore.

Lying there under the canvas with my wits still scattered by my experiences in No Man's Land, I found myself thinking about conversations I'd had with veterans who'd been out there for a long time, perhaps longer than was wise. Ask them what shelling sounded like and they'd say, 'bad'. Ask them what it felt like and they'd answer, 'worse'.

There was one sergeant I'd had a beer with during furlough, man called Morgan, and I believe he came closest to describing the truth of what it felt like to be under enemy fire. He said he'd been a stoker on the Cheltenham and Great Western Union Railway before volunteering. He listened to the rest of the boys describe whizz bangs, then cleared his throat to get their attention and cleaned his pipes with a mouthful of beer before leaning forwards. His audience sat expectantly waiting, the stoker was a renowned storyteller. Silence fell on our little circle.

His voice was surprisingly gentle and his English archaic. He said, "That whizz sounds to me very like a steam train when it slams on its brakes while sounding its whistle just as it enters a long tunnel. What a racket. Like the shriek of a damned soul begging for mercy on its way to Hell it is, echoing down that line as far as you like. The driver would do that a'purpose sometimes, just to wake up they rough travellers in the goods wagons. Give 'em a little bit of a jump like. There was always one or two getting a free ride, and they dirty buggers don't know no difference between a C&GWUR goods wagon and a khazi. Shit everywhere they did. Stink was worse than the jakes here. Nearly. As for the bang, imagine if that tunnel ended in a solid rock wall and the train roared into it full tilt, like enough to a bull at a gate. That would bounce the world back on its heels right hard enough I'd say. Yes, it would, right hard enough. Bang!'

A few weeks after that he found out how hard. He got blown up into a splintered tree by a near miss and was run clean through by a dozen branches, all sharp as bayonets. They had to saw him free. I saw what they brought down from that tree; even the poorest butcher would have rejected it for cheap sausage. His punctured corpse was no gentle St. Sebastian, let me tell you. No, he was more a mess of minced meat, shattered bone, and wooden spikes. Funny thing, he had lost so much of his body and his head was torn up – part of his scalp was gone, one of his eyes and most of an ear – but he still wore that gentle half-smile with which he had always greeted the world. I wondered what his last thought had been?

He was a loss I can tell you. He always had time to chat with the guys and he had his own way of talking with them that helped them find what little peace there was in that terrible place. Yes, he was a loss. What made me think of him again? Yes, that's what it was, the landscape. It wasn't shattered and torn the way they described it, it was more like his poor body when they peeled him down from that tree. The land was all soft and formless, a blanket of mud beaten into shapeless, pockmarked waves. Filthy, dirty, and stinking. It was no fit place for men to die. No fit place for men to live. I was feeling very down. My soul was in a bad place. And then, a voice close by my side interrupted my sombre thoughts.

'Good, you're awake. How are you feeling, Captain Cahoon? Please, no need to sit up.'

I knew the man standing over me. Tall, lean, and dark he was the chief surgeon and a top type called Spindrift. One of those old pilgrim father family names I guessed. Sound fellow and not afraid to get his hands dirty. Had a beautiful dog too, incredible hound. Black as deeds and bright as a child's prayer. Big beast, some sort of crossbreed by the look of it, part wolfhound, part German shepherd dog and part genii. I honestly believe that dog would have been worshipped in a more primitive society. Its eyes were black on black and vigilant. It was uncanny. When it entered a room, every man would swear it was watching them, every man, no matter where they were standing.

Like the dog its master was intimidating without being threatening. They had a close relationship. The dog never made a sound unless Spindrift spoke to it and then it would answer with a whine, a growl, or a huffing noise. Never heard it bark, but I swear I understood that dog better than some of the good ol' boys who thought the chow in the army was the best they'd ever eaten. They were good men who could lay a straight track, and they were brave as lions, but would you ask a lion to deliver a message without writing it down first? Their speech sounded like geese gargling gravy to me, but they seemed to understand each other well enough.

'Colin, did you hear me?'

'Sorry, Doc. I was wool-gathering fit to strip a whole flock of sheep. What did you say?'

'I asked how you were feeling. You took quite a tumble out there. You've been unconscious for three days and you cracked a few ribs, plus you suffered some serious bruising. How are you feeling?'

'Okay I guess,' I lied. 'But I can't move so much as a finger. Tell me Doc, is my neck broke?'

'Oh, right, yes. Wait a second.'

He leaned down and put his hand out of my eyeline beside my neck. I felt a sharp tug and then my whole body seemed to relax. I could move again. I tried to sit up and grunted with pain when intense agony shot through my back. I couldn't breathe. Spindrift shook his head.

'Best not try to move too much just yet, Colin.' He poured something from a neat silver flask into its cap. 'Here, drink this. Let me help you.'

He tilted my head slightly forward and poured cool liquid into my mouth. I swallowed. Its effect was almost instantaneous. The pain ebbed away and a soporific sense of wellbeing flooded through me. The pain was still there, but instead of being a tormenter it had become a friendly warning. It was no longer incapacitating. I could breathe freely again.

'Thanks, Doc,' I whispered. 'That hit the spot right on the nose. Where am I?'

'Hospital. You're one of the luckier ones. Our regiments lost about seventy men in the barrage, which is bad enough, but the British believe they lost more than forty-four thousand during the battle. The Germans caught us out in the open with our pants down and gave us a sound whipping. You'll be fine in a few days, Colin. Rest and recuperation, the tincture of time, is your best medicine and that's what I prescribe for the next three days. I'll pop in to see you whenever I can. You try to get some sleep.'

'Okay, Doc. Be seeing you.'

He moved to another of the beds in the long tent. I looked around. His dog was sitting by the tent flap. It was watching me.

~3~

Thanks to the Preacher I was up and about sooner than I expected. Did I call him Preacher? Well, that's what he was and that's what the men called him, although never to his face. Under his white doctor linen, Spindrift wore a dog collar and a pair of crucifixes next to his captain's pips. We had other clergy attached to the regiments and they were called 'Padre' or 'Father', but to us Americans he was the Preacher, and that was it. And he made time for everyone. Even the good old boys would talk up a storm with him in their gargling goose fashion and he would answer as if he understood every word.

I had always been a devout *Holy Bible* man myself. But, I was not a Sankey and Moody advocate. I was the lay Eucharistic Minister for the Episcopal Church of the Good Shepherd back home in Dallas, Texas, but I couldn't match his knowledge of the texts. Not even close. He had insight. I swear on the good book that Preacher talked the holy testaments as if he'd been there. He didn't read the gospels by rote he bore witness with a passion that inspired his listeners. Hallelujah.

Don't get me wrong, he was a great physic too. His manner with the wounded and the sick was nothing short of miraculous, as was his attitude towards general staff. He treated everyone as an equal and everyone treated him the same way. He didn't demand respect like some officers did, he *earned* it. He knew when to 'sir' and when to 'sergeant', but saints and scoundrels, colonels, and corporals all thought of him as a very fine fellow. It didn't matter which 'us' he was dealing with, he was always one of them. Preacher Spindrift they'd say, fine doctor, one of us. One of the lads. A true gent.

And then came the day of the phosphorous soldier.

I was sitting up on a wooden chair and out where I could see the sky. Spindrift and his dog were with me, enjoying the unusually mild weather. He had discarded his white coat and was wearing his uniform and dog collar. He was a man with a mission, and I was very taken with his fine military bearing. He was every inch the soldier.

'Doc,' I said. 'You may be a man of the cloth, but it strikes me you appreciate the colour of that cloth to be khaki. Same for you as it is for me.'

'Colin,' he answered, 'I've been a soldier of the Lord for more years than I care to remember, and God's colours are always worn close to my heart.

But if khaki is the colour of mud then yes, I'm afraid I wear it every day in this sodden place. If not with pride, then at least with resignation and resolve. Perhaps one day the world will no longer have need for such colours.'

The way he pronounced the word 'God' had a distinct familiarity about it; almost as if he was on personal speaking terms with the Almighty. I don't mean that brand of loud, tub thumping, *Bible* bashing, evangelism that claims to be on speaking terms with the Lord, shakes pulpits, wrestles serpents, drinks poison and puts the mortal fear of hellfire into men's hearts, no, not that. Nor the sly, snake oil faith of the backwoods charm sellers. His faith was something unique to him. Something quieter.

In all my years of church going, whether listening from the pew, preaching from the pulpit, talking in the chapel, or discussing the gospels with scholars, I had never heard such profound yearning for the Lord's grace in a man's voice. He sounded as if he was talking about a valued old friend who was sorely missed, or a beloved member of his family too far away to visit but never forgotten. I could hear how much he wanted to return to the dear bosom of his friend. I found it charming but sad. His was a soul yearning for heaven, a heart craving to bathe in that most blessed light and like a hart panting for the waters of the blessed Jordan.

Wait, hold hard, I'm painting a false picture. My description makes him sound like a prayer-kneed martyr, a man seeking death with every living breath, and such was not the case. Not by a long, long chalk.

Spindrift was a dark, slim, well-built man with broad shoulders and a lean muscular face. His eyes were piercing and sometimes looked stormy, but only when he was faced with stupidity or ignorance – and no, stupidity and ignorance are not the same thing – although one will often lead to the other.

He had a crescent moon smile that added a wicked tilt to his potent personality, and a hearty laugh that could light up a room. Does it sound as if I was infatuated with the man in the 'modern' way? If so I have once again given the wrong impression. I loved him yes, but in the same way I love the beauty of math or an elegant idea or a cast iron truth. I admired and respected him as the best man I've ever known, and, from the moment he gripped my hand in congratulations when I finally rose whole from my sick bed, I thought of him as a most excellent friend.

And the day would come when he would save my life, not as a doctor but as a soldier. There's a saying, old as the hills, 'I would follow him, even unto the gates of Hell itself'. Well, I believe I did, and had it not been for Spindrift

I also believe I would have lost both my life and my soul there. Truly, lost my immortal soul for eternity.

Our journey along the road to Hell began that afternoon when an orderly rushed up to us and broke into our conversation. He seemed to be in a state of considerable agitation.

'Captain Spindrift, sir. The corpsmen have brought in an English mining engineer. He fell into one of our trenches and looks terribly burned.' The orderly's eyes looked around wildly. 'We think it might be some new gas or chemical weapon, wicked stuff. But, sir, you must look at him. Now, sir. He looks like he's been infected with something. We've never seen anything like it. What are the Heinies up to now? Come and see, sir, please.'

Spindrift's lips stretched taut into a thin line across his clenched teeth.

'Would you be so good as to scrub up and assist please, Colin,' he said. Then he added, enigmatically, 'Now it starts.'

I had been in my third year of medical school when I volunteered. The army, thanks to its very individual brand of logic, had put me in the corps of engineers. When Spindrift learned of my training he contacted my colonel with a request that I be seconded to his team, reasoning that I would be of much more use with a suture needle than I would with a cross tie. My colonel replied through his adjutant, who agreed, saying I would 'doubtless be of more value healing the injured than becoming one of them himself, don't y'know'.

His adjutant was from Boston and considered himself infinitely more British than anyone who had ever sailed from old 'Blighty'. I didn't know where the colonel hailed from and never got the chance to find out. The few times I met colonel Peacefarthing he might very well have come from Alice's Wonderland. Or maybe the planet Mars. He sure wasn't from Dallas, Texas.

The hospital unit was back away from the shelling but near enough to the front for injured men to be rushed there and receive treatment as quickly as was humanly possible. It was made up of a patchwork collection of structures consisting of an old stone farmhouse, its outbuildings, and rows of tents, one of the longest had been my home while I recovered. Smoke from charcoal burners smeared the air with soot. On the burners sat kettles constantly filled with boiling water. The orderlies had told me that since the Preacher had joined them the recovery rate for the sick and injured had more than doubled, yet even so, he had remained a martinet about cleanliness and personal hygiene. Woe betides any man who was caught coming into the wards from the jakes without first scrubbing their hands. And he always knew. Repeat offenders found themselves transferred, usually to the front or one of my old engineer regiments.

Spindrift always worked with his own kit, which he personally prepped in a spotless white enamel bowl filled with freshly-boiled water, to which he added a sharp smelling fluid that turned the water white. None of his scalpels, probes, forceps, bone saws and suture needles were military issue. They were beautifully made, practically works of art, and he wielded them like a magician. His skill as a surgeon had become legendary, and he was certainly the finest cutter I've ever seen. It was almost as if he could see directly into his patient's body before he started, find the injury, bullet, or piece of shrapnel, and then follow the most direct route to its treatment, repair, or extraction. Others just opened the patient and rummaged around, Spindrift went straight to the problem and resolved it. On other occasions, he would know when not to waste his time, and would make sure his patient's last hours were as comfortable as possible.

The British burns victim had been placed in a smaller tent hard by one of the farmhouse's inner courtyard walls, away from the house itself and the other tents. It was as close to an isolation ward as we could get. The dough boy standing guard at the tent flap recognised us as we approached. As we were not in full uniform he didn't salute but instead raised a hand in greeting. He had a sour expression on his face and as we got closer I quickly worked out why.

I had smelled a lot of vile things during my time at the front line. Sometimes the cause was the cooks' stew pots, sometimes it was the stench of decay coming in off No Man's Land. Sometimes it was the result of bringing too many people together in one place when there wasn't enough jakes. You can only dig so many latrines, and what can you do when there are many more backsides than shovels? But the stink coming from that little tent was a real nose twister, and I couldn't say why but it filled me with foreboding.

'Scarecrows and scare-me-jacks,' said Spindrift enigmatically. He led the way into the tent's gloomy interior.

~4~

The man on the cot was still moving, which at first I took to be a good sign. Where there's life there's hope, they say. Then I looked a lot harder and the patient returned my gaze. I almost stopped breathing in shock.

His face was dissolving. It seemed to be collapsing in on itself. I was reminded of a lump of sugar in a spoonful of hot coffee. And his eyes. Even though he seemed to be looking straight at me he must have been blinded by the hellish brew that was melting his flesh and bone. His eyes were enlarged. They were black and shiny and looked as if they had been poached in filthy liquor. His breath came in an oily rasp. He was sucking air through an open maw where his nose and mouth used to be. I wondered how I could look at a face like that without feeling so much as an ounce of pity, but I felt nothing but revulsion and fear. He seemed to radiate malevolence and his eyes were like an insect's, they glittered with terrible hunger. Even with that sucking crater where his mouth used to be he gave the impression of a man licking his lips.

His body was covered with a thin blanket, and that seemed to be writhing as if some creature was scrabbling around under it and trying to push it away. I leaned forward with morbid curiosity and reached out a hand. The Preacher pulled me back. He shouted 'Colin, get out of here. Get out now! And tell the guard to move right away from the tent. Move, man, move!'

I saw him take a glass globe filled with fluorescent liquid from inside his jacket. He glared at me and jerked his head towards the tent's exit. The patient's head began twisting furiously from side to side and the movements under his blanket built to a frenzy. The blanket began to slide to one side. The Preacher roared, 'Get out, man, for God's sake,' just as a boiling mass of twisting guts slapped from the cot to the floor. I swear they were wriggling like eels in a bucket. They spilled across the ground towards us. I got the impression that huge amber blisters covered them, blisters in which wormlike shapes coiled and twisted. Blisters that looked set to burst.

Preacher threw his globe at the cot underarm then turned and pushed me bodily towards the tent's flap. I was frozen in horror and nearly tumbled to the ground by his shove, but I stumbled out into the fresh air. He followed and then at the last moment he turned, drew his service revolver, and fired back into the tent, just once.

I got a peripheral image of a hulking mass rearing up in the centre of the tent before a searing white light blinded me and my vision was dazzled into a confusion of dots and sparks. It was a few seconds before my sight returned but I had to shade my eyes to protect them from the crackling torch the tent and its contents had become. And then, over the hissing, spitting sound of the flames and roasting flesh, I heard a dreadful, shrieking voice bellow just one word. 'SATAAAAAN!'

And then the tent collapsed and the white glare sputtered out and was gone. A drift of grey powdery ash was all that remained. Preacher holstered his pistol and turned towards me as if to speak, and then looked around us. We had become the centre of quite a crowd. Soldiers and orderlies had come running from all over the unit. Some had bought buckets of water that now hung uselessly from their fists. A quiet breeze eddied the grey ash and they stepped back.

The dough boy turned to Spindrift. 'What the fu... sorry, sir. What the goddamn heck was that, sir?'

Spindrift wiped fine ash from his cheeks. 'That, private Hellman, unless I'm very much mistaken, was a new type of German boobytrap. And you listen to me soldier, we haven't seen the last of the wicked things. Not by a long Texas mile.'

...

Colonel Peacefarthing had established his headquarters about a mile further back from the front line than the hospital, which put him a good three miles away from the worst of the war. The gates of Hell, also known as the front line, opened onto a strip of land just a few hundred yards wide but several miles long. The artillery was sited anything up to half a mile behind the trenches where it was considered safer. Men were expected to march and die under the barrage, but the means to deliver it had to be protected at all costs. I sometimes wondered why we had troops in there at all. Why not leave the guns to shoot it out and award the pennant to the last one firing? It would have saved millions of lives. But then I suppose the men with scrambled egg on their hats would have been denied the pleasure of drawing lines on their maps. It seemed to be their favourite occupation. They sent men up in balloons and flying machines to make sure the lines were always in the right place. It was an obsession and men died for it.

I know war is more complicated than that, of course I do, but too many men I've talked to and got to know, some as friends, have ended up in smithereens or as bullet-riddled corpses in the mud. Some of them are still out there, melting into the landscape they glorified with their blood. What a pointless waste of youth. Lest we forget? I never shall. God knows I've written enough about it. Enough to know I'm no Wilfred Owen or Rupert Brooke. I can't order my thoughts enough to pierce through my anger and find the truth – find an honest reason for it all. Sometimes, too often, even my prayers turn to feathers in my mouth. I asked myself, could we blame the good Lord if He stopped His ears and closed His eyes in horror at what we were doing to each other? Our President Woodrow Wilson seemed a good man but he admired the navy's anthem, the song called *The Star-Spangled Banner* a song filled with the perilous fight, the ramparts and the rockets' red glare, the bombs bursting in air. Nothing has changed.

And then I recalled that He gave us his own son to be scourged and to die in agony on that bitter cross. And that Jesus Christ walked for three days in Hell amongst the damned before He was resurrected into the light. And then? Well then, I realised my prayers would be heard and my suffering understood and I would feel myself to be touched by ineffable grace. I would bow my head once more. Amen.

I forget myself. The colonel. We had an appointment. The Preacher and I walked the mile to the colonel's headquarters through safe trenches and along peaceful roads. We found ourselves in a soft winter's dream of normality and calm. It wasn't quiet, just calm. They told me people could hear the guns over in old London town and I believed it. We could hear them grumble behind us like a bad-tempered grizzly while we walked up a tree-lined avenue towards the colonel's billet. I've lodged in smaller hotels. The French call these buildings chateaux. We had nothing like it in Dallas, except, I guess, the new Union railway station that had opened the previous year. That came close. The chateau was only one room deep but they were big rooms. A Texas farmhouse could find room to wave its hat in the entrance hallway alone. We were directed on our way to the left.

As we moved further along the building we had to show our invitation three times, each time to uniformed guards who looked too clean to be real. They each examined our soiled boots warily. The last guard made us remove our boots and then wash our hands and faces before handing us each a pair of slippers. They were black velvet with red piping trim and clashed mightily with our khaki. When he was completely satisfied that we weren't going to dirty up the nice clean colonel's billet, we were finally ushered into the great personage's audience chamber.

My principal memory is of great, elegant windows between which hung gilt mirrors and gold sconces. I wondered briefly what a general's office would look like. It would probably dwarf the White House in Washington DC. Colonel Peacefarthing was also wearing black silk slippers with red piping, but his matched the voluminous dressing gown he was draped in. I think he was wearing the same pearl-grey lounging pyjamas in the life-sized, full length oil portrait hanging over the massive and delicately carved stone fireplace.

In the painting, which was quite fine and looked to have been done by the Englishman, Sickert, Peacefarthing looked slender and refined. Perhaps a little foppish and a bit vain but otherwise perfect for a literary gathering. He only lacked an orchid. I had heard tell he knew Oscar Wilde and had taken wine with Siegfried Sassoon. This latter's name sounded a little too Teutonic for my tastes but he was a recognised war hero. I wondered by which side.

In the flesh, Peacefarthing was meaty and pink. His skin folded loosely from his bones in a fashion that belied his portrait's willowy profile. He looked dissolute and oddly feminine. Hovering like a faithful dog at his side was his adjutant, a man I had vaguely known since training. Captain Ida Wolseley. He had always been a well-dressed, sharp looking man, but now he looked as if he had been ironed into his carefully tailored uniform. His handsome face shone and his full head of hair was artfully curled. Naked and painted marble white he would have made a fine addition to any classic collection of Greek gods. *Perhaps that was why the colonel had collected him,* I thought, then chided myself for my unkind notion.

Wolseley spoke with a trained musicality. 'Cahoon, Spindrift. Good to see you. The colonel has ordered us sandwiches and coffee. Would you care to join us at table?'

~5~

Wolseley pointed us to a freshly laid table and four chairs gleaming in the cool light of one of those enormous windows. The window was the height of the room, which I judged to be fifteen feet or more. After we each offered the colonel a wordless nod, the Preacher and I took our seats side-by-side. I noted the quality of the table settings. Polished sterling silver, porcelain cups and flatware, and lead crystal glasses. There were also carefully folded linen napkins in ebony grips. In the centre of the table was a neat cushion of bright greenhouse flowers.

Just over three miles away the colonel's men were washing enamel mugs and mess kits in spit to conserve water. I felt embarrassed enough to sit comfortably for my meals, on a bench by a rough plank table in the hospital refectory, but at least we used the same mugs and stew cans as our men. This colonel was evidently a creature of an entirely different kidney.

He sat at table and tucked his napkin into the neck of his pyjamas. Wolseley strode smartly to a door in the opposite wall to the one by which we had entered. He opened it. Pinkly scrubbed dough boys dressed as footmen wheeled laden trolleys into the room. They carefully placed dishes on the table under the colonel's watchful gaze, and then they departed. When they reached the door, they stood in a row and bowed like lackeys, then closed it silently behind them.

We were alone once more.

'Shall I be mother?' Wolseley poured excellent coffee into tiny, paper-thin cups barely fit to be thimbles and then handed around dainty sandwiches and cakes. He also filled our glasses from a crystal jug beaded with condensation. The water was fresh and cool with none of the chemical taste normally associated with military drinking water, which was usually transported to the front in petrol cans. That tasted so vile most of the men would only drink it as strong tea. I downed the fresh water as greedily as I would a fine wine. It was very welcome.

Wolseley waited until his colonel had popped his first sandwich into his mouth and issued a mewling grunt by way of permission before he nibbled the crust-less corner of a triangle of soft white bread.

He turned to me. 'Colin,' he said. 'I understand you know something about police work.'

He carefully placed two buff folders on the table beside his child's toy of a cup. I saw the names printed on the fronts and realised they were Spindrift's and my personnel files. I raised my eyes to his in curiosity.

Without opening my folder Wolseley quoted, 'Medical training with Johns Hopkins which latterly included a year working with the forensic pathology and evidence team of the Baltimore City Police Department. Colonel compared your work there with that of Mister Sherlock Holmes.' He chuckled, 'He will have his little jest. He loves detective novels. He especially enjoyed "The murders in the Rue Morgue", but doubts many apes will have made it all the way from Paris to Flanders. I told him they may have done so. They might easily have disguised themselves as infantry, where they could pass undetected. Oh, how we laughed.'

The colonel made a noise as if he was clearing his throat. It was the only noise he made during that entire eccentric interview, unless you count his constant munching. I wondered if Wolseley wanted me to hunt down the cat that had evidently stolen his colonel's tongue. I also decided not to disabuse him regarding the principal detective in the 'Rue Morgue' story. I was certain that neither the author, Edgar Allan Poe, nor his creation, C. Auguste Dupin, would be troubled by the case of mistaken identity.

Wolsey tapped the other folder. 'Doctor Spindrift, the colonel understands you have seen evidence of a troubling new German initiative. He has recently been informed that the Hun has found a way by which he can not only burn our troops with some ghastly form of chemical acid, but he can also infect them with a virulent disease. And that when colleagues go to the victim's aid the poor devil explodes like a firework. If this is true it is an alarming development. Before I discuss the police matter with captain Cahoon I wonder if the colonel might ask you to elucidate?'

At that moment, the man in question was gazing vaguely out of the window and chewing stolidly on a trimmed cucumber sandwich. He snapped at it like a basking lizard chewing a locust. His eyes remained unfocused and dull. His personal plate of dainties was as large as the one we three had to share.

He ate like an automaton, with disinterested and relentless greed. I began to wonder if he even knew we were there. I had to fight an overwhelming impulse to wave my hand in front of his vapid face just to see if he would react. I turned my attention back to Wolseley and Spindrift. By contrast they seemed animated and exciting. All the while they talked I was aware of a wet snap, snap, snapping noise in the background, the sound of the colonel's interminable mastication.

Spindrift politely addressed his answers to Wolseley's questions in the direction of the colonel, who had just discovered his plate of cakes and meringues and was attacking them with equally bored vigour. I remember the cakes to be small, soft, and pink. There was something disturbingly flesh-like about them.

The Preacher explained, 'The German secret weapon is a form of phosphorous gas that impregnates the victim's skin and will explode – as we have seen.' He looked across at me and I nodded in agreement. He continued. 'The victim in this case was a poor British mining engineer – and he has been the only victim to date – or at least so we believe. The gas is certainly worthy of note, but, as I am sure the colonel will readily appreciate, it is not our primary concern.'

Wolseley raised a curious eyebrow. 'No?'

The colonel continued clearing his plate. Snap, snap, snap.

'No. I'm more interested in the infection that afflicted his body. In fact, may I ask an impertinent question?'

'Perhaps.'

'Are we due a major offensive in the next several days?'

Wolseley looked at his colonel.

Snap, snap, snap.

He turned back to Spindrift. He sighed. 'Nothing is planned during the next ten days. At least not by us and not in this area. What are you suggesting?'

'With the colonel's permission?'

Snap, snap, snap.

Spindrift took that as a yes. 'The hospital is in good order and can afford to be without both of us for at least a week, allowing for surprises and disasters. I would like to assist captain Cahoon with his task, whatever that might be, and perhaps he might also help me with my research into the disease? Of course, that would depend on the nature of the captain's commission and I would perfectly understand if he didn't require my help. I will be advised.'

Wolseley looked from Spindrift to me with an arch expression on his perfect face. I could almost read the thoughts written there. *Oh*, he was thinking, *is that how it is?* His gaze flickered for the briefest moment towards the snapping creature in black silk, and then back towards me and the

Preacher. He smiled ruefully for a fleeting second, and then regained his composure.

He nodded, 'Very well. The colonel has been approached by concerned local parents. You see, children are going missing, a good number of them. They have always disappeared out here, it's a simple fact, you know? People breed children, children go missing. But just recently the numbers have peaked. There's been a positive spate of disappearances. Adolescent boys,' he swallowed, 'and young girls. All of them distinctly pretty in the, ah, local fashion, you understand?'

I asked, 'How many?'

He tilted his head towards me. 'The colonel doesn't know. *We* don't know. There is a war on you know. Some of these children might just have become innocent victims of le guerre. If you, ah, see what I mean?'

We nodded, he continued.

'The locals have turned to us because we are outsiders and relative newcomers. We've only been here a few months and they trust us. The colonel appreciates that. He chooses not to disabuse that trust. He depends upon you, Colin.'

We all looked at the silk-robed eating machine. He had pulled a plate of cookies towards himself. Snap, snap, snap.

'The details are all in this dossier.'

He handed me a slender, buff folder. There were obviously precious few details to work from.

He said, 'The local gendarmerie has been appraised of your, ah, interest in the situation. They will offer all the assistance they can.'

'Why didn't the locals turn to them?'

'They are not, ah, trusted.'

'Oh. I see. But, why not take this to the British? They've been here much longer than us.'

Wolseley smiled bitterly. 'The increase in the number of children vanishing began to peak just a year after the British arrived, perhaps less. The locals believe the British might be the culprits. They say, "Only a fool reports a robbery to a thief". Of course, the colonel would prefer such opinions about the British to be kept completely discreet. I'm sure you, ah, concur?'

The colonel stood, dabbing at his lips with his napkin. A litter of empty plates was all that was left on the table. We stood as well, it seemed fitting. The man dropped his napkin on the dishes, turned, and paddled to the door at the back of the room through which the dough boy footmen had arrived and departed. He opened it and left us without even a backward glance.

Wolseley looked after him. 'A dedicated man,' he said without a trace of irony.

'Yes, yes indeed, a dedicated man,' I echoed. Spindrift said nothing.

We shook hands and mouthed our goodbyes. We collected our boots and surrendered the slippers on the way out. When I pulled the creaking leather back onto my feet it felt as if I was slipping back into reality and I was grateful. Even if it was the stark reality of war I much preferred it to the mad place where Ida Wolseley had made his home. I pitied him his luxurious, silk-slippered prison.

~6~

'Sergeant Kirby, good to see you again. How's that calf muscle coming along?'

'Doctor Spindrift, sir. Pleasure it is to see you too. Me leg's right dandy it is. You have a gift, sir, a gift. And it's a gift that many more than a simple plain fellow such as meself can be proper grateful for.'

Kirby had taken a lump of shrapnel in his left leg, and lost almost a quarter pound of finest Chicago Irishman in the process. He would have a fine deep scar to show his grandchildren. He would probably have ended up showing them his stump if it wasn't for the Preacher, and Kirby knew that. They shook hands warmly.

'Captain Cahoon and I need the use of a pair of saddle horses, if you have some spare?'

'For you, doctor, I'd steal them from under a major, so I would.'

Spindrift grinned, 'I sincerely hope that won't be necessary.'

Kirby still walked with a pronounced limp but he moved at speed to saddle our mounts, chattering all the while. His accent had more of County Clare in it than Chicago west side. His language had a fine poetry to it that took God's English on a ramble through the hedgerows but always arrived at its destination. Eventually.

It was the morning after our interview with the colonel and I had agreed with Preacher Spindrift that it would be best not to let the grass grow under our feet. And so, we had put things in order at the hospital and made our way to the stables to see if we might make our rounds of the local villages on horseback. That meant dealing with Sergeant Kirby. Kirby would never be back at the front line. He couldn't move fast enough to run at German machine guns thanks to his injury, but nor was he injured enough to go home. He had fallen into the army's arms as a disabled yet useful man who must be found a useful job. The army had listened to his accent, heard the Irish lilt, and pointed him at the stables. The Irish, it was well known, have a gift for looking after horses and an inborn penchant for all things equestrian.

Kirby, meanwhile, had been a postal worker in Chicago and had never been near a horse in his life – unless it was pulling a coach or a wagon along the street where he was making his deliveries. He didn't complain about his new role just counted his blessings that he was whole, alive, and away from the front. He had never been involved with the fighting, he had been an engineer like me, but he had been close enough for the shell burst to get him. He was safer in the stables.

It turned out he *had* inherited a way with horses after all. He liked the big beasts and they liked him, and with the help of the other stable hands he had soon found his feet.

He placed a stepping block to help me climb into my saddle. While I did so Preacher swung up onto his horse with effortless grace. Kirby grinned and whispered, 'That fine man surely stepped down from the heavens to join us here on Earth. If there's anything he can't do like an angel I'll be the runt in the litter, so I will. And I won't because I'm not.'

I grinned back, 'No, Kirby, you're not the runt and never will be. See you later this afternoon, and don't forget to rest that leg.'

Spindrift lifted an arm in farewell and we cantered away from the stables. We were soon picking our way along an earthen road that had been badly rutted by transports heading to and from the battle lines. Spindrift looked back and then forward. He said, 'Well, Colin. Where shall we start our police action?'

I had studied the scant notes Wolseley had given me and could give an informed answer of sorts.

'The disappearances have been recorded in the villages of Natres, Rocquiguy and Equancourt, all of which are southwest of here. Natres is the largest and has a gendarmerie. A captain Morel has been informed we're coming and I'm told will be happy to see us.'

All street signs had been removed for several miles in the district around the front to confuse the enemy. It didn't help us much either, but we rode until we found some workers labouring in the fields and they happily directed us when they discovered that we weren't British, and that Preacher spoke the language like a native. At least I think he did. He made rapid and pleasant noises to the people in the field and they made rapid and pleasant noises in return. It was enchanting, and I had to ask myself why I wasn't surprised. He thanked them and they waved until we were out of sight.

'You speak good French?'

'I rub along well enough.'

'You're a godsend!'

He looked at me steadily with a strange smile on his face. 'Thank you,' was all he said, but his eyes seemed to speak volumes. I felt as if there was a question that needed to be asked, but I didn't know what it was. Then something very odd happened. I had a sudden flood of sensation. It was as if I was on the brink of something vast and strange. I felt as if I was at the very edge of an immensely high cliff and teetered in my saddle, suddenly feeling faint with vertigo. As quickly as the sensation had begun it ended and I found myself secure, my arm held firm in Spindrift's grip. Concern was writ plain on his face.

'Colin, I'm sorry. Are you, all right? You looked as if you were going to pass out.'

I took a deep breath of cold, crisp air. 'I don't know. I felt dizzy. Silly of me.'

'You're not long out of a hospital bed, old chap. Maybe you're pushing yourself a little too hard too quickly?'

'No, no, I'm fine, really. Touch of the vapours, silly of me. I forgot to breathe. I'm fine.'

'Give me your hand.'

'What?'

'I want to check your pulse.'

'Oh, yes, right.'

I held out my right hand and he took it firmly in his own. He held my wrist in the fingers of his left hand. A warm shock bloomed up my arm and surged into my chest. A sense of intense wellbeing momentarily overwhelmed me. The sky brightened perceptibly. I sat straighter in my saddle. I grinned.

'What did you do? I feel marvellous.'

'Old Chinese medicine. They use needles of course, but you can do it with pressure points if you know where they are.'

He released me and I rubbed at my wrist, which still tingled. There was a small drop of bright blood welling up directly over one of my threadlike blue veins. I looked at it with surprise. Spindrift drew out a white kerchief and dabbed at it.

'There you are, gone. Strange, never heard of that happening before. Have you?'

'I've never heard of *any* of this happening before. It seems like witchery and magic to me. But who could care on such a fine, beautiful day as this.'

I looked around me at the cobweb silver hues of a misty December morning. Birds were singing in the hedgerows and the good rich earth slept its winter sleep. There the landscape was gentle and unscarred by conflict. The birdsong leapt to my heart and I felt myself grinning like a loon.

Spindrift smiled back. 'Come on, Colin. We have work to do. The landscape will still be here later. Let's go.'

We urged our horses into a gentle canter.

'Spindrift,' I said. 'I've never heard anyone use your first name. Could I perhaps be too familiar and ask what it is?'

'Never too familiar between friends, Colin.'

'Yes, thank you. Honoured. But what is it?'

'What?'

'Your Christian name?'

'Oh, that. Maybe later. Spindrift is good enough, old lad. It's what I'm used to. That or doc. Not Spinny though, never Spinny, if you see what I mean.'

A loud honk split the air. My horse acted a little skittish at the sound and I took its reins more firmly then patted its neck to calm it down. Spindrift's horse looked around with a bored expression on its long face. We brought our mounts over to the side of the road as a Ford Hunka Tin gussied up with British red cross markings rattled past. I was surprised to receive a radiant smile from the young woman at the wheel and she waved as she drove past. Dazed, I waved back, and this time caught the attention of a slightly horse-faced woman in a nurse's uniform who was gazing out of the open rear of the truck. She offered me a blank stare, and then bent back into the shadows. We cantered after the ambulance but it quickly disappeared into the distance. Some half an hour later we caught up with it when we reached the little town square of Natres and discovered a makeshift medical centre there. A harassed looking doctor was crouched down and questioning a heavily bandaged man on a stretcher on the ground. I counted twenty-seven injured men lying silently in a row. Some were smoking tobacco. The doctor looked up as we approached. His black scowl told us that whatever we wanted he didn't have the time to deal with it. Spindrift dismounted and handed his reins to me. He strode briskly to the doctor.

'Do you need a hand? You look a bit outnumbered there.'

The man eyed him with exhausted exasperation. His gaze rested on the crucifixes on Spindrift's lapels. He sighed, 'Forgive me father for I have sinned. It's been more than three years since my last confession and I've seen too many men die since then to be in the mood for another one. I'm busy just now. Sorry, but you'll have to excuse me.'

Spindrift indicated me and then himself, 'We're doctors. I'm a surgeon. We can worry about the condition of your immortal soul later; can we help you with your patients now?'

The medic stood up and shoved out a bloodstained hand. 'You'd be a bloody Godsend!'

'Yes, so I'm told. Where can we wash up?'

The medic, who's name turned out to be Michael Worsnip, was from Cambridge. The original one over in England. He job was to assess his patients' medical condition to decide if they could be quickly patched up and made fit for duty, or needed to go elsewhere for more intense care. He also had to decide what to do about those who were beyond help. He called it triage, a word that was new to me. He told me he'd learned it from the French doctors at the aid stations just behind the lines. We joined in with the examination of the supine men and once we were done he invited us to have a mug of tea. It was strong and had been sweetened with liberal amounts of condensed milk. It had a faint yet very unpleasant chemical aftertaste. Worsnip drank as if his life depended on it and then smacked his lips while pulling a face.

'Ahhh, that's horrible. The drinking water here is foul don't you think? Is it the same for you Yanks?'

I answered, 'Strictly we're Rebs. The Yanks live up north and we're both from Texas. And yes, the water is foul. We had some fresh yesterday, it was delicious, but you have to be a colonel to get it.'

He grimaced, 'Officers!' He waved his mug at the line of injured men. 'Poor bastards. The army takes them in and chews them up then asks idiots like us if they can be mended. We fix them up until they're ready to take being chewed up some more. Talk about have your cake and eat it too. I've had men back here two or three times. Recognised the sutures. I patch them up so they can either go back to the front or survive the journey to a proper hospital before they go home. If I had my way they'd all go home to spend time with their families.' He sipped some more tea then made a face, 'Gaaah! I'm thirsty enough to drink my own weight in ale, and they serve a fine brew in that café bar over there, but I can't touch alcohol until I'm done. Daren't. Can't afford mistakes. But I'd swap all the beer in the village for a decent cup of tea made with good fresh water. Joke is there's a sweet water spring just a few hundred yards from here. Pissing the lovely stuff day and night and we can't touch it. Can't go near it.'

I asked, 'Why not?'

He pointed up the hill towards an imposing walled building almost completely hidden by pine trees. 'It's in there. Sacred spring of the Lady of Grace in the convent of the Sisters of the Weeping Heart. Fine bunch of women I'm told, but God forbid you should drink their bloody water. Sorry, father.' He poured his dregs onto the ground. 'Well then, what brings you chaps to Natres? It can't just have been to help me. Can I point you in the right direction?'

Spindrift was gazing at the convent. Something in his expression sent a cold shiver through my bowels.

I told Worsnip we were looking for the gendarmerie and outlined our mission.

'Children going missing, is it? Isn't it bad enough we've brought the war to their doorstep, and now you say they're losing their little ones too. Funny thing, there's a new one coming into the world even as we speak. That's where my nurse has gone. She came back with the ambulance and scampered straight to madam's bedchamber. Hope it's all right. I can't leave here to go look. She'll be fine I'm sure. Good sort.'

He pointed down the main street and past the clock tower in the square.

'See that black and white building with a flagpole on the roof but no flag? The one with three steps leading up to the door. That's where you'll find your captain Morel and his happy band of bluejackets. You've been a great help to me today. If you're still here later join me for a beer. I'd be right pleased to stand the first round.'

We made our farewells and as we left Worsnip headed back towards his charges with leaden steps. Before us was our interview with Morel, by then long overdue. We led our horses towards the black and white building and I became very aware that all the while we walked, Spindrift's gaze was turned repeatedly towards the convent. I wondered what he was thinking.

~7~

Captain Morel sat at his desk behind a magnificent moustache. His eyes were large and a liquid, chocolate brown colour. He leapt to his feet and saluted when we were shown into his office, then strode forward to clasp our right hands in both of his. Spindrift said something in French and the gendarme's eyes widened in delight. He turned to me and said something to me.

Spindrift said, 'No, I'm afraid Captain Cahoon does not speak your language.'

I shrugged, 'Sorry. I wish I could, it sounds beautiful.'

'No matter, mon ami. English is the new lingua franca of the world. Le Français l'était bien à une époque également grâce à lui...' And here he pointed to a fine framed etching of Napoleon on horseback. 'And once it was Latin of course because of...' This time he pointed to a gravure image of a man's head crowned with laurel. This was clearly inscribed 'Jvlivs Caesar', with 'Vs' instead of 'Us' in the ancient Roman fashion.

Spindrift asked, 'You admire fighting men, captain?'

'Mais oui. Successful commanders.' This time he pointed to the framed black silhouette of a man with a distinctive aquiline nose who was wearing a two-cornered hat pointing front to back. 'Maintenant, thanks to le Duc du Wellington – and Admiral Nelson of course – the world learns English instead of French. History, pah, the moving finger writes and then she moves on. If the Kaiser had his way we would all be speaking en Allemand, n'est pas?'

He busied himself at a corner table and turned back to us with two large glasses of dark crimson wine. He indicated a cluster of comfortable chairs around a table and placed the glasses in front of two of them.

'Please, asseyez-vous. Sit down.' He claimed his own glass and joined us. Once seated he raised his glass and said, 'May we hope l'armee Française learns from the allies and never again shames us with mutiny. Why can't they realise that les Allemands are the enemy not their own generals! Are the generals raping our women and bayoneting our babies? Non! It is the Kaiser's army on devrait leur faire la leçon if it takes a hundred years.'

We all sipped the excellent red wine. Morel clucked and then uncovered a large platter of small slices of salty fried bread topped with a grey paste. I tried one. It was delicious and I said so.

'Ah, Captain Cahoon,' the corners of his glossy black moustache raised slightly and I guessed he was smiling. 'You are too amiable. This is un peu d'affection of mine. These little croutons are spread with morel mushroom pâté. It pleases me to serve them to guests with a fine Château Mouton d'Armailhac. Une petite touche de civilisation dans des moments troubles. Amusez-vous.'

I needed no second invitation. The wine and the croutons washed the taste of Worsnip's horrible tea from my tongue, and I felt much more relaxed with our policeman host than I had with my snapping colonel the day before.

It took a while for us to broach the subject of the disappearing children. The croutons were little more than a savoury memory and we were on our second glass of wine when I finally brought us back to our main reason for being there.

'Captain Morel, your hospitality makes me forget our mission. Our colonel has asked us to consider the increased number of children disappearing from the villages in this area. We were told you would help us. Thank you for your welcome but we must now return to this matter.'

To make my point I placed my almost full glass of wine on the table. Spindrift followed my lead, but Morel cradled his glass and gazed down at it as if seeking an answer in there. Then he looked at me with anger burning in his eyes. His voice became sharp and clear.

'The peasants in the fields, the villagers and the townspeople, they think we are crooked because we stop their little mischiefs sometimes. If a man beats his wife, they say it is his business n'est ce pas? No. When the English doctor tells me that the woman has a broken nose and cracked ribs, and he says to me that if *I* don't do something about it, *he* will, then what must I do? Il est de mon devoir de faire quelque chose. I talk to the husband. I try to be amiable. He spits on my uniform and calls me un petit coq de dindon! Do I arrest him? No. Do I slap him? No. I am a captain of the gendarmerie. We are a military unit. I march away avec autant de dignité que je pourrais rassembler. I return with a squad of my men. The peasant is still there, where I left him. There is a slender tree. I have my men take the peasant and tie him to the tree. He is shouting and making threats. Then I have my men form an escadron de tir, you say "squadron of shooting". The peasant stops shouting. I raise my arm. The peasant begins screaming. Then I say "Prêt, en joue, tirez!" The man drops against his ropes. Il a pissé dans tout son pantalon. Il pue. I have my men cut his ropes. He falls on his face. Next time you beat ta femme, I tell him, the rifles will be loaded. Tu as compris?'

Morel's face became flushed. He drained his glass of wine.

'Since then we are treated avec beaucoup de respect, mais personne ne nous dit rien. Je suis autant étranger dans ce lieu que vous, mes amis. Children qui disparaissent? Oui? Shameful, but I know as much as you, mes amis, as much as you. S'il vous plaît comprenez que je suis ici pour vous aider, mais je suis dans le brouillard. Je suis désolé.'

We finished our wine and made our goodbyes. Morel showed us to the door and promised us what little help he and his men could offer. He firmly closed the office door behind us. One of his men stood to attention and saluted. He led us out onto the street where we had hitched our horses to a post by a stone trough. He shook our hands and smiled sadly, then turned away and returned to the black and white building without saying a word.

I stepped on a block of stone by the trough to swing myself back into my saddle. Spindrift began to climb into his, and then stepped down. He examined the trough more closely, sniffing at the water it contained.

'Colin, the day hasn't been a complete waste. I believe we have some excellent news for our friend Worsnip. Look here. See? Fresh water is coming into this trough through that groove there and it runs away through that notch over there. This trough is ancient, see how the notch has been worn smooth, almost round, by the action of the water. You know something? I think this is a Roman sarcophagus put to good use. Look at the garlanding on its sides. Wonderful. We can tell Worsnip he can have his fresh water from the sacred spring any time he likes.' He pointed towards the convent up the hill. 'The good sisters probably don't even know their spring has been shared with thirsty horses for centuries, perhaps even longer.'

'That's just grand for Worsnip,' I said. 'But it isn't helping us find those children.'

We began to ride back to the medical station. 'No,' said Spindrift. Then he discreetly held up a tightly folded sheet of paper. 'But perhaps whatever's written on this will give us a clue. That young gendarme pressed it into my hand while he was shaking it. I don't think he wanted Captain Morel to see what he was doing. I wonder why?'

'What does it say?'

Spindrift tucked the sheet into a breast pocket. 'Not here, Colin. Let's give Worsnip the good news and have a fresh cup of tea with him. Then we'll put some space between us and the town before we read the note.'

'But why all the cloak and dagger?'

'Look over your shoulder, my friend.'

I did. Morel was standing in the open doorway of the gendarmerie smoking a cigarette. His gaze was directed precisely at our retreating backs. I lifted a hand to him, he made a gesture with his cigarette. I turned back.

Spindrift nodded, 'I think a little discretion is called for around notre ami Capitaine Morel, êtes-vous d'accord?'

'Yes, I do, d'accord.'

~8~

'I've been here three years and I didn't think of that. You must have the eyes of a cat, Captain Spindrift!'

'Curiosity, friend Worsnip. If I was a cat I would have been dead several times over. I give thanks that curiosity is not a sin, at least not yet.'

Worsnip was on his third mug of tea. We had baulked after the second. The horse-faced nurse was back from her midwifery duties and had reported a bonny boy, healthy, and weighing in at seven pounds twelve ounces. We had brewed tea for us and the patients who were allowed it. Spindrift had advised Worsnip that the men with gut wounds should only be given plain water and not much of that. Just enough to freshen their mouths. The English had a bad habit of treating tea as a general panacea, and men who might otherwise have survived their wounds had succumbed to infection because of milky tea leaking into their body cavity.

We learned that one of the injured had died since our examination that morning. He was one of the men Spindrift had assessed as being beyond help.

'At least it was peaceful,' offered Worsnip. 'Just after you left he dropped into a coma and passed away a few minutes later. He had been in a great deal of pain. It was a blessing that he had at least stopped suffering before the end. A blessing.'

'A godsend?' asked Spindrift.

'Listen to me. A few hours with a man of the cloth and I'm beginning to sound like a choirboy again. Spindrift... look, what I said before about confession. It *has* been over three years. Do you think, you know, with your padre's hat on, d'you think you could hear my confession?'

'I have no stole, no wine or wafer.'

'Leave that to me.'

Worsnip scampered to the café bar and returned a few minutes later with a bottle of wine and a packet of biscuits.

'Helen,' he said to the nurse, 'have you got that long scarf you wear on cold days?'

She nodded and fetched it. It was plain and dark red.

'That will do nicely,' smiled Spindrift. 'Now we just need some privacy.'

Worsnip giggled, looking much like the eager fresh-faced choirboy he must once have been. For the first time, I realised how very young he must be.

'Shall we step into my office?' he said. He was back a moment later and fetched a cup of fresh water. 'Father Spindrift must bless this.'

An hour or so later Spindrift and I were on the road back to our quarters. He had been thoughtful and quiet ever since we had mounted our horses. The light was beginning to fade into the west. He watched the light dim with sober solemnity.

Then he spoke. 'The old legends had the land of the dead over to the west. They believed the sun died every night in the west, travelled through the underworld and was reborn every morning in the east. Some tribes sacrificed prisoners of war in the belief that the blood would appease the gods who had killed or captured the sun, and so they would release it and there would be morning once more.'

He was silent for a few more moments, then said, 'They were wrong of course. Death is everywhere. The land of the dead is anywhere you can find the living. Without life, there can be no death, and sometimes death is a mercy.'

In the gathering gloom, I realised he was regarding me.

He continued, 'Michael Worsnip and you have a lot in common, Colin. Of course, I can't break the sanctity of confession, but I can say that if caring for his fellow man and offering peace to the suffering is a crime then Worsnip is a terrible, wicked man and damned to hell.'

An inky shadow flowed out of the gathering gloom and resolved itself into Spindrift's dog. It fell into step beside the Preacher's horse. In my determination to find an answer to the case of the disappearing children I had forgotten the man's most constant companion and hadn't even noticed it was missing.

'How was your hunt, old friend?'

The dog answered with a throaty growl and a huffing noise.

'Thank you. I have some sweet water for you.'

We had filled our water canteens from the trough at Natres. It was a measure of his regard for his animal that the Preacher had chosen to share the precious liquid with his dog.

The dog whined and panted.

'Yes, I thought you would. Perhaps later?'

Huff, growl.

I chuckled, 'I've met dogs who understand every word their master says, but you're the first master I've known who understands the dog's answers.'

'You just have to know how to listen properly, it isn't hard. Dogs have been our companions for tens of thousands of years. After all that time, there must surely be room for commonality, wouldn't you agree? Ours is more of a two-way conversation than a master servant, order and obey relationship. Master and subject? No, that is too blunt an instrument to dissect the bond enjoyed between my dog and me.'

'I have to say I can definitely see what you mean.' I changed the subject. 'By the way, aren't you aching to find out what's written in that note from the gendarme?'

'I am curious, yes. But we must wait until we're back to the hospital and behind the blackout before we strike a light to read by. Our own snipers are just as liable to take a potshot at a strange light out here in the darkness as the Germans. I wouldn't want to risk it, would you?'

'No, no I don't. Stupid of me.'

'We'll be there soon enough. Rein in your love of mystery for just a few more minutes and we'll be able to ponder the young policeman's words at our leisure – and in as much safety as this sorry place affords.'

He was right. Within ten minutes we had returned our mounts to Kirby and made our way to the doctors' mess, which was in the farmhouse. I fetched us both a glass of beer and signed the honesty docket. Spindrift had found a bowl for his dog's water. We all three drank with relish, the dog lapped at his bowl with refined silence. Supper wouldn't be served for an hour or so but the darkness made the hour feel much later. The beer, which was French, had been stored outside and was pleasantly cool. I felt myself begin to relax. Then Spindrift reached for his breast pocket and fetched out the folded piece of paper. He opened it. My heart began a rising beat of anticipation. His dark eyes ranged across the note, then he handed it to me. I took it eagerly and then dropped it in frustration.

'It's in French!'

'Of course, it is, Colin. The young gendarme probably has a smattering of spoken English, but I doubt he can write it. Please, give it here.'

He smoothed the paper with his thumbs while he studied it.

'My dear friends,' he read. 'I must be brief. If you truly wish to find out more about the missing children you must visit the convent and talk to the Mother Superior, sister Honoria Pietas. Mention my name, Albert Fournier.

My sister is one of the nuns there, sister Matilde. If you see her give her my love. Good luck.'

He folded the note and replaced it in his pocket. He patted the pocket.

His dog placed its massive head across his knees and made a deep huffing noise. Spindrift stroked its head thoughtfully. His eyes closed. The pair remained like that for several moments. The dog's eyes were also shut. I would almost have thought them both asleep were it not for that rhythmic movement of the Preacher's hand across his dog's head. Back and forth, his fingers slightly bent. Then their eyes opened. The dog stretched out on the floor and the man rubbed his eyes. He looked as if he was returning from somewhere, as if his mind had been distracted in the middle of a profound notion.

He smiled, 'Sorry, Colin. I got carried away by a train of thought. I would be mighty grateful for another glass of this excellent beer, please.'

I refilled our glasses, signed the docket, and then brought them to the table. The dog emitted a gentle snore. Preacher looked at it affectionately.

'She's had a long day too, poor old girl.'

My stomach rumbled. The beer had sharpened my appetite. I belched and caught a faint taste of morel mushroom pâté.

'Excuse me,' I muttered, 'beer on an empty belly. Perhaps not the best idea.'

'You're right. Let's go wash up for supper.'

We got to our feet and took our glasses to the pantry hatch. The dog roused herself and got drowsily to her feet.

I said, 'I guess we're back to Natres tomorrow?'

'No, Colin. No, we have somewhere else to be tomorrow. I'll explain later. Let's eat first.'

~9~

The following day saw us lightly breakfasted, scrubbed, cleanly shaved, and heading towards the British front lines. We were on foot. That close to the front line, riding on horseback would have proved far too risky. Any kind of height above the firing line in daytime would be lethal. German snipers had had years to practice and we were in officers' uniforms, making us the top targets on the shooting range.

Spindrift's dog pattered along a few feet ahead of us, almost merging with the long, early morning shadows. I watched the landscape change from the soft, arable hills of northern France to the cratered, muddy hills of war. Mankind had wrought havoc on the land and then planted himself plumb in the middle of it. And there was that stink, a stink I had once become inured to, like a baby sat in its own shit for too long can't smell it after a while. I heard the sharp crack of distant sniper fire and some insanely optimistic birdsong, but otherwise the place was quiet.

The British trenches had been there long enough to take on a settled, beaten look. There were signposts pointing along the trenches declaring them to be 'The Mall', 'Rotten Row' and 'Piccadilly'. The signs looked as if they had been there a long time. Longer than their creators had intended. The humour had worn off but no-one had the heart to take them down.

A fine drizzle started to fall. It was going to prove another dank and murky December day. We got moved from one sentry to another until we found ourselves in front of a Major Maitland of the Royal Engineers, who invited us into his dugout for tea. His batman fussed around like a little bantam cock and presented us with tin mugs of the customarily dreadful brew. We sipped at it gingerly and thanked him. I wished we were back in Natres with its untainted water.

Maitland nodded towards Spindrift's dog, which was sniffing warily at a bowl of water. 'Your hound, is she? Fine looking beast. She was nosing around here yesterday and the chaps made a fuss of her. Ha, you were lucky to get her back. She had her fill of tid-bits before she disappeared again. Friendly pup, aren't you, my beauty?'

The dog looked hard at her owner and he fought back a smile with obvious effort.

Maitland continued, 'Interested in my sappers, is it? What have the rum blighters been up to? Wouldn't have thought they'd have the energy for mischief. They've taken to sleeping down their blessed holes these days. I was going to send a squad down today to see what they were playing at, don'tcha know. Not had a report for two whole days. Not since Cuthbert came up and asked to see the quack. Said he'd been bitten by something, looked damn queer...'

Spindrift raised a hand, 'Yes, major. That's why we're here. He came to us, you see. He was in a very poor state. In fact, he died.'

'Died, is it? Poor fellow. He was a good chap, don'tcha know. Mining stock like most of the clay kickers down there. Suppose we'd better have his body back so we can send it home to his people. Least we can do. Not much of a Christmas present for them, is it? But at least he'll get a hero's grave they can visit on his birthday.'

'Sorry, no. I'm afraid not. He was much too infectious, we had to cremate him. It was the only safe way. We've stored his ashes in a pot. You could have that.'

'Too infectious, is it? Too infectious you say? What, plague, is it? Filthy thing if it is. Saw something of it in India, God, bubonic plague, yes, must be twenty years ago, in Bombay it was. Poor buggers went down like flies. Filthy thing. You saying it's here?'

His eyes seemed suddenly haunted by terrible memories.

'No, major. It isn't bubonic plague. I'm afraid that, if anything, it might be a lot worse. We need to go down and see your sappers, if we may. They may need our help, if there's still time. Or they may need to be put into isolation for the sake of your other men. An outbreak of this disease in the trenches with so many men so close together would be catastrophic. We must contain it here, and quickly.'

'Worse? Worse, is it? Bloody hell! Really? What is it? And what can we do about it? How can I help?'

'It's a virulent tropical infection called Sha-aneer. It's passed by a type of small worm. Its symptoms are very like a hugely accelerated form of trench nephritis and mortality is almost invariably one hundred per cent. Your men are probably fine, but we must go down and see. We need to make sure.'

'I'll send a squad down with you, make sure you're all right. Those clay kickers might get a little shirty if strangers come down and start bossing them around, can't take the chance.'

'Who's the senior man down there?'

'Durham chap, ah, Bowles, yes, Lance Corporal Bowles, solid enough type. Good lad, Bowles.'

'Well, we're both captains. Do they know how to take an order?'

'They do, yes. They're sound fellows.'

'Then I don't want to risk more personnel than I have to. Captain Cahoon and I are enough if men have to be lost, we won't need more.'

I looked askance at the Preacher but said nothing. It almost seemed as if I was being held in thrall to his will. I'd never heard of a disease called Shaaneer, but it sounded 'pretty filthy', as Maitland would say. I thought back to the man called Cuthbert and the black-eyed hole where his face used to be. A cold fist settled around my heart and my guts churned. I was glad we had breakfasted lightly.

'Brave men. Fine fellows, I shall pray for both of you.'

'Thank you, major. We appreciate it. We too shall pray for God's grace in our endeavours; but first, how many men are down there?'

'There were twelve, but now you say Cuthbert has gone, so, just eleven.'

'That's enough. Major, we only plan to be in there for an hour or so. If we haven't emerged after two hours I need your men to standby with a couple of buckets of the latest Mill's bombs. If they see anything strange coming towards them tell them to use the grenades, but if what they see looks like two men running as if the dogs of Hell are at their heels, that'll be us. Tell them to hold their fire.'

'Do you want us to look after your dog while you're down there?'

'Thank you but no. She's specially trained for this sort of thing. She can see in the dark.'

'With her nose, I expect? Wonderful sense of smell, the hound.'

'Yes, sir. If you like. Now, with your permission, could we be shown to the tunnel mouth?'

'Take you meself. Proud to be your guide. Sounds like a filthy business, least I can do.' He turned to his batman. 'Vickery, round up a few volunteers and a couple of buckets of Mill's bombs. Fetch them here, will you? There's a good fellow. Quick as you like.'

The little bantam stood to attention, rigid as a poker. He was vibrating with eagerness. He saluted. 'Sah, yes, sah! Right away, sah!' And he marched away, his arms swinging to shoulder height and his feet pounding the damp duckboards with a precise rhythm.

'Wanted to be in the Coldstream Guards,' said Maitland regarding the man's disappearing back with obvious affection. 'Volunteered for it, you know. Got turned down. Too short, they said. Stupid. I think he's the perfect height for a man charging the enemy. Most of the machine-gun bullets fly straight over his head, and he's a demon with a bayonet once he's amongst the Boche. Coldstream idiots said he was too short, and I got him instead. That was my good luck. I call him my fighting cock. Heart bigger than an oak, ha, and an English oak at that.'

He sang a few quiet lines of 'Hearts of oak' until Vickery returned with his team of 'volunteers'.

Maitland thanked them for their courtesy and explained their mission.

'Vickery and I will be by your side the whole time while our American friends are in the tunnel. You must do nothing without my express orders. Understood? We shall be on friendly soil but must take nothing for granted. Very well. Captains Spindrift and Cahoon, please follow me. Vickery and the rest of you, bring up the rear. Forward march.'

He led us down the trench named 'Piccadilly' and then along one signposted 'Regent's Street'. Men hopped crooked backed onto the firing platforms to clear our way. It was a practiced manoeuvre that kept their heads below an enemy sniper's eye-line. We followed a curving path called 'Old Kent Road' and then arrived at what looked like a heavily sandbagged shelter. We had to climb up to the entrance.

Maitland muttered, 'Built up like that to stop water flooding in from outside, wet enough in there without help from the weather.' He stood to attention in the drenching drizzle and pulled a face. 'Locally they call this weather "the peasant's bathwater" because the poor peasant thinks its light enough to carry on working in, and gets soaking wet. They should also call it the "soldier's shower" because we're just as daft. Happy to join you, chaps. At least it will be dry in there.'

Spindrift sniffed at the mouth of the mine, 'Thank you, major, but no. We'll see you soon, God willing.'

We entered, and I heard his dog whimper. It didn't make me feel any better.

~10~

What had become known as 'tunnel warfare' was largely ended by the middle of 1917. By December and all along the line, clay kickers who had once been employed to dig battle tunnels and mines under the static German positions were turning their hands to creating underground hospitals and accommodation for the vast numbers of men massing for the 'next big push'. They carved through the blue clay and stone common to Northern France and the Pas de Calais to hollow out mess rooms, bunk rooms and surgeries connected by corridors four feet wide and more than six feet high. The tunnel we entered that morning was dry underfoot, which was very unusual. I had heard stories about advanced cases of trench foot the British medics had been treating thanks to mining engineers working eight- to twelve-hour shifts while wading in a foot or more of muddy water. The tunnels were a monument to perseverance and misery. The stoic men who dug them fully deserved their daily ration of rum.

In the intense gloom that gathered as soon as we stepped away from the entrance, I saw a little narrow-gauge rail track that ran down the centre of the tunnel. Just a few feet ahead of us everything was pitch-dark. It was darkness with real character. I could feel it waiting for us to walk into its clutches. I hesitated. Spindrift whispered close to my ear, I felt the touch of his breath against my cheek.

'We'll be fine, don't worry. Here, drink this and wait for a few moments.'

He handed me a silver cylinder after unscrewing its top. Then he looked down, at his dog. 'Okay, old friend, I'll need your good eyes and ears. Off you go. See what you can find out for us.'

I drank from the cylinder as the dog disappeared into the blackness. The liquid was icy cold in my mouth and then seemed to evaporate into my sinuses rather than trickle down my throat. After a moment, my head felt light and I experienced a slight sensation of dizziness.

'All of it, Colin. Drain the cup. It will do you no harm I promise.'

I did as I was told. My whole body tingled and a warm glow developed behind my nose. It was as if I had taken a mouthful of hot English mustard. The warmth filled my head and then spread down into my chest and belly. I felt immensely calm and peaceful. I exhaled and then breathed deeply. Questions should have been crowding my mind and clamouring, demanding to be answered. *What had I just drunk? What was it doing to me?* But instead I regarded the Preacher with profound sense of serene trust. I handed back his cylinder. He screwed the cap back on and it vanished into one of his inside pockets. He smiled without humour, 'How do you feel?'

'Good, fine, thanks.'

'Are you ready?'

'Yes. Ready'

He nodded and we moved deeper into the tunnel. We had gone a good few yards before I realised that I could see quite clearly. The walls of the tunnel were bathed in a ghostly phosphorescence. Even the floor glowed with silver light. I could see tools that had been left leaning against the walls, a woollen cap someone had dropped. There was a small table in a deep niche to my left on which sat a collection of tin mugs.

I turned to Spindrift but he put a finger to his lips. He tugged at his ear, and then touched his nose. At first I thought he was silently asking me if I understood that I was to remain quiet, and then I smelled it. A stink that was both fetid and alien on the still air. I heard a distant muttering of oily voices, but I couldn't quite make out what they were saying. I felt the hairs on the back of my neck begin to rise. The Preacher squeezed my shoulder and whispered close, 'Do you want to wait here?'

In truth, I did, but I couldn't let him down. I shook my head. We strode towards the sound. I spotted the dog sitting facing down the tunnel towards a point where it seemed to open out. The voices had become louder. They were hissing and gurgling like water seeping into a drain. They clarified.

'The host is ready to move out and seek more of the delicious Eden flesh. We smell it on our tongues. It is above us and around us. We shall feast and feast and feast until all have joined us.'

'We will seed the Earth. Our seed will reach down to the First in its nest, reach deep into its sleeping belly and quicken it. The Earth shall be made in *our* beautiful image once more. It shall awake and rise, *rise*. We shall be whole once more and our world will be made complete and beautiful – as it was before the Eden filth soiled it.'

'But the Eden flesh is soooo delicious! Soul and marrow and blood melts on the tongue. Delicious fare for us. Juicy morsels of man meat shall make the worm of the deep earth grow strong, strong and stronger.'

'The Sha-aneer shall devour the sweet Eden flesh, the host will thrive! We shall suck the souls from their bones. Suck them and devour them.'

'Feel the hunger. Feel the lust grow, feel it...'

'Wait, wait, someone watches...'
'Who watches? Is it him? Is it him?'
'Is it that creature, Satan?'
'Is it the Eden beast, Satan? Is it him? Is it the bastard, Satan?'
'SATAAAAAN! SATAAAAAN!'

The noise had become deafening. And then *something* boiled out of the end of the tunnel and flowed towards us. It reared up like an evil wave of putrid grey flesh. Thick strings of muscular limbs like tentacles stretched eagerly towards us. There was no time to get away, there could be no escape. I reeled back in shock and then saw that Spindrift already had two of his crystal globes in his right hand. He threw them towards the roaring mass and drew his pistol with the other hand in a single fluid motion. His shots rang out like cannon fire in the confined space. There followed an intense flare of white light and I was blinded. A rising shriek of pain and horror battered my ears. I pressed my hands to my head, trying to block the agonising sound, but it got louder and louder until I thought my ears would burst. The piercing squeal bored deep into my brain like a drill on an exposed nerve. I know I was screaming too, my throat was raw with it. And then the entire world exploded.

I was thrown several feet backwards by the force of the blast. I landed hard, winded, and nearly knocked senseless. Not very lucky I thought. Almost instantly something massive landed on top of me and smothered me. My first thought was that the grey monster had caught me and I would be devoured. I struggled and lashed out. My hands were caught together in a powerful grip and I was pressed down flat. I howled in futile anger, and then I heard a calming voice right next to my ringing ear.

'Colin, relax. It's us.'

Something rough and damp swiped at my face, and I realised Spindrift's dog was licking me. It whimpered in greeting. I attempted to rise and Spindrift pressed his hand against my chest.

'Stay down, this isn't over yet.'

Then came a concussion like a shell burst, and the length of the tunnel lit up like the heart of an exploding star. A bank of white fire rolled towards us. Spindrift covered all three of us with his long coat and put his hand above my head. He placed his mouth over my mouth and nose. I was so shocked I didn't think to protest, I just took in a sharp intake of breath. And I tasted cool, fresh air. The inferno raged around us and I felt my feet become uncomfortably hot for a long moment. And then it was over.

The Preacher stood up and helped me stagger to my feet. I wiped at my face with a trembling hand. My ghost sight had been scattered into red blobs and sparks until I was more blind and confused than I had been in the darkness, but slowly it returned. Eventually I could see the empty tunnel and a drift of fine silver ash all around us. Spindrift and his dog walked down to where the tunnel opened out. He looked keenly around and then returned to my side. The dog's tongue lolled thirstily from its mouth.

He said, 'It's over. This place is clean.'

There came a clatter of running feet and we saw a feeble light bobbing towards us. Behind it came Maitland and his men. They paused a few feet from us, illuminated by the bullseye lamp in Vickery's fist.

'You chaps all right?' the major asked. 'Not infectious at all? Not... burned?' He examined us as if expecting to see something vile crawling under our skin.

Spindrift answered. 'Thank you, major. No, we're fine. Can we get out into the light? I'm afraid your men didn't make it. I'd like to report.'

'Yes, good chap. Shame, about the men, filthy business. Where are the bodies?'

'I'll tell you out in the open air, if I may.'

'Of course, let's get out of here. Smells damned odd, don'tcha know.'

I wondered how much of the truth the Preacher would reveal? How much he could reveal?

~11~

That was when the earth began to buck and tremble under our feet. Some of Maitland's men fell to their knees and I was thrown hard against a wall. My uniform was taking quite a battering, as was the tender flesh under it. Spindrift pulled me upright and hauled at the men.

'Run,' he yelled. 'Aftershock, gas pockets. Move!'

Maitland and crew hesitated, confused.

'Bombardment, is it?' stuttered Maitland. 'Safer here under cover, surely?'

'No, major, no. Explosive gas! We have to run, NOW!'

The major's men got the message and scrambled for the exit, Spindrift pushed me after them and I ran. When I looked back I saw him seemingly wrestle with the major, and then hustle him back up the tunnel. The major seemed to be trying to fight him off. That was when the Preacher picked the man up and draped him across his shoulders. He sprinted towards me.

'Come on, Colin! Get a move on.'

I needed no second invitation and picked up speed, lifting my knees high and pumping my arms. I had been something of a track star back in high school and at University, so I believed I had a tidy turn of speed. However, even though he was carrying a bulky, full-grown man on his shoulders Spindrift easily caught up with me and egged me on. I heard the major huffing in baffled surprise. He seemed to be repeating 'Wha, wha, wha...?' As if trying to question his treatment at the hands of the tall American captain.

I looked back over my shoulder. Something new was rising and flooding from the extreme rear of the tunnel. Even with my ghost sight I couldn't make it out. It was dark and fluid, a dancing black spectre moving in the ebony shadows. I almost slowed to take a closer look. Spindrift pounded me on the shoulder and I automatically strained once more towards the exit, which was just a few yards away. Suddenly, hot, foul breath stung at my nostrils and caught at my throat. The air took on a sticky, poisonous quality. I couldn't breathe and began to choke. I staggered, faltered, almost fell. Spindrift thrust me forwards and sideways with a powerful shove and I found myself outside, sprawled on the duckboards of the trench. We had made it to the open air! The icy drizzle tasted like nectar on my parched lips. I looked around. Several feet away on the other side of the tunnel mouth I saw the Preacher press Maitland hard against the trench side and cover him with his body. The Englishman looked appalled and frightened. And then a plug of thick, hot slurry vomited from the tunnel and spattered hard against the trench's opposite wall. It sounded like a sledgehammer striking a tree, splintering some of the boards. I expected it to smother and drown me as it roared out the trench, but instead it solidified instantly at the touch of the cold, fresh air.

I found myself separated from my friend and Maitland. I climbed unsteadily to my feet on the other side of a smooth black wall that completely blocked my path. I stood frozen and stared at the steaming, dark barrier. How had it happened? What was this mysterious stuff? Curiosity clawed at me and I edged closer, my hand outstretched. I could feel its heat against my palm. It was like glass to the touch. I muttered to myself while I stroked the enigmatic stone, barely daring to breathe due to the strong stench of that sulphurous vapour that had almost stolen my breath during those last moments in the tunnel. I wondered at its miraculous appearance. Was this stuff thrown up from the burning pits of Hell? The liquid manifestation of evil frozen by the light? Was this some demon's foul exhalation made solid? I thought of those oily, ghastly voices we had heard in the tunnel just before the conflagration and my spirit quaked. Had I heard fiends from hades screaming out for their master? They had chanted, Satan, Satan... there was no mistaking the name. What place had we entered in that tunnel? What evil had we disturbed?

It was then that Spindrift's raised voice finally penetrated my confused and circling thoughts.

'Colin? Hello, Colin? Are you, all right? Colin, answer me!'

He sounded worried. I answered straight away. 'I'm fine, Spindrift, fine. What is this stuff?'

'Good, that's good. Now, stand well back from it. Stand well clear, you hear me?'

I took a few steps away from the plug of stinking stone.

'Are you clear?'

'Yes, well clear.'

'Good, now keep your head down, there's a good fellow.'

I crouched. Behind me some of Maitland's men had returned, no doubt to find out what was happening to their major. I gestured at them to stay back at the zig-zag of the trench and to keep their heads down. I had no clue what was about to happen, but kept a wary eye on that steaming black wall from under the rim of my tin hat.

Then a wonderful sound began. It started low and then strengthened until it resonated like a song, but a song sung in a strange, musical language. It was quite lovely in an unearthly fashion; and it reminded me of something I'd heard before somewhere, but I didn't know where. Or when. It was almost as if my mind had been opened to someone else's memory. It was the memory of music from a life long ago, music both ancient and beautiful. It conjured a spirit realm of raw magic and sorcery. It made my heart ache with deep loss – without disclosing what great treasure had been lost to me. I fell into a waking reverie and surrendered my senses to the song. Crouched in the trench and frozen like a statue, I dreamed. My mind's eye travelled deep into the music.

I was flying like a bird. I saw great seas and rising swells, stone islands rising sheer from foam flecked, green waters. Great, grey winged, white birds, silent as thought, floated like dreams across the rising peaks. Scraps of foamy spindrift were snatched and blown away from the mountainous crests, scattered froth glowing whitely under a sky like polished steel.

And then the view changed with the tone of the song, and the seas became suspended in time, frozen. My eye now traversed an infinite mountain range. These were not the softly weathered pinnacles of our time, but immense raw spires of new stone wrenched from the body of the Earth and thrust up into the sky to scrape at the highest clouds. Deep gashes, and fresh wounds were still clearly visible across their razor-like, granite shoulders.

The song rose and my imagination soared with it, climbing swiftly up towards the summit of the highest peak. The sound was so high now it was almost beyond hearing, yet it was still clear and pure like a horn blown by an angel. I swear my teeth vibrated in my head. And then in a soundless shock the mountain erupted.

Once more I found myself being thrown backwards like a sack of bricks. I landed heavily and bounced against a wall of sandbags, adding new bruises and scrapes to my already painful collection. My vision was blurred and clouded, and I feared my optic nerves had been jarred loose. Then a figure strode through the cloud and I found the Preacher standing before me, his half-moon grin gleaming white in his dark face.

'Colin, I'm sorry, but I warned you to stand back, old fellow. Let me help you up.'

He was coated in a liberal dusting of greyish-white powder, as, I soon discovered, was I. Maitland came into view, batting futile hands at his begrimed uniform. He wiped a fist against his moustaches and sneezed hard, three times in rapid succession. He drew off his dust laden peaked cap and looked at it mournfully, then beat it against his thigh before returning it to his head. His every action added more dust to the air.

'Damndest thing I ever saw. Damndest thing. Really. Captains Spindrift and Cahoon, I should be very grateful if you would both accompany me back to my quarters and explain exactly what has been happening over the last half hour or so. Damndest thing. Wouldn't believe it if... Well, saw it with my own two eyes, don'tcha know. Damndest thing.'

He edged past us and then hesitated. He looked straight at the Preacher.

'I believe you just saved my life, sir. Saved my life. Good man, thank-you. Bottom of my heart. Mean it. But I would be grateful, most grateful, if you could explain what you just saved me from? Damndest thing.'

He coughed a string of clay-like mucus. 'Something to cut the dust is called for, yes?'

The powdery cloud was settling and clearing. A small group of astonished faces appeared at the corner of the trench.

'Vickery, you there?'

A stiff little figure stepped forward, stamped his right foot down hard and saluted. 'Sah, yes sah!'

The major returned the salute. 'Stand easy, there's a good chap.' He indicated us and then himself. 'We're heading back to my quarters. Sort out some of the good stuff from home, will you please. Wet the whistle, cut the dust. Good man, thank-you. That's all, off you go.'

The batman vanished and we followed at a more leisurely pace. Maitland kept looking back at us, especially at Spindrift, and shaking his head. Every breath of wind lifted a trail of silvery powder from our bodies. The soldiers we passed gazed at us with open curiosity, and I couldn't blame them. I would have done the same. We must have looked like wraiths freshly climbed from the tomb and making our silent way through the world of the living.

~12~

Whether drunk from a tin mug or a tankard, I'm sure the major's cold ale would have tasted just as good, even without the dust. Vickery had apologetically brushed the worst of the pale dust from our uniforms before allowing us to enter his governor's dugout. A great, earthenware jug had met us when we entered. Maitland fetched his tankard and two tin mugs then served us himself, having first excused his batman from his quarters while we talked. We were silent at first while we sipped deep. When we had drained our cups, he topped them up again, a major acting as servant to two lowly captains.

I offered, 'Thank-you sir, but there's need, we can help ourselves. This beer is excellent by the way. Delicious.'

'Glad you think so, Cahoon, glad you think so. My family brews it on the estate. We make a rather good apple cider too. I say "we", ha! What I mean is, we have people who brew it and they know what they're doing. I couldn't brew a decent cup of tea until I came over here, never needed to, but I thought I should learn how to fend for myself against an hour of need. Vickery taught me a few essential survival skills. Clever little cove, salt of the Earth! Don't know what I'd do... anyway, you catch my drift. Cut the dust enough for a little parley? Really keen to find out what happened in that tunnel.' He indicated the earthenware jug. 'Help yourselves, please. More where that came from, tapped barrel in my sleeping quarters. Mum's the word though. Men get thirsty for a little foaming ale to ring the changes from tea and grog. Best not to put temptation in their path. What they don't know won't bother them.'

He settled in his seat and raised his pewter tankard.

'So, then, what just happened in there? I've been here since Mons in August fourteen, seen some rum business, but I'm damned if I've seen anything like that, damned if I have. What's the damned Boche up to now? Was it the Boche?'

I glanced at Spindrift. He drained his cup and leaned forward to place his head between Maitland and me.

'Major, what we just experienced was more likely geology than German, but I believe that a new German weapon may have been the trigger that sparked it off. There's a new type of phosphor gas they've started using.'

He spoke at length, explaining how one of the men must have been unwittingly infected, or more correctly saturated, with the gas, and introduced it into the tunnel. He posited that it was a heavy dose that had become even more concentrated in the confines of the tunnel.

'It was a primed bomb just waiting for a spark, and I'm afraid we may have created that spark when we called out to your men. We may have startled them into lethal action. It would have taken little more than a spark, metal against metal such as a bayonet blade against a rifle barrel... But, then again, if one of the men had lit a cigarette or pipe...'

He looked at Maitland, who blinked like a man recovering from a dream.

'What? Well, yes, some of the men smoked, course they did. Helps clear the lungs, don'tcha know? They get claggy with all the damp in the tunnels and a blast of healthy cigarette smoke helps bring up the worst of the muck. They should know better than to light up in a gas-filled tunnel though. Silly mistake.'

'It may not have had a smell.'

'Then the bird would have told them. Who was it? Yes, private Westerman, he had a bird in a cage. Little thing would have keeled over. They looked after that bird like a child and it looked after them. Little thing had popped over twice already. If it popped over again it got to go home, retired you know. Cruel to keep gassing little birds.'

I couldn't help myself, 'We seem happy enough to do it to our men.'

Maitland gazed at me for a moment without saying a word. Spindrift took up the thread before I could dig myself in deeper.

'That tunnel must have been dug above an old strand of fine soil, perhaps silt from the earliest seabed held in a stratum of sedimentary rock. The gas explosion in a confined space must have compressed it and it was held under extreme pressure until it found a flaw in the strata...'

He sounded very credible and sincere, yet every part of his tale was as fantastic as the work of Mr H. G. Wells. Maitland kept nodding as if he was agreeing with every word.

'...Major, as an engineer, I'm sure you understand the effects of flow dynamics on certain types of soil when it's been held under intense pressure. As you know it can, and will, flow like water, and then revert to a solid when the pressure diminishes. What we saw today was a classic demonstration of that effect. It was only because I felt the first faint traces of the tremblor that heralded the eruption that we could escape, otherwise we would have joined your poor miners in their tomb. It was pure luck that I've seen such an event before, in Italy.'

'Italy, is it? God smiled when he sent you to us, captain Spindrift. He smiled indeed. Where was it, you know, in Italy? Beautiful country, spent some time there as a young fellow when the current Italian King's father was still on the throne, Umberto the first. There was a man who appreciated the importance of a good moustache. Lends authority to a face, erm...' He glanced at our cleanly shaved faces and weighed his next words carefully. 'Yes, lovely country. Lending its good right arm against the Austro-Hungarians, don'tcha know. So then, captain, where was it you felt your first "tremblor"?'

'The foothills of Vesuvius, not far from a town called San Giuseppe Vesuviano. Land moved like water and swallowed a peasant and his mule whole, even while I stood watching. Nothing I could do for the poor fellow. I was in Naples the day after that, when the volcano finally erupted. More than five hundred souls lost their lives and I heard that a good number died in San Giuseppe when the weight of volcanic ash caused the roof to collapse on two hundred people attending mass in the church of Santa Anna. They were asking for God's help in their hour of need, as so many have done here, in Flanders Fields. But the Lord is not a manservant to run around at every man's disposal. He gave enough warnings for those prepared to listen. There are none so blind as those who will not see, and none so deaf as those who will not hear.'

He grinned, 'But I digress. It was back then, before that peasant and his mule had vanished into the earth before my very eyes, that I felt the exact, self-same tremor that I felt in the tunnel. I knew I had to get you and your men out into the open before it was too late. I would not stand by and let you perish.'

Maitland offered Spindrift a hand, 'And thank-you for it. My men and I are extremely glad you know your, hm, "flow dynamics". Extremely glad.'

It was a good half hour before we could shake off the major's gratitude and make our way back to the hospital. The light was already fading from the sky so I missed the moment when Spindrift's shadow darkened perceptibly and I realised his dog had returned to his heel. Where it had been, I didn't know, I might ask later, but I had a more pressing question to raise before then.

'So, then, doctor Spindrift,' I said once we had left the trenches and the guards and had returned to the gentle road heading back to our billets. We were alone on the road. 'So then,' I repeated. 'What really happened back there in that tunnel?'

'My explanation to the major didn't convince you then, Colin?'

'You know it didn't, you weren't speaking for me were you. When were you near Vesuvius, by the way?'

'The last time? 1906. The ruin wrought by war is shameful, but that created by nature can be just as terrible. Very well, you deserve the truth. Let's get some dinner and then please, join me for a drink in my rooms. I have a tale to tell that requires a glass or two.'

'The truth?'

'Every word, I promise. Every word.'

'And will you also tell me why Maitland didn't ask you about your singing?'

'My singing?'

'Yes, just before that plug of black stone exploded.'

'You heard that?'

'Of course, I did. It was wonderful, quite swept me away. Right up to the time the stone shattered.'

'We have much to discuss, yes, much to discuss.'

And he said no more.

Curiosity burned in me like a fire all the way back to the hospital. We changed and washed up before dinner, then I rushed my meal of beef and tinned vegetables. Soon we would be eating turkey on Christmas day, as we had on November twenty-ninth for Thanksgiving, but boneless beef or pork was the staple every other day. I was hungry but it wasn't my belly that needed feeding it was my hot curiosity. At last we retired to the Preacher's rooms and he uncorked a bottle of red wine and fished out some glasses. Wine, unlike ale, does not suit tin mugs.

'Very well, Colin,' he said at last. 'Time, you heard the truth.' He raised his glass, 'Cheers, my friend.' His dog was lying by the fire and its tail thumped on the rug at this. 'To you too, old friend.' He grinned. 'Enough, the tale from beginning to end. Prepare yourself.'

And he began talking.

~13~

When he was spinning his yarn to Maitland I had compared his imagination to that of Mr H. G. Wells. Well, what Preacher told me that evening would have set the great author's hair on fire. His said his story began on a far distant world called Eden. This brought me up cold. I studied his dark, earnest face to see if he was playing the giddy goose, but his eyes were as sober and reflective as when he was discussing the war. Whatever he was telling me, he believed it to be the truth. But accepting it was going to be tough. The longer he talked the more I felt like a python trying to swallow an adult elephant whole.

He explained that Eden was a mature and civilised planet. Its people had conquered many of the travails that blight Earth. War, disease, famine and, to a degree, death, had been vanquished. Its people were long lived and prosperous. They were wise, and noble. They had learned how to share their planet with all its flora and fauna, and had built sophisticated spaceships in which they had explored their neighbouring planets and moons.

But even this great race of people could not span the vast distances between stars in a single lifetime, and all their attempts to put a crew into a state of what Spindrift described as 'artificial hibernation' had failed with tragic consequences. Volunteers had been anaesthetised and 'cryogenically' frozen, whatever that meant, but once thawed they couldn't be revived. I asked Spindrift what had driven the people of Eden to such desperate measures.

He replied, 'Nature at its worst. You see, their sun was being steadily leeched away by the approach of a great black hole, a kind of immense gravitational magnet that can swallow stars and planets the way we eat soup. They faced extinction unless could find a way to preserve their species. Of course, the Edenites would never meekly surrender to their fate and would doubtless have continued looking for fresh avenues of escape until their time ran out, but they needed to do something quickly with the technology they had to hand. They decided that even if they were to be wiped out with their planet, somehow their seed must live on.

'Their greatest intellects and engineers worked together on what would probably be their last and most important project. They built six giant spaceships and crewed them with artificial intelligences, beings largely held in thrall to the guiding super-intelligences built into the cores of the ships themselves. Those beings were fashioned in the likeness of their creators, and shared some degree of their wisdom and nobility. Each ship was designed to provide its crew a beautiful environment in which they could thrive. A garden if you will. Another Eden. The crew had been manufactured for incredible longevity, they must survive the long years their task required, but beyond obedience to the ship minds they also had free will. They needed to be able to adjust to whatever their destinations threw at them.

'Those superb ships gave them a home in which they could travel immense distances between the stars without becoming insane over the centuries. The crews regarded their ship homes as "Heaven", but the ships' official title was General Organism Development Systems, or GODS, for short.'

He paused and eyed me with concern. I was coiled forward in my seat. I had a tightness in my chest and my fist was gripping my glass as if it was my only lifeline and I was adrift in a cruel sea.

'Colin, I can stop if you like. If this is too painful for you.'

I raised my glass to my lips but lowered it without drinking. I had emptied it while he was talking and hadn't noticed. I had questions for him, there were things I had to know. I tried to keep anger from my voice.

'How did you learn all this? How can you be so sure that everything you're telling me is true? It sounds like some late night tall tale, the kind of mad invention best saved for a midnight session after a coney hunt. A story told around the campfire after a good few beers too many. Sure, I wouldn't expect to see any of it on the front pages of the *Houston Chronicle*, but come on. Do you really think this tale is true or are you just taking a roundhouse swing at my faith? Eden, heaven, Gods? What are you telling me? Is it mischief and devilry? Are you trying for a joke? If you are, well, I'm sorry, doc, but I can't say I see the humour of it and that's a solid fact. I hope you'll forgive me my opinion, but this sounds like a pile of shee-it.'

He took the glass from me, refilled it, and returned it without a word. I took a long draw on it. I was not doing his wine justice, it could just as well have been water. I guess I wanted to numb my senses to help make his tale more bearable, or at least calm my outrage. I respected Spindrift, but he was asking me to exchange everything I believed in for a story worthy of Mr Jules Verne or Edgar Allan Poe.

He took a steadying breath. 'May I tell you the rest of the tale? Imagine a campfire and a string of coneys if it makes it easier for you.'

I nodded, feeling nauseous. I looked at my glass, empty again.

The Preacher continued. 'Each ship had a specific and separate destination. Even across the vast stretches of interstellar space the people of Eden had subtle devices that could identify new worlds that might support their progeny. Earth was just one of the potential targets, but it was a promising haven for the Eden seed...'

'The what? I'm sorry, for the what?'

'Sorry, I didn't explain. Each ship was a repository for the seed of the people from Eden, the Edenites. They couldn't freeze a person and then resurrect them, but they could successfully freeze fertilised seed, ovum. They might die but they hoped a new host could found to provide a home for their seed. On Earth, we found two species that had a lot of promise: a very intelligent ape and the precursor of the modern dolphin. Both species were seeded and evolved. The dolphin, however, proved an evolutionary cul-de-sac. It was having too much of a good time in the oceans to take anything other than poetry and song seriously. It plateaued out at a certain level of culture. The ape, on the other hand...'

I gestured that I had another question. 'Sorry, but what exactly do you mean by, seeded?'

He explained that the great ship had positioned itself securely out beyond the orbit of the planet Mars. Several seed delivery technicians – or husbands – had travelled to Earth in pods fabricated from precious metals. All of them were directed to fall into the oceans. The pods dissolved and the husbands destined to seed the apes swam to shore, while the others sought out the dolphins. They were 'equipped', his word, to place the specially treated Eden seed into the wombs of the chosen species. It was identical to the sex act, except it placed a fertilised egg into the uterus and a nutritional fluid that would feed it until it had successfully anchored to its 'mother' and she would take over.

The image of these alien creatures having congress with apes and dolphins did not sit well in my mind. Spindrift cited passages from the *Bible* to support his revision of history. He quoted whole sections from the book of Genesis, that there were giants in the world in those days and that angels had come down unto the daughters of man. Race memory from the time of the seeded apes. Evolution, at least as I understood it, based on the survival of the fittest, was placed firmly to one side. I do believe if Mr Darwin had heard him he would have begun spinning like a top in his grave.

'And where are they now?' I asked. 'Those husbands and the results of their Eden breeding program? What has become of them?'

'First I must explain why it was so important to preserve the line of the Eden born. It was more than vanity that drove them to ensure their species' survival, much more. You see, Colin, the people of Eden had evolved to become unique on their home world, and perhaps even in the universe. They had received a special gift from God. Each of them had developed an immortal soul, and thanks to that soul they could, albeit as if through a glass darkly, they could sense the hand of the original creator and worship Him and His works. The Edenites believed that such an awareness had to be worth saving. It had to be worth sending the seed out into the void in the hope of planting it in fresh, fertile soil. Find it a haven, somewhere it might prosper and grow strong once more. Here on Earth, only one race has that self-same soul. The dolphins might have developed it too, they had the potential, but their minds are focused purely on earthly pleasures. They would rather perform a double back-flip in mid-air than ponder the ineffable. They will never feel touched by the love of God or strive to earn His grace. They sing songs about sex, the sea and swimming, and those are fine enough if you know how to listen, but they couldn't countenance Gregorian plain chant and nor would they understand the Lord's prayer. Only man, Colin, only mankind, has inherited an immortal soul that first bloomed under unimaginably distant skies. Only you and your people can one day know your Creator and hope to find redemption.'

'I,' I almost choked on the words, 'I... Look, I want to believe you. But how can you possible know all this?'

And then I felt it again, that sensation of being near something enormous. It was as if I was being pulled from my chair by an irresistible force. I suffered vertigo and experienced deep confusion about what was up and what was down. I found myself falling out of my chair and dropping to my hands and knees, my empty glass still held in my quivering grip.

Spindrift stood up. He looked down at me with an odd expression on his lean face. I perceived his pity, but also his profound resignation and something else, something unknowable.

'As I said, the crew who manned the GODS ships were designed to be very long lived. Most of them have returned to the ship, but the few who remain here on Earth are tasked with protecting those born of the Eden seed.'

With a shock, I suddenly realised that he was hovering in mid-air, suspended over a foot from the floor. Intense energy filled the room and seemed to crackle like lightning around us.

'And I have been given a great task,' he continued. 'Something was here before we arrived, and it looks upon the Eden born with terrible envy and hatred. It would destroy us and all our works. That must not be allowed to happen. It *will* not be permitted to happen!'

Fierce energy poured from him like a physical force and struck me down where I knelt. My mind reeled and my breath came in choking gasps. My sight became dim and a red mist threatened to overwhelm my scattered senses.

It was then that we both became aware of an urgent pounding at the window. Spindrift settled back to the floor and gently dragged me reeling to my feet. We stood side-by-side. The noise got louder, we heard a voice. Spindrift looked briefly at the fire, decided it was safe, then hurried over and tugged back the black-out curtain. I squinted through the windowpane trying to see who was trying to attract our attention. In the slight wash of firelight that still illuminated the outer darkness I saw a slender woman staring back at us. She looked furious, and her burning eyes were aimed directly at the Preacher.

~14~

Spindrift lifted his arms away from his sides, palms open in a universal gesture of greeting.

'Rowan,' he said, 'you are very welcome to join us.'

And suddenly the woman was in the room. She was a spitting hellcat, a force of nature. She lashed at Spindrift with a savage tongue and stabbed at him with an accusative finger.

'What are you playing at Satan Spindrift? Are the guardians of Eden bullying the poor brutes born of the seed now? This poor creature can't stomach such a rich diet. What, will you turn him inside-out with your tricks or do you just want to maze his simple wits and bend them to your will? I'll stop that game, see if I don't. I'll put some juice in his spine and he'll be able to stand up to the worst you can throw at him.'

Without hesitation, she turned to me and grabbed my face in both her strong hands. Her head darted forward like a striking cobra and she kissed me, hard on the lips. I was too shocked to resist but my mouth opened in protest. That was when a gush of cool sweet liquid flowed onto my tongue and I swallowed on reflex. It happened twice more, and twice more I took the strange draught down my welcoming throat. I doubt I would have been so careless had the method of delivery been less attractive.

I felt dizzy strength course through me. Spindrift had given me his elixir in the tunnel and I had felt revived, but that flavourful kiss delivered a much headier brew. I remember thinking that I must now know how a young god might feel when the stars were favourable and fortune smiled on him. Without thinking I took the woman in my arms and kissed her back, all thought of my ex-wife Rachel sent flying to the four winds. And then I found myself foolishly leaning forward with empty arms and puckered lips. I almost fell flat on my face again, and staggering a little I straightened up, letting my arms fall my side. I was blushing and had a sheepish grin plastered on my crimson face.

The woman was standing several feet away by the fire and regarding me with arch delight, her fists at her hips and a glint in her eye. For the first time, I had the chance to truly appreciate her tawny beauty, and she took her time in studying me.

'You have the stance of a married fellow,' she said with a flash of bright, white teeth under full, saucy lips. 'Behave yourself, now, sir, or I'll give you reason to regret such flirtatious shenanigans.'

'I was, but not anymore. She left me for another fellow,' I mumbled. 'She said we had married too young and she had come to realise that I would never amount to anything. She said I would never get my head out of the *Holy Bible* long enough to smell the java, and that she had a life to lead and had met a man who knew how to make his way in the world – and it wasn't on his knees.'

I looked up and smiled weakly, 'I'm told he trades in pork futures and his name is Clarence; Clarence Archibald Mathers. Rachel and I were divorced before I boarded the *USS Henderson* and sailed here from New York. I've no doubt she is Mrs Mathers by now and I wish her well of it. I pray pork will be the settling of her future and that she will find the happiness I couldn't provide her. I do.'

The woman pulled a face. 'I shall never eat another pork chop so long as I live.'

'Please, not on my account.'

'Never you fret, I never liked the stuff anyway, prefer chicken or a tender coney. Crow breast on toast is delicious too, if you know how to climb a tree to the nest and your knife is sharp. I wish you luck in your loss, mister...'

'Cahoon, Colin Cahoon. Please, call me Colin.'

'I shall, Colin. And you must call me Rowan. Poor man that you are, to lament the loss of such a foolish creature. Forgive me, but she must have soaked a cake in her virgin's water and made you eat it to bewitch your heart from its rightful place. Or did she offer you a blood sausage? Did she now? Let's not go there, eh? Let's not. That's dusty old magic used by crones and bitter women to entrap good men and strip them of their senses. I hope that foolish ex-woman of yours gets saddled with a future as a Mather's mother milch cow, I do. I curse her with rampant fertility and wish her blessed with a busy womb.'

She made a gesture. 'May the woman become known only as Mother Mathers, that'll teach her. And may her days be filled with squawking babies and filled nappies – and may her proud dugs be stretched and baby chewed until they hang from her ribs like spaniel's ears. And may her babies make her belly grow big and sag to her flabby thighs like a masonic apron!'

Rowan was grinning like a fox chewing sour berries from a thorn bush, she was getting into her stride.

'And may she always smell of shit and sour milk and her hands grow red and chapped from the constant washing and cooking. Ha, yes! Her ears shall never again enjoy quiet conversation and laughter but always and only the wails of fretting, colicky cubs. How long will it be before Clarence Archibald realises his porky future would be better with a newer, fresher gilt?'

'No, no please,' I protested. 'I loved her once. Please, let her be happy.'

'Leave a good man for a pork future? She's already got eedjit written across her arse in scarlet letters a foot high! Her future is nothing of mine, Colin, but if she's willing to swap a good Cahoon for pork futures, well, I for one know she's doomed to half measures from now on.'

At this she turned to the Preacher. 'And what were you thinking of, Satan Spindrift? We could hear your blessed racket all the way from the hills of Paris to the painted caves of Lascaux. Are you trying to wake the dead or browbeat this poor man into submission?'

Spindrift answered in a language like music. I recognised it as the same beautiful language he had used to destroy the barrier in the trench. Rowan gasped, then she answered in kind and tilted her fine head to one side. The saucy girl vanished from the room and she became a solemn priestess while she spoke. I regarded her with fresh eyes. I was out of my depth with this woman and wading still deeper, but at the same time I was aware that while my mind spun like a loose wheel my body felt better than it ever had before. My sight was clearer, my hearing sharper, and those niggling twinges across my shoulders that had plagued me since I had been blown-up at the front and injured, were gone. I had somehow been revived and refreshed and made whole. I had missed Rachel it was true. Yes, I had mourned her loss, but Rowan's verbal portrait of a baby-ridden old harridan in an exhausted body had brought a smile to my face. Something rotten jarred loose in my chest and floated away on the new tide. I was ready to face my future now, and I wasn't on my knees. Not yet.

Spindrift leaned towards Rowan and brushed his lips chastely against hers. I felt jealousy leap up in a hot spark and almost spoke out in protest. But then he stood back and cupped his hands together. Rowan brought the palms of her long-fingered hands together as if in prayer. She closed her eyes and lifted her face towards the ceiling. Her lips parted and she took a deep breath, then she intoned words of such breathless purity, and looked so lovely while speaking them, that I found tears of joy burning freely on my cheeks.

I felt like a child once more, a child on Christmas day come to see the nativity at chapel and keen to see the holy infant cradled in his mother's arms. I had never been that child, never looked up at my mother's face to see only care and love in her eyes. I had never been an innocent buoyed by trust in the warm containing arms that held me. But in that moment, I knew what it felt like to have a new, trusting soul. I was washed clean. The long years of battering, adult experience spiralled away from me like a great flock of black bats roused from their nest. I felt myself become lighter as the swarm of darkness drifted up and away from my spirit, carried away on the Preacher and Rowan's sublime voices. The songs of the choir in our church had always been able to unman me, the songs of children would take me by the throat and fill my heart with rejoicing. This was different. This was the promise of the immortal spirit given voice.

I lifted my eyes to the couple silhouetted against the fire's waning light and realised I no longer knew who or what they were. We were in place outside of time and beyond the mud and blood of Flanders. There was enchantment in the room and its inky shadows sparkled with colour and movement. They were no longer creatures of the flesh but beings of light. Something flowed between them, and Rowan moved like a graceful acolyte in a temple. She bowed her head and dipped her hands towards Spindrift's. A stream of clear fluid flowed from her to him. He spoke words over the fluid and I was reminded of the Catholic prayer of sacrament over water and salt, or perhaps something much older.

Then he drank.

Rowan remained still as a post, her hands pressed together and her sweet mouth open in song. Her body quivered like some alert young doe's, taut as a bowstring. She was clothed in a russet dress that glowed like leaves in the brightest flush of autumn, but I was very aware of her womanly body under that dress. Spindrift stood tall as an oak and placed his hands either side of hers. His baritone joined her lighter voice and then the music soared. Grace touched me, and I felt myself to be in the presence of God. If my heart had failed me at that single moment in my life I couldn't have been happier.

I fell to my knees, shut my eyes, and clasped my fingers together in worship. Rowan's exquisite contralto wove around Spindrift's powerful baritone like a phoenix around the sun and filled me with sacred fire. I realised that until that moment I had been but a poor empty vessel, a hollow reed driven by a careless current along the river of life. But there, in that room before the ebbing fire in a forgotten grate, I was washed and blessed by spiritual flame. Their song had filled me with love and awe, and I was scorched by it, burned by joy. I found myself kneeling at the raw brink of eternity and even with my eyes squeezed tight shut I saw God's work written plain across the universe. My soul bloomed and unfurled like a banner of joy. My mouth opened like a funnel and all the filth that had soiled and weighted my spirit spurted out. I hadn't realised how much darkness had stained my spirit and held me down like a man of clay, rooted to the mundane ground. Years of carefully husbanded pain, fear, and misery poured from me and was burned away in that righteous fire.

The stars looked down upon me and I regarded them as equals. I had become a passage for light, a sword in the hand of God, a fire burning in His love. My immortal soul was swept up by the song like an eagle in flight and I flew to the very limits of the sky. I saw stars scattered like jewels across the firmament. A red world swept past me, a dust storm raging in its thin atmosphere. Massive, irregular boulders and flying mountains rounded by time swam around me, turning majestically as they tumbled through the void. And then amongst them floated an oddly symmetrical and spherical dark shell. I drew nearer. As I approached it grew until it filled my sight and stretched horizon to horizon. It was enormous. Its surface looked burned, ashen black, and it swallowed all the light that touched it.

And then I felt an awareness that stirred and looked out at me. I sensed a wave of intense curiosity at it finding me there, followed by cold shock. A sudden blaze of alien anger scorched away my sight, and I heard a cold voice snarl, 'Satan's plaything.' And then there was nothing. Nothing.

~15~

My scattered thoughts came slowly back to me. It felt as if they had been made to travel a vast distance. They seemed to coalesce in my mind like condensation on a cold window. My body was a blank page run through with lightning strikes of white hot torment. Nothing was written there but pain. My awareness hovered above my body for a moment as if it wanted to escape the torture, then I fell downwards like a stone into a dark pool and I found myself locked once more in my too solid flesh. It was very strange. My body was wracked with pain but my head was strangely comfortable. I opened my eyes and looked up. I had myself a close-up, albeit oddly angled, worm's eye view of a woman's upper body, and if it hadn't been for a sudden shock of agony I would have been able to appreciate its firm curves a lot more. What I could see looked just fine, and was wrapped in a flimsy, tawny fabric that had complex veins of metallic thread running through it. I watched her breathing for a while, the gentle rise and fall of her chest. It was very soothing.

I had no memory of anything leading up to that moment, but decided I was content to remain where I was, at least until I could bring the confusing mess of recent events back into proper focus. I was in no rush to move. I snuggled my head deeper into its warm nest.

I then realised that a pair of large amber eyes flecked with gold and surrounded by a pixie-like face and a shock of hazel hair were looking down and regarding me with evident concern. *Rowan,* I thought. The name sprang out of my mental undergrowth like a startled squirrel. *Rowan! She's real!*

She turned her glorious eyes away. 'Satan, he's waking up.'

A tall, lean figure came into my field of vision. My eyes blurred momentarily and I seemed to see a dark halo around the man's head, then it was gone.

'Doctor Spindrift,' I groaned and tried to sit up. Rowan pressed a hand against my chest.

'Rest a moment, let Satan look at you first.'

Who was I to argue? I remained still while he prodded at me as if he was thinking of buying me for a Sunday roasting joint. He didn't use his stethoscope, just his fingers. He poked in my ribs and belly, rotated my hands on my wrists and my feet on my ankles, bent my knees and elbows. His eyes glinted. It was then that I realised I was naked, all apart from a thin sheet. The fire blazing once more in the grate did little to warm me, but I could feel the heat flowing from the comely woman who was supporting my head. I realised she was resting my head on her thighs. A modern woman would be wearing a thick skirt and layers of heavy petticoats above woollen drawers. I would have felt no hint of flesh or heat through so many layers. Such was not the case with Rowan. She burned me where I touched. I could feel her raw heat. I whimpered.

She idly stroked her right hand through my hair while she watched Spindrift at work. Despite everything, despite the pain and my friend's proximity, my weak flesh began to rise to temptation. I was mortified, but couldn't stop what was happening. Something of her effect on me must have been visible through the sheet because she chuckled.

'I think he's beginning to feel a little better.'

'Please, Rowan, don't tease the poor fellow. You know what the fey can do to a mortal.'

She chuckled again, an earthy sound. Her body quivered as she laughed and I felt the movements vibrate through my scalp. I began to sweat.

'Oh, look, his ears are turning bright pink. Isn't that delicious? See now, he's blushing.'

Spindrift raised an eyebrow. Rowan bit her juicy lower lip with her fine white teeth and smiled coquettishly. 'It's all right,' she purred, 'I'll look after you.'

I whimpered again. I had an idea how a mouse might feel once caught in a cat's paws. Spindrift slapped me on the shoulder.

'Very well, Colin, you can sit up. You're solid enough, sound as a yearling calf, and I think you might feel a lot better with your pants back on. Rowan, please help him up.'

I discovered I had been laid out on the trestle Preacher used as a table, and, as I had suspected, with Rowan's thighs as my pillow. She pushed me up until I was sitting erect, the sheet gripped around me like a flimsy shield, then she slid off the table like an eel. I got a brief glimpse of what was under her dress when it moved smoothly up her legs to her bottom. No sign of any drawers. Everything under there was one hundred per cent woman. The sight fair took my breath away. She wriggled the hem back down and patted her dress with both hands, her hips swaying in a hypnotic figure of eight.

'Fair exchange is no robbery,' she grinned. 'Your turn.'

Preacher sighed, 'Rowan, be fair now, please. Give the poor man a little privacy while he gets decent will you.'

After a lingering look at the middle of my firmly clasped sheet she turned her back on me. Spindrift pointed to the chair where my clothes had been carefully folded, and I tore off the sheet. I had fixed my pants and was fumbling at my shirt buttons when I looked up and saw Rowan's gleeful face reflected in a large mirror over the mantelshelf. It glowed crimson in the firelight and her big, beautiful eyes shone. Shadows flickered there like a magic lantern show, mysterious and captivating. She licked her lips and grinned. In all my life, I had never seen anything so dangerous or so lovely. Any residual feelings I might have harboured for my ex-wife dissipated like ice in a hot skillet. I grinned back at her like a happy boy. I had nearly thirty years under the sky, but at that moment I felt right bucked, and more like an unseasoned greenhorn than a veteran. She had that kind of effect on me sure enough.

Spindrift's voice split the mood like an axe through kindling.

'I'd be happy to let you two alone once we've answered a few questions and I've finished explaining some important things to Colin here. Rowan, I'd be grateful if you let the man take charge of his senses for just a few minutes while we talk. I need to ask him a few things and he'll make no sense at all while he's sprite-touched, now will he?'

'No magic at work here, Satan. Nothing nature couldn't lay claim to.'

'Yes, well, stop lending nature such a big helping hand, the pair of you.'

I pulled on my socks and laced up my shoes, and that was when the itch in my brain burned into a fully lit flare.

'Doc, why does Rowan keep calling you Satan?'

The tawny girl chuckled fetchingly, 'Why not? It's his name. Always has been, for a long, long, long time. Is that not so, Mr Satan Spindrift?'

My mind spun like a top, 'Is this true?' I had no doubt she was telling the truth but I wanted confirmation from his own lips.

'Yes, it is. My name used to be something else, something much finer, but I lost it when I made a foolish mistake many years ago, more years than I care to remember. I am the first and original Satan from the *gospels*, and I know what has been written about me... But you don't want to believe everything you read. There really are two sides to every story I promise you. I am a true soldier of God, protector of the ancient people of the fey,' he nodded at Rowan, 'and a warrior at the wall to defend the Eden born. That's you, Colin, you and your kind.'

My legs suddenly felt weak as water and I plumped myself down carelessly, landing like a sack of stones on the chair that still held my jacket, collar, and tie. My tongue seemed thick and useless in my mouth, numb. My entire focus was on the lean man standing in the firelight, his face glowing red as a demon with reflected heat. Rowan's voice came gently into my ear and I realised her hands were soft on my shoulders. I felt the warmth of her breath brush my cheek.

'Satan is one of a kind. He is strong in the law, stalwart, honest, and trusted by our wisest council. You can accept what he says as the truth. He is a shield dog of God. A fighter. It has been a long time since I've set eyes on him, but the fact that he's here tells me that the danger is real and that it's very close. There is a creature called the Sha-aneer, we think of it as the worm of the deep earth. It is hungry and vile. You wouldn't invite it to dinner unless you wanted to lose all your other guests. But if Satan is here you can be sure it is close by. He hunts it. He destroys it before it destroys all of us.'

I stuttered, 'I've seen it, I've heard it.' I gazed open-eyed at Spindrift, the man I now knew was called, Satan. 'I knew it wasn't a disease or a gas when you were spinning that yarn to Maitland, but he swallowed the story whole. What story are you telling me, now? Can I believe you?'

'I'm going to tell you nothing but the truth, Colin. You deserve nothing less.'

'Thank-you. And may I also ask, why did you strip me naked while I was unconscious? Was it to perform a medical examination, or something else?'

'But, no, sir! We didn't do that. We didn't lay a finger on you. Colin, you disappeared. You vanished completely. One moment you were on your knees listening to us make our vow and the next you were gone! Just your clothing remained in a pile on the floor. That's what I wanted to ask you. Where did you go? Do you know? Do you remember anything?'

~16~

'I did *what*?'

'You disappeared. Your corporeal body vanished. You were gone for about ten minutes and when you reappeared you were over there by the door, curled up like a ball and shivering. You were freezing cold. Rowan warmed you with her body while I got you a sheet from my bed. We carried you to the table to get you higher up and nearer the fire. The floor in this room is stone flagged and bitterly cold as I'm sure you know. We couldn't leave you lying there.'

The words 'Rowan warmed you with her body' stood out in letters of fire. How did she do that? I held my silence but my mind ran riot. I was very glad to be decently dressed just then. My sinful flesh was heated enough to set a spark to the coldest stone flagged floor.

Spindrift continued, 'You must have been unconscious for at least another five minutes. You were dead to the world and your pulse was thready. If Rowan hadn't previously shared the sprite sap with you I doubt you could have survived the experience.'

'Sprite sap?' I turned to her. '*Sprite* sap?'

She nodded. 'It's a fluid drawn from the very sinews of the tree of life itself. It rose into my mouth like sweet liquor when our lips touched and I shared it with you. I had to. The kiss was strong and the liquor flooded my mouth. We shared three times. Once is polite between friends, just a medicinal tonic you understand, but three! Well now. That's rare, Colin Cahoon, let me tell you that's very rare. I will explain why when we have more...' She looked across at Spindrift and drew slightly away from me. 'When we have more time.'

Her eyes in the mirror had held a promise I wanted them to keep. I prayed we would find the time. Somehow, we must make the time. Her hands felt hot against my shirt. I almost expected the fabric to smoulder. That evening was taking me along a very strange and unusual path, but if that incredible, unbelievable woman was its destination I would be happy enough. I would run into the strangeness with my knees high and my arms pumping.

'Colin,' Spindrift was speaking. 'Can you remember anything of what happened to you when you left here? It is important.'

My head was empty. No, not empty. It was full of Rowan and her implied promise. I closed my eyes and concentrated, I put the spirit woman away from me with a pang of regret and tried to go back to the moment when she and Spindrift were singing. I remembered how my soul had lifted and soared with the sound... And then it came back to me. The memory fell back into my mind all in one piece. My eyes flew open. 'It called me "Satan's plaything!" I remember, I remember it all.'

Spindrift frowned. 'What did?'

'It was a moon, some kind of a great black ball. It was the size of a city, no bigger, and it was out beyond the red planet. It looked burned. It was huge and it swallowed the light. I could barely see it, even when I got close, but it knew I was there. That was it, it also knew *I* was there and it was angry. It called me Satan's plaything and then... and then...' I shook my head. 'And then nothing. I woke up here on the table.'

The expression on Spindrift's face would have frozen the spine of a tiger in that moment. It was so alien. It seemed almost inhumanly inert, completely blank. He looked like a clockwork toy whose spring had unwound and all movement had ceased at once. His was the face of a living corpse, vitality sucked from his dark cheek. And then he was back in the room and energy radiated from him once more. I could feel the force of his personality return to his body like a shell rammed into a cannon's breech. Then, in that moment, more than ever before, I understood the profound nature of his martial aspect. I understood how he was God's warrior defending the wall, as he had described himself. I sensed Rowan stiffen and stand taller beside me. She felt it too.

He looked at the ceiling as if seeing through it to the sky beyond, then back at me, his eyes little more than flickering slits. There was an awkward pause during which I heard the distant slam of a door. All else was silence. I had no idea of the hour but it felt very late.

'How?' Spindrift was trying each word on for size before uttering it. His jaw was working as if he had swallowed something unpleasant but was loath to spit it out. 'How,' he started again, 'how is this possible?'

Rowan and I waited. He wasn't asking the question of us but of himself. He began to move around the room, darting glances at me every few moments as if I was an armed grenade about to explode.

'That place you describe is real,' he finally blurted. 'It is as real as this room, solid as this table.' He slammed the flat of his hand down with a crack and I jumped. 'It is a place I know very well, Colin, very well indeed. I have described it to you this very night. What you saw is the spaceship that carried us from Eden to Earth's solar system all those millions of years ago, it was my home during that long interstellar voyage and I remember it with such deep, deep longing. Inside that black shell, inside that burned moon, is Heaven. My Heaven, my haven. And I am forbidden to return as all my brothers bar two have done. What you saw was the GODS, the General Organism Development System, devised by the Edenites to carry their hopes to a new world. It waits there in the asteroid belt until it knows that the offspring of Eden is free to thrive, and you will have built Heaven on Earth, a new Eden in which the offspring can prosper and be bountiful. Looking at what you are doing to each other here I believe it has a long wait.' He smiled grimly. 'If the Sha-aneer wasn't your greatest enemy I would wonder how long mankind could survive without wiping each other out. You spend more time and squander more wealth devising instruments of destruction than you do on medicine or caring for your elderly. How long will it be before you develop weapons that could destroy your world and everything on it? Answer me that, Captain Colin Cahoon!'

He drew a breath and flapped a hand in my direction, 'Sorry, sorry, my friend. The voice of a creature who has seen too many wars and so many promising civilisations torn down and forgotten. Not your fault. But how is it possible that you have physically travelled out into space and seen the GODS? How is it possible that it has spoken to you and you have returned here? I can tell you that a human body subject to the freezing vacuum of space would not come back here curled into a ball and shivering. It would freeze solid, or else explode when every drop of fluid in its cells expanded at once. So how is this possible? How could it happen? Hm?'

I had never heard Spindrift speak for so long or with such passion. I didn't know what to say. And how could I answer him when I had no more of an idea about what had happened to me than he did? And then Rowan spoke. I could hear the spreading smile in her voice. 'Well now, that would explain a lot of this mystery without too much of this dancing the hoop, wouldn't it. That would settle the matter right quickly and explain why there are these lovely, choice fruits hanging from the wrong tree, and that right enough.'

Spindrift almost groaned, 'Please, my lady, I beg of you, no more riddles.'

'Riddles? Riddles you say? No, not riddles, dear Satan, but answers. You want answers and I may have some for you. But first – a question.' She leaned around until her face was almost in front of mine. Her glorious eyes danced with mischief and something else, something wise.

'Tell me, you lovely man, what do you know about your mother?'

~17~

I hadn't known what to expect, but if I'd had to guess the nature of her question it sure wouldn't have been *that*. And, in fact, truth to tell, I couldn't help her.

'Nothing much, not about my birth mother. I could tell you about my *mothers*. There were seven of them. I was brought up in an orphanage.'

'And did they tell you about your parents? Anything?'

'Nothing! There was nothing they could tell me. I was a foundling. Fetched up to their door in a basket by the drovers who found me. I was told to be grateful for every day I was alive, and I was then and I still am. Something else could have found me other than those drovers, something hungry with a taste for baby meat, and then I guess I wouldn't have been so lucky. And I guess if there hadn't been the Persimmon scholarship I couldn't have gone to college, and if there hadn't been the Hayden police initiative I wouldn't have spent my year working with the pathology lab. Good luck has followed me every day of my life. Mine is a charmed life. Fortune smiles on me.'

Spindrift eyed me, 'I wonder how many other men might think that? Men who had been blown up on the front lines, injured, and then nearly burned by the Sha-aneer, I wonder how many of them might think themselves lucky? They might think fate bears a powerful grudge.'

'Well, doc, sure. Yes, I got blown up, true, but it was thanks to that, that I met you. You healed me just fine, and then you pulled me out of the frontline, *and* you protected me from the fire in that tunnel. And now, thanks to you, I've met Miss Rowan here, and that's just fine and dandy by me too. Who wouldn't feel lucky? I'll say it again, I live a charmed life.'

Rowan stepped around my chair and lifted her bottom up onto the table. Pure poetry in motion. God must have taken a long time over creating her, love of His craft shone in every fine curve.

She shook her head, 'Luck is where you find it, or so I've been told. Some seek it in a bank vault and others in a fishing boat, others in the strength of their two good shoulders and hard work. Some see food on the table as good fortune, others look for it in strong drink. Luck is only where you'll find it if you have eyes to see it. Not everyone can. The Lady Fortune can walk everywhere with some people and every waking moment she'll be holding their hand – and they never know she's there. But, tell me now, where is your heart? In the soil and the trees, the fire in the hearth and volcanoes, the water in rivers lakes, and oceans, or in the sky and the clouds? I think I know the answer, but tell me anyway.'

It was a curious question. Where was my heart? The way she said it was odd but I instantly knew what she meant. I answered without hesitation.

'I couldn't live without a view of the sky. I'm all stumped as to why I wasn't born covered in feathers. The sky is my home, it is. I love its aching blue in spring, its silver and yellow mists in winter, the golden orange of autumn, the big majestic dome of indigo in deep summer. For its every mood and every season, I dip my cup into the sky and I drink deep of it. Yes, that's the truth of it. If my heart's anywhere it's up there in the sky.'

'And your dreams?'

'My *dreams*?' I laughed aloud. 'What is this? You're reading me like a wise woman. How could you? No, never mind. In my dreams, as a child I would fly out there, under the stars and around the moon. I have tumbled through clouds, floated in starlight and breathed deep from the cold air at the edge of space.'

'And how often did you awake to find you were cold and wet?'

How did she know? How could she know? It had been my shame to rouse in my icy cold, wet bed in soaked pyjamas. The mothers had thought I had wet myself and it happened so often that they chided me severely. I had felt the paddle more than once, a paddle for a puddle, they said. They called me a baby and a piss-pot and made me stand in nothing but a diaper in class – and in the lunch-room – and I would have to go without food. I had been punished and mocked right hard in many ways, but the wetting continued, and finally I had been sent for medical examinations. But the good doctors reported that it wasn't my poor bladder that was at fault. They called it a 'condition', said it was night sweats and that it was due to my growth spurts. That was my first taste of what medicine could mean to a person. It changed my life for the better and set my mind on my future career. Even so, after my wonderful dreams the sopping sheets had been humiliating. I told Rowan so. She nodded that fine head of her's and smiled with a hint of pity. And then she blazed with fury.

'Why did we not find you sooner? We could have brought you home long ago. You grew up without understanding what you were. Made you stand in a nappy like a naughty imp, did they? Made you starve, did they? And they had the temerity to call themselves *mothers*! Where is this nightmare home for cruelty and ignorance? I'd go there right now and I'll tell them to their faces what I think of their loving care. I'll burn the bastard place down with them in it, see if I don't. Then we'll see if the old crones still want to bully a child, mock him, beat him, and starve him. I'm surprised you haven't been damaged for life. I suppose even the sweetest flowers have bloomed in the ripest shite. Sorry, but I'm that angry. They would do that to one of us? Bitches, dog bitches they are, and I apologise to dogs who would never do such a thing to a puppy.'

She had leapt from the table and had filled the air with her fists and flailing arms. Anger radiated off her like steam. I had never thought badly of the mothers before. I had been the wicked child in my wet bed. They didn't look cruel when they beat me, just tired and sad that it had to be done to strike the message home. Even in the face of Rowan's fury I couldn't find it in my heart to blame them for my faults. But once more something she had said glowed in my mind like fire.

'Rowan, what do you mean, "one of us"? What are you saying? Please, what are you telling me?'

Spindrift was looking at me with fresh intensity, his brows raised and a half-smile teasing his lips. 'I should have seen it before,' he breathed. 'It's so obvious now you point it out, Rowan. I can see the signs quite clearly. Remarkable.'

'Can you, old warrior? Can you? See his eyes? See that mop of white blond hair. Look at his carriage. He's surely a prince amongst men, or he would be if he *was* a man.'

They were both grinning at me as if I had just done something very clever, but I was feeling stupid. They were telling me something, evidently giving me clues, but I was none the wiser. Something strange and incredible was tugging at my mind's eye, but that was impossible. They couldn't mean that? Rowan couldn't be saying that? Surely, how could it be possible?

'You know what I'm saying, Colin Cahoon. You know it, sure enough. You're one of us, one of the fey, a sprite. And an air sprite from what you've told me. You have been flying in your realm when your conscious mind told you that you were still asleep in bed. When you woke up wet it wasn't from your bladder or growth sweats, it was water from the air and the clouds, condensation they call it. I must do something about this. I have to...'

And she stepped up to me, took me in her arms and kissed me thoroughly. The cool, pure essence of life flowed between us once more. She pressed urgently against me and I reacted, mashing my body hard against her's.

And then she was gone. Spindrift and I were alone in his room and it seemed suddenly a much emptier place.

~18~

It was well past one o'clock in the morning when I finally shook hands with my friend who I now knew to be called Satan Spindrift, and walked numbly back to my room. I washed my hands and face then brushed my favourite cinnamon flavoured tooth powder against my teeth. Mundane actions to conclude an extraordinary day. The tincture Rowan had shared with me seemed to roar and surge through my body. I had never felt more alive.

I extinguished my candle and drew back my heavy blackout curtains. To others that night sky would have seemed dull and overcast, but to me on that wonderful day it was a magnificent pile of massing clouds and the white moon pressed fingers of light down through gaps in the clouds, caressing the landscape like a lover. I gazed upwards, completely enchanted by the scene. I should have been exhausted. I should have found sleep beckoning at my shoulder and ready to close my eyes with a weary sigh, but I couldn't. My mind was dancing around inside my skull on wings of light.

Then the radiance of the moon washed over me and I felt its touch like a gentle caress. My skin had become so sensitive that its gentle exploration made me feel like a baby under the amazed fingers of a new mother. I stripped naked and, luxuriated in the light. I hadn't been in my room since before dinner and my fire was cold. I should have been shivering in the intense chill, but I felt nothing of the sort. The heat of the *moon* warmed my flesh while Rowan's wonderful elixir glowed within me. I half expected to see its radiance shine out of my skin and paint my walls with glory. I shut my eyes and breathed in the air of a fresh new world, one I had never even dared dream existed. I had lived nearly thirty years and yet there I was, a newborn creature naked and made whole in the light. And that was when it happened.

Without knowing how I was windborne and spiralling my way towards the clouds, arms out like wings and mouth open to the cool, fresh air of early morning. There was no taint of war up there, no carrion stink or cess reek. It was a clean place and it washed me free of care. I was beyond the reach of colonels and generals, big guns, and mines. Even the Sha-aneer's blight, the worm's fire, couldn't reach me in my realm of silver light and sweet air.

I pierced the clouds like a bullet and swam up beyond them to a magical place of clear skies, brilliant stars, and the shining, almost full face of the moon. I was soaked with cloud dew and vapour as I had been as a child, and I laughed with joy to finally understand why I was wet and would need to towel myself dry when I returned to my room.

But then I paused. Would I return? Why should I return? This was my home now, here amongst the clouds and the stars. On the far eastern horizon a pearlescent mist already promised the light of a remote dawn in a few hours. I was higher than a mountaintop and I could see the curvature of the Earth. This was my place, here. Why should I return to that humble room and that captain's khaki when I could bide here in paradise?

I remembered the intense thrill of my youthful night adventures, which I had believed back then to have been only in my dreams, but this was so much better, so much richer an experience. This time I knew it to be real, impossibly real. I was awake and I revelled in it. My heart beat against the cage of my ribs like the pounding wings of a great bird. I spread my arms and pressed my feet together, holding myself rigid as a bar. I was silver in the moonlight, and I imagined myself to be the living image of the sterling silver crucifix I had purchased back home before leaving for France. It was lying on top of my beautiful leather-bound *Holy Bible* in the top drawer of my tallboy back in my room. They had both brought me a great deal of comfort in this strange land of death and hatred. They had reminded me that Christ had died on the cross in agony that I might live, and that even He had doubted at the end. Nine hours of torture on that tree, fighting for every breath. Who can blame Him for crying out "Eli, Eli, lema sabachthani?"

And then I wondered, but what of me now, Lord? What am I to you? Have you forsaken me? Do You still hear me? Are You still with me? Are You still close to me, as I feel you to be in my heart? Do you still abide with me? What can a naked man poised in mid-air high above the billowing clouds expect from his saviour?

It was then that I felt that touch of grace once more, and I knew I was saved. It was truly numinous. Doubt is the nature of man, and faith is the nature of redemption. A wise man, a prophet, once said that the righteous would live by faith. I had the courage of faith, and whatever new experiences my changed estate might bring I knew I would meet them gladly, with my saviour at my side.

It was then that a thought came to me, and even though I hadn't moved a muscle to make it happen I found myself winging back down into the clouds. I was almost blind in the misty vapour and silvery spray streamed from my head and shoulders like a cloak with a slender, argent train. I didn't know the precise direction I needed to take or even the distance I had to travel, but something in me had calculated my journey to the inch. In the whisk of a swallow's tail I found myself circling a brooding building on the hillside above the village of Natres. The convent of the Sisters of the Weeping Heart. What had drawn me there? Curiosity I guess, that's all it was. I wanted to see this place with its holy spring water and its sisters who lived in isolation from their neighbours. I hoped that none of the sisters would be abroad at such an hour to see me. What might they make of a naked man, flying, and dripping with cloud water? I would probably have appeared to be an hallucination, or a nightmare. Or, perhaps, they might have run screaming and genuflecting to throw themselves flat before the altar. Would they be praying for forgiveness while believing their sinful imaginations had surprised them with visions of naked men. I reproached myself for such thoughts about the holy sisters, but could still feel the pert grin on my Caliban cheeks.

One small window was lit, high up in the flat, almost featureless wall facing back towards the crest of the hill. Perhaps its position tucked away from common sight was the reason the occupant felt able to ignore the blackout, or the fact that it was a good distance from the front. Most of the convent's better architectural attributes faced out from an escarpment overlooking the village, as if it had been designed to impress its neighbours with its elegance. This rear facing wall was simple and bland, almost brutally so. It consisted of flat dark stone cut with mathematical precision, and near its gables there was that single square of quivering yellow light. I had to see who was about at so early an hour. Call me nosy but I couldn't resist. I rose to the window and peeked in, expecting to see an aged insomniac nun at her devotions. What greeted my astonished eyes couldn't have been more different and the scene almost wrenched a cry from my lips.

The people on the bed were as naked as me. A kneeling woman was facing me, her legs spread wide. She was straddling a man's hips. Her eyes shut and her mouth open she was performing a piston-like action on the man's penis, bouncing up and down with her back towards the man's head. He was thrusting up into her with his brown fingers buried in the pale flesh of her hips. She had very short hair but that didn't detract from her evidently young and very feminine allure. She was slender and full breasted, and looked to be in a state of considerable arousal. The man was an anonymous actor in the performance. I couldn't see his face, the woman completely shielded his upper body, but, in any case, he didn't matter. *She* got all my attention. I watched in complete fascination, wondering how often such a scene must have been played out in the upper rooms of that holy house. I presumed she was a servant girl taking advantage of the late hour to steal some private time with her beau. Finally, guiltily, I got set to turn away and let the couple have the privacy they deserved. I admit that watching their performance had brought some sympathetic heat to my own loins, and she was certainly a sweet sight, wanton enough to catch any man's eyes, but I was an inadvertent voyeur and had to practice some degree of discipline. I would depart and leave them to their sport.

And then the man sat up to paw at the woman's breasts and press his lips against her slender column of a neck – and I saw his face for the first time. Even though it was little more than a brown smudge behind an immense and damply smeared moustache he was unmistakeable.

It was Captain Morel.

~19~

The next morning, I awoke back in my bed with a kaleidoscope of images scudding across my mind. I was still naked, but was relieved to find my bedding was dry. I reached out to grip the towel draped over the back of the bentwood chair beside my bed. It was very damp and icy. I basked in glorious memories of the night before and grinned to myself. Then the rapping sound that had roused me was repeated. I shouted out, 'Just a minute,' climbed into my robe and opened the door. Private Greenhalgh stood in the corridor looking concerned.

'Sorry, sir, I've been knocking for ages. Captain Spindrift's compliments, sir, but he's expecting you at the stables. He sent me to remind you and to bring you this.' He handed me a rapidly cooling mug of the strange, mahogany coloured liquid that we all agreed was probably coffee, or at least a distant relative. I took it and sipped gingerly. It took the gloss off the morning and added a layer of something unpleasant to my tongue. I nodded to the fidgeting corpsman.

'Please inform the good captain that I shall join him in just a few minutes, and thanks for this.'

I shut the door, opened the window, and dumped the 'coffee' onto the ground outside, my usual practice when someone brought me the stuff. I was sorry for anything trying grow out there, but rather a French weed than me. This was war after all.

I was with Spindrift a little over ten minutes later, still buttoning my greatcoat against the chill of the morning. By then he was no longer waiting for me at the stables but in the cobbled square by the outer entrance of our quarters. He had brought along the same pair of horses we had ridden to Natres a few days earlier. So much had happened since then that it seemed impossible to imagine it had all taken place in less than forty-eight hours. Spindrift placed a welcoming hand on my arm and handed me my horse's reins.

'Morning, Colin. How are you feeling? Sleep okay?' A half-moon smile played across his lips and his dark eyes glittered from under the brim of his peaked cap. The uniform suited him, he had a natural martial air. I didn't. I strongly believe that during my entire spell in the AEF I looked very much like a comedy character from an amateur revue. Nothing ever seemed to fit right. My limbs were too long and my body too slender. I didn't so much wear the khaki as flap about in it. Instead of a peaked officer's cap I was wearing one of those round tin hats that I suspected made my head look like a metal mushroom. They said those hats could deflect a rifle bullet but I knew from experience that they couldn't stop a direct hit. No matter, it was metal instead of cloth and every little helped. Spindrift's clothes looked tailor-made and fitted him perfectly.

'Fine,' I grinned back. 'Took a while to settle down, of course, but I managed a few hours before Greenhalgh reclaimed me from the arms of Morpheus and hustled me out to you. I don't remember any plans to go riding today. Sorry if I forgot.'

'No, no, you didn't forget, my friend. I just felt, after the successful turn of events yesterday, that we should pursue the question of the disappearing children and visit The Sisters of the Weeping Heart without delay. It's a pleasant enough morning, and I have the distinct feeling that we have much to do and a limited time to do it in.'

We climbed into our saddles. Previously I had always needed a mounting post, but that day I swung up easily with one foot in the stirrup. I felt strong, and despite my lack of sleep well rested. Spindrift regarded me with a grin as we trotted out onto the road once more. He waited until we were clear of the hospital grounds and on our way before striking up a conversation. He first gazed around to make sure we were completely alone.

'What did you do last night after you returned to your room? It must have been tough to come to terms with everything you'd learned from Rowan.'

I shook my head and breathed deeply for a moment.

'It was as if I'd always known I was different, but not how or why. She's an astonishing creature isn't she. Magical isn't the word. Enchanting, perhaps? Is she a species of human?'

'Human, no, but more humane than most men and women. She's no more human than you, Colin, and certainly no less a person. She's one of an ancient race, older than mankind. Think of her as a physical manifestation of spirit, the spirit of soil and the plants. The older religions would have man borne of clay after God breathed life into it, and in a very real way that's true. I think we can take the idea of God fashioning the woman Eve from Adam's rib with a large pinch of salt, don't you, but the principle holds true. Humans evolved from creatures that first climbed out of the primordial ooze countless millions of years ago – with a little help from us along the way. But the species of creatures known variously as the fey, sprites and elementals, they are truly the things of creation made aware. They are the spirits of soil, water, air and fire, each with their own particular characteristics, and they are bound together and made whole by the fifth element, perhaps the most important element of them all.'

'Iron?'

'Sorry, iron you say? No, something far stronger than iron, and more precious than gold. All such minerals are bound into the rocks and the soil and enrich the oceans and rivers. No, the fifth element is love. It's the binding that holds everything together and it's very powerful in the elementals, people like you. Tell me, did you test your powers last night or did you just dream about them as you did when you were a child?'

I told him everything, about my flight above the clouds, about my moment of doubt. And then I told him what I'd seen at the convent, about captain Morel with the woman. He frowned and squinted down the road as if he could bridge the distance and see for himself the mystery woman from the convent at Natres and the captain of gendarmerie.

'You must let me know if you see this woman amongst the Sisters of the Weeping Heart today. Do you think you would recognise her again?'

I thought back to the bucking beauty riding Morel with such intense concentration, her body pumping like the pistons on Casey Jones's *Cannonball Express* on its final fatal journey. The image of her cropped hair plastered to her finely shaped head with sweat would be forever impossible to erase from my mind.

'I'm sure of it. She was no Rowan but she was a striking figure all the same. Not a girl, you understand, but a young woman in the full bloom of early maturity. She would turn heads wherever she was. Yes, I'd know her again, even with her clothes on.'

'Good! We might find it hard to convince a group of nuns that we need to see them all naked.'

I laughed merrily. I was in fine fettle that morning but still couldn't quite come to terms with my changing fortunes. I had to ask.

'Doc, what am I? What am I really? Do you know?'

'Yes, yes I know. You are a fine person, you will be a gifted doctor, and you are an air sprite. Last night you picked up something from me, a stray thought perhaps, and you visited the place that stood out most strongly in my mind. The great GODS ship of Eden. The ship tasted my influence in you somehow and threw you back to me. I am not its favourite servant. It thinks me errant and arrogant and perhaps it is right. But I serve it here on Earth by protecting the Eden born. I just do it my way, that's all.'

A thought occurred to me and I changed my tack. 'Why are we interested in the woman from the convent? I thought it likely she was a servant and Morel her lover. I saw nothing suspicious in it.'

'You said her hair was cropped. That would be strange in an attractive and sexually active woman, don't you think? Perhaps I'm wrong but that would make me suspect she's one of the sisterhood. If such is the case she's married to Christ, and Christ makes a poor cuckold. If discovered in such an act she would likely be whipped, forced to wear a cilice, thrown out of her order or worse. Her life would be ruined. Would she risk being caught in the act in the very convent where she lives, works, and prays? Is Morel worth all that? Really?'

He was right. I shook my head. 'No, no he isn't.'

'Then what is she doing?'

It was a good question. A very good question.

~20~

We took tea with Worsnip who was enjoying a rare quiet time. He only had two customers in his care, a Yorkshireman whose leg had been fractured by a stack of sandbags falling from one of the little trains he was helping unload, and a London man who had been shot in the hand. The former was an amiable enough fellow who cheerfully upbraided himself for his carelessness, the latter was a surly, taciturn type who regarded us from under beetling brows. He made me think of an old chimp I had once seen in the Abilene zoo. The London man looked just as trapped and sullen as the poor creature in its cage. I mentioned this to Worsnip who nodded. 'Yes, I know just what you mean. Well, he's got every right to be ticked off. We've had a spate of injured hands from the front just recently and the authorities are cracking down on them. Chaps are deliberately sticking their hands in the air to get them shot at, damn poor show. Cusper there says he was reaching for a butterfly because it was so pretty! Rot! He's left-handed and was injured in his right, and that's a bit too convenient for me. Lost a finger but otherwise he'll be fine. Thinks he's going home but that's not going to happen. He'll be patched up and shipped back. Quick as spit he'll be back on the line, good as new except he'll be short one finger. He can still hold a rifle. On the other hand, Carmody's a farmhand on civvie street and honest as the day. He untied a rope when the load was too heavy for him to handle and, well, quite frankly, crunch. And here he is. Been over here since the start and done his bit. I'm going to recommend he goes home for a touch of R and R. He's earned it. Take a while for the leg to heal properly, compound fracture you know. He might as well recover over in Blighty as here. He'll probably end up in one of the medical units they've set up in country houses. I hear some of them have rather lovely grounds just perfect for a stroll, not that he'll be walking anywhere anytime soon.'

'Michael,' Spindrift interrupted, 'do you mind if I change the subject? Can I ask, have you heard any rumours connecting the convent with these missing children. Have the sisters said anything?'

'What? Well, that's a rum question I must say. Like what? Why do you ask?'

'Helen has been out amongst the villagers, has she heard anything? Anything at all?'

'Ask her, old man, she's here.' He called out, 'Helen, have you got a moment, please?'

The horse-faced woman bustled out of the building's back rooms, drying her reddened hands on a linen cloth. She flashed us a smile of recognition that softened her features with a surprisingly pleasing effect. She suddenly looked years younger and I warmed to her, responding with a sympathetic grin.

She freshened our cups from the teapot, poured one for herself, and joined us by taking a seat, crossing her legs pertly and placing her mug on one knee. Spindrift asked her his question about the convent, and then added one about captain Morel, wondering if she knew how the locals felt about him. She sucked at her lips thoughtfully and gazed at the ceiling for a moment before answering.

'How did you know I speak French?'

Spindrift grinned his trademark, half-moon grin, 'I presumed you must to go out amongst the villagers. How can you ask them about their symptoms if you don't talk the language?'

She smiled and nodded, 'Good thinking, nice observation, I like that.' Her voice was clipped and displayed the serene authority of the English upper crust, there was also an evident lilt of arch humour. 'Most people wander about in a daze and wouldn't know an original thought if it bit them on the arse. Yes, I speak the language, well enough to gossip a bit and ask them about their symptoms. Spent half my life over here, albeit considerably further east and south of this benighted place.' She laughed, 'Daddy always said French would come in handy one day. Bet he didn't think I'd be using it to shout "push" at a French housewife whose baby's due, or for asking an arthritic old peasant where it hurts. Ha, before now it came in most handy for telling some old Duke what would happen to his wandering hand if he didn't keep it to himself. Nearly as bad as the Italians, the French aristocrats. I like the common people, they have more respect for each other and for me. Yes, I like that. Sorry, listen to me rambling. Lovely old Worsnip here has heard all this before, he just rolls his eyes like the darling man he is and helps me up onto my soapbox, then off I go like a clockwork rabbit. Nice to have two fresh pairs of ears to chew at, you will forgive me while I prattle away I hope?'

We nodded. All the time she was talking Helen had been taking surreptitious glances at me. Finally, she seemed to make her mind up and turned to face me. 'Sorry to be so blunt, but have you been on the stage or on the cinema screen? You seem familiar somehow. I know I saw you here the other day, but, that isn't what I mean. I don't know, you just seem so, yes, so familiar.'

I shook my head and told her I was here fresh from medical school. I'd never even done dramatic theatre while I was at college.

'Well,' she said, blushing faintly, 'if the medical profession doesn't work out for you, you should think about the arts. I would say you could give mister Douglas Fairbanks a run for his money. My word, yes.'

She turned her attention back to Spindrift, 'The convent and Morel, two of the favourite subjects for gossip and rumour around here, and a girl has to find her entertainment where she may, don't you agree? First, Morel. His family has lived around here for hundreds of years. Most of them kept themselves to themselves, but our captain Auguste Morel is the first to come out of the sawdust pile and be seen in public. Can you believe he threatened to have a man who beat his wife shot?' We nodded. 'You know about that?'

'Yes,' said Spindrift. 'He told us about it.'

'Well, in my mind that was one point in his favour, but the villagers don't agree. In Natres, what happens between a man and his wife *stays* between a man and his wife. They resent Morel's high handedness. The women here also think there's something odd about him. They call him a "hot little fish". Some believe he has a wife, but no-one has ever seen her. Others believe he has a mistress, but no-one knows who it might be. They say he "struts around like a cock chicken looking for his spurs", and I can see what they mean. I like a moustache on a man, but there should be a level of balance between the moustache and the face behind it. Morel wears his like a barrier, a shield. He hides behind it like a fox behind a bush. Why? What's he hiding? His father killed himself you know.'

This last statement came as a shock. 'He did what?' I blurted.

'Shot himself the day after Morel's eighteenth birthday. Nice way to make sure his son never forgot the anniversary of his death. His widow, Morel's mother, sold up and left without a backwards glance. Never been back. So, yes, Morel is considered something of an enigma, for all that he grew up here, as did his father and his father's father going back generations. They say he won't let his home soil dirty his shoes, which is a neat way of putting it.'

Spindrift leaned forward, 'What do you think of him?'

'Slippery, used to the depths. Prefers the shadows, very like an eel. We had a geography teacher like him when I was at school. He used to have some of the prettier, younger girls come to his rooms for tea. Always alone. The girls never spoke about the tea-parties afterwards, even though we were jealous and asked them if there had been cakes and biscuits, and whether they drank tea or lemonade? You know the sort of thing; and you know the sort of girl. Pretty, delicate creatures, like china dolls. Very shy and very quiet. Little mice, born victims, red-riding hoods waiting for the big bad wolf to knock at grandma's door. Justin Elliot, yes, that was his name. Licked his lips when he spoke to us in class like he was tasting the air to make sure we were still fresh. Then, one day, one of the girl's fathers came to the school and horse-whipped the man and then proceeded to withdraw a military swordstick in front of his class. His daughter had sent him a letter asking whether some of the things Mr Elliot had done to her were, well, proper, and she went into some detail. And she had also asked whether she might be excused from doing some of the things Elliot had asked her to do to him in return, because she didn't like them at all. Not even for a teacher and in exchange for cakes and lemonade. I think the poor man would have killed Elliot if the terrified schoolgirls' screams hadn't brought some of the other teachers running. Can't blame the father, can you. Elliot was a filthy beast of a man, a cad, a predator. I don't know what happened to the vile brute after that, but I'd bet he was never allowed near little girls any more. At least I hope not. Well then, Morel is like that around women. You can feel his hot little lusty eyes follow you when you walk past him. Even some of the better preserved older women say the same. He always wants to be in control. They say they can feel his heat when he looks at them. They say he's sick with it, starving, but he's never been known to take a single bite from the local menu. Not even so much as a nibble. And then some days he looks like he's had a good meal somewhere and he ignores everyone, even the pretty ones. He's been getting his oats from someone, but the village can't find out who's filling his bowl for him. Ha, the town gossips hate not knowing, it's driving them mad. Some of them even thought it might be me. Sorry, but really, I have more taste. Oh, excuse the pun, unintentional I assure you. So, there you are that's Morel. A creepy little lecher in a captain's uniform. Now then, the convent, and this is where things get really interesting.'

~21~

'You made quite an impression on nurse Helen.'
'She just thought she'd seen me before, that's all.'
'I'd say she was hoping to see you again.'
'Please, Doc, this conversation is embarrassing.'
'Yes, I'm sorry, please forgive me. I needed to warn you about this. I think Rowan has reactivated something in you, something inherent to who and what you are, but it has remained quiet until last night. Elementals have certain gifts. May I ask you, what did you think of Rowan, speaking between friends? Please, be honest.'
'Rowan? As well you know, she's beautiful, gorgeous in fact.'
'Yes, she is, that's true. But, how does she compare to any other woman you've ever seen. And I mean any woman, Mary Pickford say, or Maude Fealy or Theda Bara?'
I'd been to the movies and I knew the actresses he was talking about. They were called the "stars in the movie firmament" or some such claptrap. They were fine looking women sure enough, but how did they compare with Rowan?
'No-one else comes close. She's wonderful, the purest beauty I've ever seen. Flawless.' In saying it I realised it was true.
'Yes, yes she is. A perfect example of her race, and they are all noted for their beauty, not just the women but also the men. Elementals also have a talent called "Glamour". I've seen it at work without understanding quite *how* it works. Luckily, I'm immune, but humans are prey to it. You see, Helen wasn't just seeing you when she looked at you, she was seeing the most perfect version of you, the ideal Colin Cahoon, a sublime vision of masculine magnificence. Still you, but with all your little faults wiped away by Glamour. I don't know what mister Darwin would make of it as a survival trait, but it's there and you've got it. God knows what you'll do to a bunch of nuns, my friend, but you've made a hard-boiled English nurse go weak at the knees. Ah, good, here we are, the gate. I'll do the talking.'
Helen had spent another half hour filling us in about the nuns and the convent. It had proved very illuminating. Few of the nuns had come from the local villages, and the few that had, had been hand-picked and invited to become aspirants and then postulants. The first process had been accelerated

from two weeks to a long weekend. Girls who returned home on the Monday spoke of the hard work and silence they experienced over the three nights. Once accepted and voted into the community as a postulant, the girls were never seen in the outside world again. They were cloistered for life, and after a year would enter the novitiate before next becoming a sister and then a nun of complete consecration. At that point, the woman would become dedicated to the church and a recognised spouse of Christ. The idea of telling others about the Word of the Lord seems to have been completely bypassed by the sisters at Natres in exchange for prayer and contemplation. Helen didn't know if they were a silent order, but, she said, they might as well be for all the communication they had with the outside world. Most of the Sisters of the Weeping Heart were outsiders, a fact that rankled amongst the people of the little town. They appeared to be a tightly closeted community and I increasingly doubted we would be allowed to pass through the gate, let alone pass Albert Fournier's love on to his sister. In fact, I doubted if we would be allowed to talk with anyone at all and wondered what our plan would be if that proved the case.

Spindrift dismounted and walked to the gate where he pulled at a long thin chain on a pulley. We heard a bell toll in the distance.

He looked at the sky. 'It's about ten or just after, so they shouldn't be at prayers until Sext in around two hours. We should be okay.'

I drew out my watch and examined it. 'I make it six minutes after ten precisely.'

He grinned, 'The sun needs no minute hand, my friend. Ah, here comes somebody now.'

A girl in a white veil scurried to the gate and peered short-sightedly at us through the bars. The white clashed badly with her muddy complexion and highlighted a scattering of painful looking, white headed pimples. She looked at us in horror and recoiled. Making a strangled sound like a rusty hinge she turned and hurried back the way she had come, panting with exertion. She had uttered not a single word and neither had we.

Spindrift raised his eyebrows. 'I don't think we were the people she was expecting to see, do you? Perhaps sisterly compassion doesn't stretch as far as common sociability.'

He lifted his hand to take another tug at the bell, and then lowered it again. A broad woman in black was stamping towards us. She had an inordinately large chin and badly needed a shave. I wondered if mirrors had been banned from the convent. On the evidence to date it would have been a kindness. She barked at Spindrift, her voice a rasping lower register. He answered gently which seemed to infuriate her.

'What do you want?'

'An audience with your Mother Superior, if she is free.'

She tilted her box-like head back and glared at him from behind gun barrel nostrils, which she had trained squarely at his chest. I had received barely a fleeting glance and a cursory sneer before the woman's powerful personality had been turned on my friend. Whatever had struck nurse Helen so forcibly was evidently not working here. I decided to be grateful for the fact, and remained safely mounted on my horse. Strangely enough the horse, which had been carefully trained to remain calm in the face of gunshot, artillery fire and even tanks, was acting skittish as a fresh pony when confronted with the anger flowing from this sister of Christian compassion. I had to pat my horse's sleek neck and talk quietly to her before she would settle.

The nun's next words were delivered with what sounded like a coarse, Scottish lilt.

'American, is it? Well, what are you doing riding up to my gate and scaring what few wits my girls have still got clean out of their empty heads. And you can tell the pretty boy on the horse to stop gawping at me like a fish. I remember when a gentleman would never have remained seated while a lady stands. Those were better times.'

Spindrift took off his cap and offered a little bow, while I climbed from the saddle and peeled off my tin hat. He smiled.

'Have I the honour to be addressing sister Honoria Pietas?'

She made a snorting, choking noise, which I realised must be laughter.

'And are you stupid enough to think the mother superior answers the door to strangers? Even pretty ones and their masters.' She grunted and turned her burly jaw in my direction, but her pink eyes remained firmly glued on Spindrift. 'What do you want? Why are you cluttering the path? And if your horses shit on my road you can clean it up! Understand!'

'Understood,' said Spindrift in a gentle, considered tone that merely shovelled more fuel onto the woman's burning rage. She was literally quivering with the force of it and bared her big, yellow teeth at him. Spittle flecked the corners of her mouth.

'Then you can damn well understand you're not wanted here. Clear off and take your pet monkey with you.'

'We would like, sister, to speak with sister Honoria Pietas on a matter of some importance.'

'What matter of importance?'

'We will discuss it with your Mother Superior. If she wishes to I'm sure she will share it with you after Sext at your midday meal. You and your sisters might indeed be able to help us, but first I must speak with sister Honoria Pietas. I should be very grateful and I promise we won't take up too much of her time.'

'Grateful, are you? Well, we'll see, won't we. What are your names? I won't think she'll want to see anonymous soldier boys no matter what message you have for her.' Spindrift introduce me and then himself. She snorted. 'Wait here,' then glared at me, 'You, pretty boy! I hope you've brought a shovel.'

She stamped away laughing just as a redolent odour reached my nostrils. I turned and watched as my horse raised her tail for the second time and more tight balls of steaming faeces joined the pile in the centre of the dusty path. I wearily unshipped the little shovel from my horse's pack and cleared the mess into the shrubbery. Spindrift spoke to his animal and stroked its nose. It nodded its head and backed delicately off the road into the hedges where it voided its bowels without soiling the path. Spindrift grinned.

'Pick your jaw up, Colin, or our friend the sister sergeant major will want it on a shovel.'

We turned at the sound of a polite cough. A younger, completely different, black robed nun was opening the gate to us and beckoning us in. My heart took a lurching leap into my throat. Her downcast eyes and demure stance couldn't disguise her face. It was her. It was the woman I had seen in bed with Morel.

~22~

Her voice had an utterly charming French musicality. It was light and cultured, and, thank God, she spoke excellent English. Much better than her lover, Captain Morel. I could easily see what had attracted him to her, but completely failed to understand what she saw in the little "turkey cock". Spindrift had told me what the peasant had called him when he spat on Morel's uniform, and I agreed with him. It was very apt.

'Please, come in and welcome, and please forgive sister Bridget who was here just now, she's very defensive of our privacy and can become a little over-enthusiastic when dealing with strangers. I promise you her bark is much worse than her bite, although when you watch her at mealtimes her bite is also quite ferocious. I pity anyone who gets between her and the soup.'

I saw a slight smile curve her delicate lips. Her beauty was quite radiant.

Spindrift said, 'Thank-you, sister. Forgive me, are you sister Honoria...'

The woman shook her head, 'No, no. I have just been sent to get your horses taken care of and bring you to the Mother Superior. She is waiting for you in her office. No, I am sister Matilde.'

'Ah, yes,' I sputtered, 'we have a message for you from your brother, Albert. He sends his love and asks if you are well?'

'Albert? *Albert*? Which Albert... Ah, you mean Albert Fournier? God bless the man, he is not my brother.'

'But he said...'

'No, no he isn't. After my family moved here to Natres we lived across the street from the Fournier home. He and I played together and shared secrets – as little children will. I think he became, what do you call it? Ah yes, he developed a little passion about me. A hook to the heart. Poor man. Thinking of me as his sister was his way of dealing with the situation. I liked him well enough, but, poof, there you have it. My heart was elsewhere, you understand?'

She fingered the crucifix at her throat, but thinking back to what I had seen through that small, high window I thought I understood very well indeed. A white veiled girl arrived to take our horses in hand, and sister Matilde directed us into the chill convent interior. There was a lot of gentle light flooding through the large windows, but the stone floors and walls it illuminated were Spartan and a little unwelcoming. I thought of the warm woman by our side living is such a soulless place and felt my first real pang of pity for her. She existed in a grey world of smooth stone and shadows, perhaps Morel brought some much-needed colour to her nights.

Spindrift looked around him, 'I have always thought of the Catholic church as being a colourful, creative, vibrant place. Your convent seems, forgive me for saying so, a little bleak.'

She raised her head, 'Ours is a contemplative order, captain Spindrift. We need no trivial distractions from our meditation on the perfect beauty of God's work, as it is shown to us, His poor servants, through the intercession of the blessed virgin.'

She indicated a shadowed niche that held an ancient Madonna and child. The wood was black with age but both Mary and the baby Jesus had eyes fashioned from inset, highly polished mother of pearl. The eyes had perfectly round, jet black pupils. Both mother and child also had fan like gold rays emanating from their foreheads. The piece was lovely yet also disturbing. It repelled me, but I couldn't understand why. I think it was those strange eyes, they looked out at me with the same blank coldness as a shark's.

That was when I became aware of a stench on the air, faint but pervasive. It was familiar and yet... And then the short hairs on the back of my neck stood on end. I knew that stink. I opened my mouth to comment but Spindrift gave me a guarded look followed by a brief nod, he had noticed it too. Matilde silently led us deeper into the building and we followed like wary hounds expecting the wolf to pounce at any time. Finally, she halted by a tall, green painted door.

'Here we are.'

She knocked and we heard a clipped response. She opened the door and stepped through into the room. 'I have Captains Spindrift and Cahoon who wish to see you, Reverend Mother.'

'Thank you. Bring them in, sister Matilde, I shall see them at once.'

She had a distinct accent and it wasn't French, but her English was clipped and precise.

I followed Spindrift into the book-lined room. Every wall was covered with rows of leather spines, all the same height and thickness. I gaped at them in amazement. The black robed, stick thin figure standing beside a massive wooden desk smiled broadly at my discomfort.

'Captain Cahoon, is it? Yes, you were described as the blonde one. I see you are interested in my library. Are you a bookish man, captain?'

'I enjoy a good read when I find one and have the time, ma'am.'

'No need for the ma'am, captain. Reverend Mother will do. Thank you, Matilde, you may go. I shall call you when the good captains are ready to depart.'

Matilde nodded and backed out of the room closing the door as she went.

'Please, take a seat, gentlemen. Can I fetch you a drink? It is a little too early in the day for alcohol but we make a rather wonderful lemonade here in the convent.'

We both said yes please. She gripped one of the vertical uprights of her bookshelves and pushed. The whole row slid sideways to reveal another bank of shelves. These too contained books but of a more natural looking type, different sizes and thicknesses clustered together or in little piles. She pulled out a tray containing a pottery jug and tall glasses. The weight seemed a little too much for her and I leapt to my feet and took it. I held it over her desk and regarded her quizzically. I couldn't see anywhere else to place it.

'Please, captain, that will be fine.' I put it down and regained my seat. She lifted the jug and said, 'Shall I be mother?' She grinned, showing large yellowed teeth. 'You must excuse me, I am infected with a streak of whimsy that forty years under the veil has failed to curb. The sisters are sometimes a little too solemn, but I believe the occasional bon mot helps relieve even the weariest soul. We have taken vows of chastity and poverty, but that needn't mean poverty of the mind. And if we can make little luxuries for ourselves, such as this fine lemonade, well, why not? They are the results or our labours, and taste much better than the sweat from our brows.'

She brought our drinks to us then returned to her chair behind the desk. She lifted her glass in a toast and then drank deep.

'Ah, so refreshing, even on a cold grey day. If you are still here, you must join me and try it on a warm spring afternoon; then it is pure nectar.'

I sipped the cloudy liquid, then took a good long draught. It was delicious and I told her so. 'My mothers used to make something they called lemonade during the summer, but it was never as good as this. You could bottle this stuff and make a large profit in the good old U S of A, Mother Superior.'

'Killing? What do you mean by "killing"? And what do you mean by "mothers"? How many did you have?'

I launched into a long explanation. I was just reaching the part about my being a foundling when Spindrift entered the fray.

'Reverend Mother, sorry to butt in, but we know you're a busy woman and we're taking up too much of your time and generosity as it is. We came to ask a question not share our personal histories, may I come to the point?'

She nodded, her face expressionless. He continued, 'Thank-you, you see, we wondered if you might be able to help us with our enquiries about children who have vanished from this area. The local people have spoken with our superiors and Captain Cahoon here has been tasked with investigating the matter. We've been advised that you might be able to help us.'

'By whom?'

'I would rather not say.'

'Very well, Captain Spindrift. Very well. Let *me* make some enquiries. I shall see if the sisters can shed any light on this sad matter. Could I be so bold as to ask you to return tomorrow at the same time? I might be in a better position to help after twenty-four hours. Is that acceptable?'

'That would be just fine, Reverend Mother. Most grateful for any light you can shed on the matter, thank you.'

'Then I shall see you tomorrow.'

She rang a handbell such as a school teacher might use to end recess. Ten minutes later we were mounted and back on the path the other side of that gate. I blew a low whistle.

'Well, that question poured cold water on the party. I got the feeling you didn't like her much, and I don't think she took much of a shine to you neither.'

'No, you're right. Do you think that was why she started lying?'

~23~

'You noticed that smell in the convent?'
We had put several yards between ourselves and the gate before Spindrift asked the question. We didn't want the nuns to know we had spotted anything suspicious. Something unsavoury was afoot with the Sisters of the Weeping Heart that had set enough alarm bells ringing to jar my spine loose. The back of my neck tingled and I turned in my saddle to look back. A black-robed, stick-thin figure stood tall behind the bars of the gate, watching us.
I quoted, 'Something is rotten in the state of Denmark.'
'No doubt, but I'm afraid we haven't time to play giddy goats like young master Hamlet. The Sha-aneer relates to that place somehow, directly, and physically. Close enough that, even in winter, we could smell its stink like a midden on a hot day. Scarecrows and fiddle-me-jacks, shadows, and mirrors. What's behind it all? Those women are playing dice with their immortal souls. We must save them from whatever they're doing if we can, but Natres and the whole of France is at risk if we don't act soon. How is Morel involved? What's really going on between him and sister Matilde? What's all this to do with those missing children? What's sister Honoria's true agenda. We're digging up more questions when we should be finding answers. What was all that nonsense with the fake bookshelves and her wittering on about whimsy? "Shall I be mother?" Really, Colin, I've seen better performances on the penny stage. What's the darned woman playing at?'
'Good lemonade, though.'
'Yes, and I suppose she always has a jug and glasses hidden away in that crazy bookshelf just in case a pair of thirsty Americans drop in for a chat after fighting their way past her Rottweiler at the gate.'
'That lemonade was fresh and cold; did you notice that? It was put there just so she could show off her sliding doors. I'd bet a golden eagle that it was brought from the kitchens specially for us while sister Bridget was giving us a hard time at the gate. Something sour then something sweet. And all the while we're being played like guitar strings to keep us off-balance so we'd miss anything unusual while we're there. Everything looked normal because we were being distracted the whole time, but all that was missing was a white rabbit with a watch. We didn't walk through a gate we fell down a rabbit hole. Should have asked to see Sister Alice.'

Spindrift said nothing but he reined in his horse and stood tall in his stirrups.

He looked around, concentrating hard, then settled in his saddle once more.

'When you visited this place last night did you have time to study the surrounding terrain?'

'No, I'm afraid I was distracted by the novelty of the situation. My first time in the air when I didn't think I was dreaming, so no, I wasn't looking around so much as you would notice. Why, what have you seen?'

'Nothing, and that's what worries me. I'm thinking about the Sha-aneer and how it works. How it always works.' He flicked a glance back the way we had just come. 'The stink back there was a mature worm and one of those is never close to the surface. They prefer holes and caves, or tunnels, like the one we met back at the British trenches. They spread by seeding an area with little red and white maggots. All you need do is touch one of those things and you're infected. I've only known two men survive infection. The first I got to before it was too late, if I'm quick enough I have ways to remove the beast before it spreads. The other man burned his own arm off to stop it taking hold. Insanely brave fellow. You would have liked both, especially Caleb, Caleb Sawyer. I'll tell you the story another time. So then, the Sha-aneer, the worm of the deep earth. For tens of thousands of years, the worm has been quiet. It still struck when it could, of course. I've met its victims often enough that it's learned my name. I can tell you that it hates and fears me, but not as much as I have learned to hate and fear it. It is an evil thing. Maitland was right to call it filthy. There can be no parley with the worm, no mercy. History is full of stories about demons and witches who had to be burned to cleanse them. Some of that was me releasing the poor infected devils, as you've seen. Other times it was thanks to misbegotten fools burning their neighbours, or hanging a harmless old woman living alone with a pet cat, or drowning a girl with a third nipple which the idiots thought was for feeding her familiar. Humankind's ingenuity in finding new and better reasons and ways to kill each other has never ceased to astound me, and yet most of them wouldn't let a dog or a cat come to harm while they watched. You heard Maitland talking about the birds his men took down the tunnels. If they were gassed and fell over three times they were retired to a five-star bird sanctuary. Fair enough, but what about the men? Tot of rum and back down they go until they're so sick they get sent away to recover. Once they're fit, down they go again. The birds have a better time of it.

'Mankind is subtle and sets strange, see-saw standards for itself. But the worm is more primitive so it works in straight lines. It has done what it does for millions of years, longer, and now, although it's become more ambitious and it's upping its game, it won't alter its methods.' He took a deep breath. 'Listen to me ramble on. Sorry, Colin, I needed to talk to help me think things through, and you listen so well. We have another question to answer, my friend. How did the seed maggot get from here to the British tunnel? The mother worm is here somewhere, under our feet or deep in the hillside, we can be sure of that, but somehow the infection travelled four or so miles and got to the clay-kickers in their tunnel without infecting anyone else along the way. How is that possible?'

To me it seemed obvious. 'It couldn't have, we'd have followed a trail of worm infection all the way from here to there. Those poor devils must have dug their way to the worm. It must have been like that, it must be, it's the only way. It got to them underground.'

Spindrift looked north-east towards the distant battle lines. 'If that's the truth we can expect more cases unless we can put a stop to the thing now. But, we can't, not yet. We must find out where the thing is. Once we have it we can kill it. And we must work soon. You saw what a dozen infected men looked like in that tunnel. Can you even imagine what two armies would become, with the infection racing like a terrible plague through the trenches until every man jack of them has been devoured and subsumed into the Sha-aneer. And it wouldn't stop there. It would grow and spread across the globe until one day the last group of humans on some remote island would see a strange ship coming towards them. They would row out to meet it carrying things to trade with the passengers. But there wouldn't be any passengers, just the worm waiting to welcome them to the host. And that would be the end of the Eden born on Earth, and the worm would be master once more.'

'We can't allow that to happen.'

'No, we can't. We must act, and soon.'

~24~

Worsnip was waiting for us when we got back to the little town square. He was patently agitated and sprinted towards us as soon as he saw us.

'There you are, thank God. I thought something must have happened to you.'

Spindrift dismounted and shook the man's hand. Worsnip nodded at me then continued. 'No bally time for niceties I'm afraid. You must get back to the hospital. The Boche mounted a shock offensive. They must be crazy. Middle of the day, no artillery cover. They just came running at our lines like madmen. Our chaps had no warning and barely had time to see them coming, only a few of the machine gunners opened fire. I've only heard reports but I'm told there was some bitter hand-to-hand fighting in the forward trenches before the bastards were stopped. I'm afraid you'll have some customers when you get back, but you must get a move on, they need you.'

Spindrift nodded, 'Thanks, Michael.' He leapt into his saddle, 'Come on, Colin. I've been expecting this. Come on man. Ride as if the very Devil's at your heels. It's started.'

We rode like Pony Express men, leaning low and forward against our horses' necks, urging them to run faster and ever faster. A black shadow flowed from the hedgerows and kept pace with us with almost arrogant ease. Spindrift's dog had rejoined us. When we finally reached Kirby at the stables, our horses were blowing hard and flecked with foam, but he took them from us without a word of protest. We ran to the wards. Worsnip was right, we had customers. Dozens of them. Even so Spindrift insisted we wash thoroughly and don fresh gowns, even though men were groaning and even screaming for help, some of them in English but with German accents.

I joined him in performing triage, selecting the men who needed help first, those who could wait, and those who were beyond care.

Machine gun bullets and artillery can make a mess of a man, but hand-to-hand fighting is a cruel killer, dirty and desperate. It takes a lot to shove a bayonet into another man's guts and twist it, then pull it out and move on, but that's what a modern soldier has been trained to do. They learn to do it without thinking, to do it fast and first. They practice on straw bales and sacks of hay, and they get good at it. I guess the alternative is to think about it too long and give the other guy enough time to get his killing thrust in first.

Of course, I'd rather our guys survived to go home, and we hadn't started that stinking war, they had, but it doesn't mask the horror at what war does to a man's mind. Can the same hands that pushed a bayonet into another man's belly hold a woman or a child with tenderness afterwards? Will the woman feel a chill at their touch?

A bayonet wound creates its own problem, part of the bowel is pulled out with the blade. Spindrift would make the wound bigger so he could exteriorise the gut, clean it up and suture it before closing the incision. He would feel around to make sure there was nothing he'd missed, especially pieces of cloth. Bullets and blades would drive pieces of people's clothing into a wound, filthy scraps of shirts, jackets, and greatcoats. I'm told it was always worse in winter, there were more layers. Leave those behind and you might as well put a bullet in your patient's brain, it would be much quicker and kinder. The scraps fester and then you get gangrene, the black killer, or ulcers that erupt internally and cause sepsis. Old school said, work fast and sure, Spindrift said, work fast and clean.

He washed his hands between patients and sterilised his instruments. He cut, cleaned, repaired, and closed, rarely taking more than ten minutes on a wound. I began to lose count of how many men we had treated, all the while his steady, calm voice explained the situation while a clear flow of instructions told me precisely what to do.

And then, finally, it was over. Cleaning and bandaging superficial wounds could be left to corpsmen and our plucky little band of FANYs, British First Aid Nursing Yeomanry, women who the men called 'angels in uniform'. The last thing Spindrift and I did was spend time making sure the dying men's last hours were as comfortable as possible. And then at last we could strip off our surgical gowns and wash the last of the blood from our hands and faces. German, Canadian, American, French or British, the blood was always the same colour, red.

Spindrift asked me to fetch him a beer and wait for him in the mess, which I was pleased to do. There were few men in there, exhausted officers who had arrived with their men, other members of our overstretched medical team. Few of them had the energy to do anything other than raise a hand or nod a head in greeting. I fetched two beers in pint mugs and sat at a table with two chairs. Spindrift joined me just as I was thinking of drinking his beer and fetching him a fresh brew. He drained his pot in one long draught, sighed and fetched us both a second pint, all without saying a word. He sat down and tilted his lean head towards me.

'How are you feeling, Colin? Been a long day, I know. You bearing up?'

'Good thanks, Doc, fine. Seems an age since we rode out this morning I must admit, but yes, fine thanks. How about you?'

'Hungry and footsore. But we need to go out again. We have a job to do.'

I must have gaped at him because he reached out and touched my arm.

'It's okay if you don't want to come with me, but you're a good man in a tight spot and I'd be grateful for a little help tonight.'

I started 'Where...' but he gestured for me to keep my voice down.

In a quiet hiss, I asked, 'Where are we going? The convent?'

He shook his head, 'We'll talk on the way. The convent can wait, this is more important.'

'What's happened?'

'Let's grab something to eat first. Our patients are comfortable so we've earned some hot food in our bellies. It's going to be a late night, maybe an early morning. Best we eat first. Doctor's prescription.'

We got ourselves around a plate of stew pork and potatoes with a mess of greens. We ate and we talked about everything in general and nothing specific, the way you do when you're burning to broach a subject but you must hold fire for some reason. Spindrift was taking me somewhere to do something he considered more important than the nuns and the missing children, and even the creature we believed was under the convent. Whatever it was, he had learned about it since we got back to the hospital. My mind was spinning, and then suddenly things began to fall into place. He had been talking with the injured German prisoners. There had to be a connection and the only connection was the worm, the Sha-aneer.

'The Germans,' I said in a hushed voice. 'They weren't running towards our lines today, were they? They were running away from their own.'

He nodded, gazing at me across his plate as if we were discussing the weather.

'Finish your food,' he advised. 'You'll be grateful for it later.'

'We're going over to the German lines on a worm hunt, aren't we?'

He barely nodded his head.

'We don't even know where the bastard thing is!'

'We do, or at least we have a very good idea. Look, we can't leave the worm free to rampage around the country like a wild bull. We need to contain it here – and kill it here. Destroy it, before it can spread its seed. I must go out. I've got to find it and kill it, I have no choice. I'd be grateful for your company, Colin, very grateful, but whatever happens I'm going to track the worm down tonight and I'm going to burn the heart out of the foul beast. Then I'm going to have another chat with our friend the Mother Superior, and this time I don't want any bloody lemonade.'

'Well, why didn't you say so in the first place.' I stood up and reached for my greatcoat. 'What were those green things with dinner?'

'The leaves? No idea. The British grow them behind the lines to bolster their diet. They say it's something the army learned from the navy, helps keep their boys healthy. Sounds like a good idea to me.'

'You know what worries me?'

'What?'

'The Brits have been in this warfare business so long they've become really good at it. What if they decide they want the USA back? Once they've given the Boche a thrashing what's to stop them coming after us?'

'Don't be daft, Colin. The Brits don't go about starting wars, that's not their style. They go about finishing them, and that's a creature of an entirely different kidney.' He stood up and put his hand on my arm. 'Ready?'

'Sure, why not.'

'Let's go to work.'

~25~

At that point in the war there were no frontline American trenches on the Pas de Calais, so we chose to return to Major Maitland's dug-out and start from there. He was surprised to see us back so soon but he made us very welcome and quickly fetched us mugs of his family brew. We chinked our pots together and drank while Spindrift explained the purpose of our mission behind German lines. Maitland wiped foam from his moustache and belched quietly.

'Pard'n me. Good idea, I'll send a squad of my lads with you. We could do with a recce party out there after all the shenanigans today. Bloody Boche came screaming at us like hungry hyenas. Madmen and lunatics every one of them, out in plain sight like that, makes no sense. They must be getting desperate. Stopped their little game though didn't we, ha, yes, we did. They came a right cropper when they fell into the trench. They came face-to-face with British steel and British guts, stood against them like a wall. Proud of the men, bloody heroes all of them. No give in them, no give at all. Just the finest stuff.'

Spindrift raised his mug of Maitland's beer, drained it, and sighed appreciatively.

'There's not much I'll miss about this place, major, but your brew is amongst the best I've ever tasted.'

'Open invitation, old lad. When this business has been tidied up and Kaiser Bill gets his marching orders you must come to the hall and have a few days en- famille. Both of you. Very welcome. The womenfolk would love to have a couple of dashing American captains to fawn over, and if you think this stuff tastes good over here, you should try it looking out over a few hundred acres of Capability Brown's handiwork. Adds salt to the recipe, tears of joy don'tcha know, tears of joy. Wish we were there now, love the old place. Missed it when we were in India, missed it in Africa, miss it now. Bloody war.'

He was becoming misty-eyed with memories. Spindrift eased him back to the here and now.

'Thanks for the offer, major, but we have to go alone. We think that plague we told you about might have struck the German lines and we need to look for ourselves. Fewer the better on a mission like this, we're sure you agree. Rather lose two than a platoon.'

'If the rest of the Yanks are like you two it's the Boche I feel sorry for. Backbone I call it. We built an empire on determination and backbone. No wonder you Yanks won your independence. Not sure it would have happened if we hadn't been up against that little Corsican Corporal Bonaparte at the same time, but gallant all the same. Good chaps. Sure I can't send a few handy lads with you? No? Right. When's the off?'

'Right away. It's dark and overcast, there's no moon. There couldn't be a better time. We'll be there and back before breakfast.'

'You'll need a password, something short and easy to remember. The chaps will take a pot shot at anything moving on a dark night, and we can't blame them if they don't know it's you. Still, can't have you shot down by friendly fire can we. Embarrassing, yes? I know, "pint pot"! They'll remember it well enough. I'll get the word passed down the line.'

'Pint pot it is. Thank-you, major. We'll be on our way.'

Corporal Vickery showed us to the most forward position, the far end of a trench that stuck out like a finger a short way towards the German lines. He silently shook our hands and touched the rim of his tin hat with a salute, and then he vanished back into the relative safety of his major's dugout. Spindrift tapped me on the shoulder and we climbed up into No Man's Land.

He had offered me a draught of his tonic that helped me see in pitch darkness, and I had swallowed gratefully. What with his concoctions and Rowan's kiss my insides should have been boiling and brewing away like the beer vats at Maitland's hall, but the fact is I had never felt better. At some point, I would have to come to terms with who and what I was, and what it might mean to my future, if I had one. And whether Rowan would be with me. This last subject was taking up a lot of my waking hours. I couldn't be sure of how she felt about me – but I knew exactly how I felt about her. I was keen to explore our relationship further.

However, the best time to be thinking about a woman was not when you're trying to pick a cautious path through the slime-filled shell craters, splintered debris and lines of wicked barbed wire that gave No Man's Land its name. No matter how beautiful. She would prove a lethal distraction.

To me the moonless night glowed with a silvery patina, almost a ghost light. The world was drained of colour but I could see the landscape clear as day, shadows shone and outlines were picked out with an intense clarity. A German soldier was stretched across the wire like a sack of clean laundry, his hatless head dark and leathery in the eerie light. Straps of kit and neat, square pouches hung around him. He believed he had been ready for anything when he left his trench that day, and then we had killed him. Now there he was, him and his carefully chosen equipment, entangled, his blood blackened face poised inches from the mud. A few yards further on a British tank loomed out of the shadows like a murdered steel beast. It was tilted to one side, one of its caterpillar tracks torn away and the other buried and useless in the churned earth. Scratching sounds came from inside it and we ducked down and hastened past in case they drew the attention of a sharp-eared sniper. We reached the German wire. It was better than ours, vicious and razor-sharp. The men were more afraid of it than they were of the Boche soldiers, except, of course, the brutal machine gunners. They said that wire would scratch your eyes from your head if you looked at it too long. We found a stretch that had been pressed flat into the ground and picked our way gingerly across it.

Spindrift pressed his mouth to my ear. 'If the Germans came running we'll need a clear path back through this wire, but don't worry I've got cutters if we need them.'

I nodded, I hadn't thought to bring them. My head was too far into the clouds during those confounding days. I was a stranger in a strange land, a place that looked like home but was throwing fresh mysteries at me from every corner. I wondered why the capable Preacher needed me by his side, he was better alone. He had more soldier in his little finger than I had in my whole body. Even so I stiffened my resolve and tried to stand taller.

'Get down,' Spindrift hissed. 'We'll see what we need to see soon enough. Let's not make a target too soon. Right?'

I swallowed bile at my foolishness, crouched lower, and followed him into the silver darkness. The shades and shadows resolved into horizontal lines. I found myself reminded of a calm midnight sea I had once watched on an equally moonless night in California. Flat waves had rolled over each other making almost perfect black bars that slid forward and disappeared onto the phosphorescent sand. It had been hypnotic. The memory soothed me for a moment, and then I realised that when I had sat so still and dreamed gentle dreams on that beach all those years ago, it was a different time and a different place. I was not threatened with the sudden, savage bite of an enemy bullet. Nor by something else, something much, much worse.

And then we were climbing down onto a firestep in a beautifully finished trench. Like everything the Germans did it was clean and well organised. Where the British had simply piled sandbags against raw soil in long makeshift ditches, then floored them with duckboards, the Germans had erected neat wooden walls of carefully placed planking. I supposed there was some cultural lesson to be learned from it.

Spindrift sniffed the air and stood silently, his head tilted to one side. He was listening intently and scenting his prey. He turned and beckoned me to follow, then began loping along the perfectly laid planks of the trench floor. That was when it hit me hardest. We had reached the enemy frontlines – and they were empty. And then Spindrift was running towards the thing, or things, that had emptied them. He was tracking down the creature that had scared battle seasoned troops out into machine gun fire, and I was running at his side. My head spun. Who was the greater fool? The man who runs where angels fear to tread – or the lunatic who follows at his heels like a faithful puppy?

~26~

All pretence at secrecy had been abandoned once we reached the German lines. From that moment on, we were on a mission to find the enemy as quickly as possible and destroy it before it could unleash a nightmare plague on France and the rest of humanity. We had no way of knowing how many German troops had been infected and subsumed by the worm. It might have been dozens or even hundreds before the survivors finally risked their mad dash towards the British lines. The poor devils must have been terrified if they preferred to face hostile gunfire rather than stay where they were, safe in their strongly built and comfortably appointed trenches.

I didn't need to ask what horror had driven them to take such a fool's gambit, I already knew. I'd seen it before, close-up.

I had no idea how we were going to kill the beast, but if the Preacher wanted me by his side while he did it I was there for him, lickety-split. We were no longer afraid of German snipers, although British ones might have been a problem, so we weren't worried about making noise. We ran and our feet pounded on the wooden boards and the lonely sound clattered and echoed around us. We were greeted by silence and an eerie emptiness, a hollow stage waiting for the star act to appear.

The British trenches were always alive with humanity and activity. Someone was always smoking a cigarette or pipe, boiling a kettle to make their dreadful tea, or frying bacon on a little Primus stove. There was laughter where little groups swapped stories in shallow corners, and the sound of coughing while a Tommy tried to clear his congested lungs. To traverse a trench, we would have to clamber over and around huddled bodies or reclining forms, answer murmured greetings and enquiries, all the while threading our way through the long and narrow defensive nest of an army at rest.

This empty wooden tube was uncanny and frightening. It sounded of nothing but the clatter of our boots on hard boards and the sound of our breathing.

And then suddenly I heard it. That dreadful sound I had heard in the tunnel but amplified a hundredfold, a grinding host of sibilant voices, all whispering and oiling their way into my ears. We were close. The Preacher slowed down and held out his hand to stay me. I could see nothing ahead but the flat lines of the trench's planks stretching away to the next zag after our current zig. He touched his nose. Yes, I could smell it too, rank and raw like rotten fish in a bucket but laced with that alien undertow of hot tar and sulphur. And something else, a high, chemical stench that burned at my sinuses like acid. My eyes began to water and the rank air caught at my throat. It was as if we were swimming in the stink of the worm, drowning in it.

And then, impossibly, the stench and sound was all around us. Somehow the still invisible host had managed to surround us. But where was it? We looked along the empty trench and saw nothing. And that was when the boards under our feet began to swell upwards and the walls of the trench bowed inwards towards us.

Spindrift yelled, 'Fly, Colin, fly!'

What did he mean? The hissing chatter was deafening and the stink a physical force that numbed my mind. The trench was closing in on me like a fist and I cowered in mindless shock. The planks began to buckle and split. Long splinters like white daggers opened out and stretched towards me, starving mouths ready to bite. And then grey flesh oozed around the wooden shards and reached out, sending boneless fingers to touch me, to grab me and take possession of me. Its incomprehensible, hissing chatter was a crescendo battering at my failing senses.

And then I felt myself gripped with unbreakable force. I screamed defiance as the life was squeezed out of me and I was lifted helplessly into the air. My life was finished. I expected to be subsumed, crushed, devoured. To become just another hissing voice in the host, a soulless mind amongst the many. My flesh would be added to that of the great worm of the deep earth. My senses had been strewn to the winds, swept away by a hopeless, sick horror. I looked up to snatch one last glimpse of the beautiful sky before it was lost to me forever.

And I saw Preacher Spindrift's calm face outlined in silver against the darkness. His strong arms held me as we soared up and away from the roaring worm which was lashing around below us, rendering the neat wooden trench to a shattered ruin. It was screaming in baffled fury and mottled tentacles of thick flesh stretched out like covetous fingers towards us. Spindrift had wrapped me in his long coat and I felt a hail of objects strike against it then fall away. And then we were clear.

'Colin, listen to me. I need you to fly for me, I can't do what I need to do while I'm supporting you like this. Can you do that? And try not to lose your clothes this time, that might take too long to explain if anyone sees you.'

I thought back to my flight a few days before, no, with a shock I realised it had been just the day before, and I nodded. Spindrift opened his arms. And I fell like a stone. Below me the rapidly approaching worm opened its maw in welcome, but at the last moment I reeled to one side and sped away from its embrace. I looped up to where the Preacher stood in mid-air like a sentinel, his arms folded and his coat whipping around him like a cloak. His half-moon smile gleamed whitely in his shadowed face. We looked down at the beast. It looked like a distended grey belly, inflated fit to burst. Its hide was stretched smooth, it gleamed and pulsated in the ghost light. And then Spindrift reached inside his coat and pulled out a handful of his glowing crystal globes.

'Get ready to move as fast as you can.'

I nodded.

He dropped the crystals and followed them down a short way, drawing his pistol as he fell. He aimed and fired three times. Three distinct and sharp statements that split the air and silenced the hissing racket of the worm for the briefest moment.

And then it was as if the world had exploded and a shockwave almost struck me from the air. I was blasted upwards on a tide of boiling white fire, my eyes dazzled, and momentarily confused. And then my eyes cleared and I watched events unfold beneath my feet. I held my breath. Where the belly of the worm had once been, a splashing lake of brilliant white fire flared and seethed, a broiling, living inferno. Long strings of sticky burning material spattered and arced around it, scorching the earth in black stripes. I could feel the intense heat sear my skin. The carefully constructed stretch of trench had been consumed in seconds. A vision of pure hellfire replaced it, blazing in the formless night.

Spindrift hovered at my side, his eyes reflected the conflagration and glowed like lamps. 'Careful, Colin. We don't know how big it is. This could get very dangerous. Watch, see there!'

And that was when I realised that the immense burning thing below us was just the tip of the beast. The fire had started to seethe along the trench, getting whiter and hotter as it accelerated. It followed the zig-zag lines precisely until it reached a fortified mound and entered a long straight length of trench, at which point it seemed to stop. Nothing happened for several seconds and I began to wonder if it was all over and the worm had been consumed. I wanted to cheer. And then came an intense whistling sound, rising until it reached the very limits of my hearing but still drilled into my brain and wrought exquisite agony. The longest section of trench bowed upwards like a bridge, rising towards us, and something unfathomably huge burst from the ground and reared up darkly, blotting out what little light was available other than the sorcerous glare of phosphorous fire.

The tortured scream of the great worm tore the night to tatters. I thought they must surely hear that right across the Pas de Calais and I wondered how many eyes would be turned towards the titanic creature's death throes. And then the chemical stink of burning offal became chokingly powerful. I couldn't breathe.

Spindrift and I climbed higher to reach cleaner air, climbed away from the white-hot conflagration of alien flesh.

We watched as veins and arteries of spitting light climbed the screeching mountain of heaving tissue, peeling its blistered hide away in blazing sheets. It began to glow internally, first like a gigantic pink lantern and then brighter and brighter. The light at the beast's core seemed to spiral down, deep down into the boiling ground. It dragged at my eye and I felt I was looking along an immense stretch of glowing gut burrowed deep into the earth. And now it was lit like a fuse leading to the biggest cache of dynamite I'd ever seen. I didn't need the Preacher's warning to tell me to get out of there. I was already hightailing it back towards No Man's Land when the ground erupted for the first time and I experienced a silent concussion that swatted me hundreds of yards away from No Man's Land and out towards the canal and the town of Cambrai. I tumbled like a leaf in a gale and darkness bloomed forward from behind my eyes.

~27~

I fought to keep my wits about me while I fell like a comet across the sky. It was hard, but eventually I managed to regain control and spiral up and away from the town's buildings and the long, arrow straight, silver line of the canal. Everything around me was thrown into shocking relief by the geyser of white fire erupting behind me. The light seemed to intensify and brighten, as if it was determined to engulf the world and everything in it.

I had heard tell of the great mines the British had exploded under the German lines earlier in the war. They had blown huge craters out of the raw earth, craters so wide it took a man a good while to walk around them. They were said to have been the largest man made explosions ever seen and had sent fountains of soil dozens of yards into the sky, punching holes in the ground eighty feet deep. The great worm was much bigger and dug down a lot deeper, and its destruction was creating waves of pressure that made the sky vibrate in sympathy. I began to feel as if the teeth would be jarred clean out of my head.

Like a flapping bat, Spindrift swooped towards me. He bellowed to be heard above a strange, high-pitched ululation that was issuing from narrow fissures opening in the ground around the dying beast.

'Come on, man. We must get away from here before it blows. We must get down and behind something solid or we're finished. We need a shield, a strong shield.'

He looked down at the town as if expecting to find an answer amidst its geometric complexity. An image snapped into my mind. I shouted back.

'That tank, the one we passed on the way here. A few tons of hard steel should do the job.'

'Good thinking, follow me, I remember exactly where it is.'

We turned and looped around the raging inferno that was sending thick plumes of dense, liquid flame dozens of yards into the air. I thought of images I had seen of volcanic eruptions but this looked hotter and more violent. It the heart of that fearsome conflagration was a living creature and it was scattering strings of burning flesh in hot sticky loops around it as it tore at itself in agony. A white ball of flame shot skywards. We accelerated, certain that there could be little time before the end. Spindrift and I got out of the sky and behind that wrecked tank as fast as we could. We had barely touched down before he dropped to his knees and began clawing at the ground.

'Dig in,' he shouted at me. 'We need to get down as low as we can.'

Using our bare hands like shovels we scooped away the gluey clay in the lee of the tank, pushing the dirt up before us to make a low wall which we compacted as much as we could. Then we threw ourselves flat in our makeshift foxhole. We were just in time.

The tank was suddenly outlined by a silent nimbus of blinding light that gushed over and around us like a wave. There followed a pause while the night seemed to hold its breath; and then the fury struck. The steel brute we were using as a shield quivered like a whipped dog, and then with a mounting sense of horror I watched as it was lifted from the ground until it teetered directly above us. I feared it must be flipped over to slam down and instantly crush us where we lay, but I had underestimated the sheer power of the storm created by the destroyed worm. In its final moments, it had exploded and unleashed an overwhelming blast of pure destructive energy that reduced buildings to rubble and flattened trees in a blast radius nearly half a mile across. We learned later that a solid wall of hurricane force wind had screamed over the British lines, caving in some of the more casually made dugouts and burying the occupants alive. It even tore one of the little trains from its rails and tipped it onto its side, ripping a great gouge from the earth in the process. One soldier, he was standing tall on the firestep to better see the incredible firestorm over the German lines, was lifted clean off his feet and slammed back against the top edge of the trench wall behind him, breaking his back and killing him instantly.

Crouched low in our scooped out hollow, Spindrift and I cringed helplessly while nearly thirty tons of steel loomed over us like a blacksmith's giant hammer about to be pounded down on the anvil. Spindrift flung a useless protective arm over me, but if that critter fell on us we were powerless as a bug under a boot. And then the full force of the blast hit and instead of falling flat onto us the tank was snatched up and thrown rolling over our heads like a great paddle wheel to finally crunch down hard and roll just once several yards behind us. As it spun overhead its projecting sponsons missed us by bare inches. Even the least touch of the hurtling mass would have wiped the life from us sure as a shell blast. With a loud clatter, it finally landed upright and settled back onto its ruined tracks. It sagged in the centre as if exhausted by its antics.

And then, at last, the storm was over. Silence fell apart from a distant roar on the British side, and total darkness returned to No Man's Land. I let out a long, juddering breath and sat up. Ghost vision gently illuminated my sight once more and rendered the tank into a battered grey and silver spectre against a grey velvet sky. I studied it for a moment longer and read the name painted on its side. Deborah.

'Thanks for letting us live, Deborah,' I said through chattering teeth.

Spindrift stood tall and helped me to my feet. I automatically crouched over, but he took my elbow and bade me stand upright.

He explained, 'Don't worry. Any sniper out tonight will have been blown clean out of his boots. Do you feel up to a short walk back to the British trenches? We'll have to be careful, they're likely to have been rattled by all the fuss we caused. What was that password again?'

I thought for a moment, 'Pint pot.'

'Ah, yes. I could certainly do with a filled one of those.'

'Amen to that, soldier. Amen to that.'

I felt surprisingly chipper after all we'd been through. More than anything else I was surprised to be alive. The world had, at more than one point that night, seemed desperate to stack the chips against us. More than once my courage had been pushed beyond its absolute limits, but I couldn't stop myself from grinning as we made our way past the stretched soldier hanging on the wire. Even the fierce winds had failed to release him, a poor human fly caught in his barbed-wire web. The bottom line was illustrated right there, we had survived, and that poor wretch had not.

I guessed I would drop into bed that night like a sack of gravel, and sleep until the birds woke me. But right there, even in that tortured wasteland that had seen so many dead, I knew what it meant to survive against all odds. Every breath was like wine, I could feel my muscles moving under my flesh. I was alive.

We began to hear voices ahead, urgent whispers that offered an uncanny similarity to the hissing sounds of the worm, but these were men, solid and real. As we drew closer the keen note of contained panic and urgency became evident.

We called out, 'Pint pot, hello, pint pot!'

We needn't have worried. Had we been enemy soldiers we could have marched down into the trench singing *Watch on the Rhine* at the top of our voices and no-one would have noticed. What we found was a scene of organised chaos. It was our first taste of the damage the shockwave from the worm's destruction had caused. Everywhere men were at work. The uninjured were tending to their injured colleagues or digging frantically to free people from their collapsed dugouts. Some stumbled around in a confused daze while others snapped orders at running troopers. We couldn't stand in any one place without getting in the way, so we battled through the crush and eventually found Maitland beside Vickery, sitting at the entrance to his quarters. The major had a gash over his left eye which was dripping blood onto his cheek. It had pooled and crusted in his moustache. He looked exhausted but his woebegone countenance brightened when he saw us and he jumped to his feet, sending a fresh spurt of blood arcing from his forehead. It flowed down and closed his left eye. He wiped at it carelessly and grinned. He had blood on his teeth.

'Never thought we'd see you chaps again. Boche used something to blow everything up, look at it! Wicked bastards. Absolute nightmare. How do you prepare for something like that? Men got blown around like playing cards. How do you fight that? Never thought we'd see you again. Good show.'

He was clearly stunned and his wits were a little loose. Spindrift spoke firmly, 'Vickery, get us some medical supplies. We'll need to see to the major straight away and then help out where we can.'

The little corporal tried to stand but his right leg collapsed under him at completely the wrong angle. He groaned and his face became a white rictus of pain.

Spindrift shook his head. 'Brave little idiot, what was he thinking trying to stand on that leg? Okay, Colin, you look to the major and I'll tend to Vickery.'

He pointed at a trooper hustling past, 'You there, find us all the medical supplies you can and bring them here. Keep them clean, understand? Good! Fetch us water, something to boil it in and a stove, got that?'

'Very good sir.' The trooper turned to run and cannoned straight into Michael Worsnip, nearly knocking him for six.

Worsnip howled. 'Watch out you blithering idiot, look where you're going why don't you?'

'Sir, yes, sir. Didn't see you there, sir.'

'Well, get along with you! Go on!'

The trooper scuttled away, muttering to himself. Worsnip came to us, just behind him was Helen, his nurse, and the pretty blonde FANY driver we had seen at the wheel of the ambulance. The three of them surveyed the scene with sombre expressions. Worsnip wiped his hand through his hair and grimaced.

'Spindrift, Colin, might have known you'd be here. One day I'll work out if you have a fine nose for trouble or if trouble has a fine nose for you. You seem to sniff each other out often enough. Righto, that's enough chat, what can we do to help?'

~28~

We bent to our task, and after a few hours I looked up to rest my eyes for a moment, and with some surprise realised that dawn had cast a pale glow to the sky in the east. We had taken a long day's sleepless journey to reach this frosty new morning. The ground was gilded with silver and frozen crystal and the massing clouds were polished like new pewter. I could taste ice in the fresh air and licked my dry lips to moisten them. I had lost track of time while I assisted Spindrift in his careful ministrations. Precise and fast. He would complete his job, check it, and move on. In his wake men who might have lost their lives or limbs could look forward to a full recovery. The stream of patients eased to a trickle and then, finally, dried up.

Bless him, Worsnip had brought enough fresh water with him in the ambulance to make tea for everyone in our little band. We were extremely grateful when the steaming mugs were finally pressed into our hands after our long hours of work.

Worsnip stood with both hands pressed against the small of his back and stretched hugely. He yawned and took up his tea in a grateful fist.

He said, 'Take a breather, chaps. We've got enough casualties without adding you to the butcher's bill. I think we're there. Take a seat, why don't you? The boys can wait a moment before we get them to the transports.'

We did and right grateful too. Afterwards we supervised the loading of the stretchers. Spindrift enjoyed almost superhuman stamina, but even he was looking peaked by the time the last stretcher case had been placed into the ambulance, rolled onto a horse drawn wagon, or carried into the trucks pulled by the little replacement train that had rolled up during the morning. It stood steaming close to its stricken sister. The stoker was frying bacon and eggs on a bright shovel and he offered us a sandwich that he described as a bacon banjo. I swear it was one of the finest things I'd ever tasted and I attacked it greedily.

All around us everyone was debating the astonishing events of the previous night. Spindrift and I listened and remained silent. Later we would learn how talk of the strange new German super weapon had spread down the line like wildfire, but enemy prisoners questioned while awaiting dispersal were as baffled as everyone else. They were still insisting that a monstrous 'demon' had attacked them and their fellows and forced them to flee their trenches. That story was ignored as utter nonsense, or at best an illusion caused by some sort of experimental gas weapon, accidently released by German scientists, that had driven their own men mad. The Boche were known to be an inventive crew and our troops would believe just about anything of them.

Nature abhors a vacuum. Imagination began to fill in the gaps about what must have happened that night. The event had injured more than one hundred men, some seriously, and killed three; one thanks to a broken back and two poor devils buried alive in their collapsed dugout.

One of the men serving under Major Maitland, had coined the handy phrase 'Dragon's Breath', to describe the effects of the weapon, and, not surprisingly, it had stuck. Following that, and as is their wont, people began to remember the sequence of events in a way that made perfect sense, or at least it did to them. Their memories altered to supply answers they could comprehend.

To the recorded facts of a bizarre, hurricane-force wind that had swept through a limited stretch of the allied lines for those devastatingly long seconds, were added numerous witness accounts of a white-hot firestorm or column of flame over the German trenches near Cambrai. These were put together with the description 'Dragon's Breath' and very soon grew into the story about an immense flamethrower, probably train-mounted, that had been tested against the British lines on the Pas de Calais.

The greatest mystery was why the Germans had not followed up their use of the super weapon with troops on the ground, and that wouldn't be answered until a solitary flier took his Bristol F.2 bi-plane over the German lines for a look-see early the following day.

What the pilot saw sent him scurrying back to his base to report, his aircraft's tail peppered by rifle bullets. He had flown over an almost perfectly circular feature that straddled the German front lines, and which he estimated to be about half a mile across. It was the centre of a scene of utter destruction, and consisted of a ring of flat, dark grey ash with a tar-black central core. Everything within that circle had been flattened, trees had been blasted to the ground and buildings toppled. He was too high to make out the finer details, but something about that circle of ash made the hair on the back of his neck prickle. He said he felt it looking back at him like a baleful eye. Within that radius nothing moved, but beyond it, the pilot said, 'Some blighter must have kicked over the ant's nest. Boche all over the bloody place. Swarms of the bastards, marching forwards from as far as the eye could see.'

He had wanted to make a photographic record of the scene, but when they spotted his biplane outlined against the pale winter sky several German troops had opened fire before he could fish out his camera. Believing discretion to be the better part of valour the pilot made his escape, and it is a credit to his aircraft's robust build that he made it back to the airstrip at all. His batman counted seventeen bullet holes in the Bristol's canvas tail and fuselage, or, as the pilot reportedly said in a heavily edited newspaper report, 'Lovely old Biff got me home with more holes in her backside than a gun dog sat in a briar patch.'

His report added yet more fuel to the Dragon's Breath theory and it evolved further. The hurricane was no longer believed to have been caused by the test firing of a train-mounted weapon, but instead by a top-secret, flame-throwing tunnel. Scuttlebutt had it that the tunnel was the mouth of a kind of cannon, a massive device that had gone badly wrong and exploded, wiping out everyone around it. If the resultant shockwave hadn't thrown our frontline troops into such a state of chaos, it was claimed they could have marched across No Man's Land and taken the town of Cambrai without a bullet being fired. As it was things soon settled down and the status quo was restored.

Captain Ida Wolseley had greeted us on our return to the hospital later that same day. We had arrived well after lunchtime in the ambulance with some of the wounded, which included Vickery but not Maitland. A spell in hospital would probably have done Maitland the world of good, the flap of meat carved from his forehead had required a lot of stitches. But the major had insisted that he refused to leave his "lads", and that might well have been true. A less charitable element in my mind wondered whether he might also be loath to leave his barrel of excellent beer, regarding which he had apologised for not offering us a taste after our gruelling morning, because, he explained, 'It's all shaken up by the storm and needs to settle, don'tcha know. Make you ill it would, can't have that. Can't afford to have you chaps off sick, now, can we?'

We had cleaned and stitched the gash on his forehead while he sat stoically on a little stool. Spindrift had offered him ether but he refused it saying, 'Need to keep my wits about me, Boche might take advantage of the situation and be on us like the wild brutes they are. Cowardly brutes!' As a compromise, Spindrift had injected something directly into the wound. It made me wince to watch and Maitland quailed a little when he saw the needle, but after that he accepted our ministrations without so much as a whimper.

The redoubtable Vickery had also fought hard to stay with his major, and it was only after Maitland had issued a direct order that he reluctantly allowed himself to be loaded onto a stretcher and placed into the bone rattler ambulance. The medical work had been completed to Spindrift's satisfaction so there was no need for the usual frantic rush to get the men to aid. We spent a few leisurely hours making sure everyone was comfortable on the train and the wagons before we swapped salutes with Maitland and accepted a lift back to the hospital in the ambulance.

Spindrift and I had been allowed to travel up front with the blonde, whom we learned was called Susan Piper and who was, she told me with a direct stare, most definitely unattached.

'Not, due to a lack of interest, of course,' she explained, with a touch of vanity. 'No, but, you see, I'm a selective girl and the boy I love has yet to reach the gallery.' At this she cast a saucy glance in our direction and smiled, 'But I'm open to offers from the right quarter, if they're willing to wave of their handkerchief.'

She was so busy casting coquettish looks at us that a small group of farm workers had to throw themselves out of the way of her ambulance, and I had to shout a warning just in time before she rumbled her wheels right over one of the poor fellows where he lay. There was a squeal of brakes and we eventually lurched past while the men hurled abuse at our retreating backs. I heard Helen shout in reply, 'Well, really, was there any excuse for such foul language!'

After that Susan applied herself to her driving and we arrived back at the hospital without further incident.

We had already treated the injured men so we had no need to tend to them further. The corpsmen would quickly settle them into their beds and I dazedly wondered if I might be allowed a few hours in mine. I was beginning to suffer from that strangely detached sensation that indicates my body had gone too long without sleep. And it had been a packed thirty-six hours since I had last seen my bed. Susan waved and smiled brightly as her ambulance rumbled off towards Natres, Helen and Worsnip now comfortably in the front beside her. I waved my handkerchief and she blew a kiss. Spindrift and I turned towards our quarters. And there stood the immaculate Captain Wolseley who was regarding us with a cool, hostile stare.

'Gentlemen,' he said as if the word was distasteful and profoundly inaccurate. 'Gentlemen, I'm afraid the colonel is displeased. There has been a complaint, no, indeed a rebuke. He has been personally, yes, personally, castigated because of your actions and he demands an explanation, and, indeed, an apology!'

'What?' asked Spindrift. 'Who complained about us and why?'

'Don't act so coy, captain. You know full well. The Mother Superior from the Convent of the Sisters of the Weeping Heart, sister Honoria Pietas. She's livid. What were you thinking, man?'

~29~

It seems that the Reverend Mother had prepared some delicious treats for our appointment that morning at ten, and that she was an impatient host when guests were late. By eleven she had dispatched her pet bull terrier, sister Bridget, on the back of an ass, sending her straight to the colonel's chateau. I fought down an involuntary smile at the mental image of the frog-faced, bloated, black-robed creature perched on the back of a strutting little donkey. I imagined field workers throwing themselves over hedges and into ditches to clear her path.

The woman had obviously lost none of her charm since our encounter the previous day. I doubt she got as far as the personage himself, but the foppish Wolseley carried all the hallmarks of someone who had suffered the deep wounds inflicted by the Scottish nun's fierce tongue lashing. She had called me a 'pretty boy' and a 'pet monkey', I wonder what she would have made of the colonel's prissy aide. He seemed very upset. I was tempted to ask but considered it best to hold my tongue.

Wolseley had taken it upon himself to make the trip to our quarters and personally demand an apology, and to insist that we make amends to sister Honoria whatever it took, because, in his words, 'She is the nearest thing these rural types have to a lord of the manor. She's regarded locally as something between a mayor and a bishop. To show her disrespect is to show France disrespect, and that is not acceptable in the current situation.'

He had been waiting for hours and the steam had evidently built up inside him until it rattled his lid. When we finally returned, he began to whistle his woes. He had taken his stripes and now we must take ours, and he went on in that same whining vein for some several minutes. I followed Spindrift's lead and stood silently, allowing the man to vent his spleen. Beside me I could feel the sheer force of Spindrift's personality building, and began to fear for Wolseley's safety if he pushed the Preacher's patience too far.

I was already light-headed from exhaustion, and my thoughts floated gently to the conclusion that Wolseley would be much safer if he were just to shut up. His face seemed to swim in front of my eyes as if I was seeing him through rippling water. *Be still,* I thought, *be still.* And then I could see his mouth moving but I could no longer hear that clipped, yapping voice of his. The silence was wonderful. His eyes began bugging out of his head and he clutched at his throat, his mouth opened in an agonised rictus. He collapsed to his knees, his face turning blue. I watched as if from a great distance.

Spindrift muttered, 'That's enough, Colin, don't kill the poor fool.'

And I snapped out of my reverie as if waking from a dream. I blinked and shook my head. By then Wolseley was gagging on all fours, roaring air into his starved lungs and coughing thick mucus onto the ground.

Spindrift stepped forward and took the man's arm, he looked at me with an expressionless face.

'Help me with the captain, Colin. Let's get him into the officer's mess and fetch him a drink. Poor fellow has had a bad turn.'

Wolseley gasped, his face red and his eyes watering. 'Couldn't breathe, couldn't breathe. There was no air... No air. Couldn't breathe.'

Spindrift answered in a calm, composed manner, 'That's all right, Captain Wolseley. You've had an episode but it's passing now. You'll be fine once you've had a drink. Come on, come with us, please.'

'Couldn't breathe, no air, none. Choking!'

'That's fine, just breathe for me now captain. Good, good. That's fine, that's fine. Good.'

We settled him in a comfortable armchair in the mess and I fetched him a beer while Spindrift loosened his collar. He drank it greedily and belched loudly before thrusting the glass back into my hand.

'More, please.'

I fetched three pints and two chairs so we could get comfortable and enjoy at least a little time of relaxation after our long exertions. My mind was buzzing with unanswered questions. Spindrift evidently believed that I had somehow been the cause of Wolseley's 'episode'. If so how? This latest demonstration of my talents was obviously another facet of my legacy as a sprite. Well if such was the case I would obviously need to learn how to control myself. I couldn't go about choking people to death at a whim. I needed to talk with Rowan. I needed advice. My life had become a chapter from a fantastic child's picture book, but I was damned if I would let myself become the big bad wolf.

Spindrift was weaving another of his verbal tapestries. I listened, chuckling inwardly behind a serious face.

'Did you suffer from fainting fits as a child?'

'I, I, what? fainting? No, not that I can recall. Perhaps I did, why?'

'Neurasthenia, a classic case. William James described it as Americanitis, you must have heard of it. You've been working far too hard, poor fellow.

You've been pushing yourself to the limit and your mind is telling you to slow down. It is a syndrome of the noble mind, Wolseley, it affects the hardworking, ethical martyr, and demonstrates itself in hysterical symptomology – including irrational anger and shortness of breath. Do you ever feel an overwhelming urge to weep when you're alone?'

'Weep? I, well, yes! How did you know?'

'Classic symptom. How's your drinking?'

'Drinking? What can I say? I enjoy a glass of wine as much as the next fellow.'

'Do you ever feel you need it?'

'After a hard day, who doesn't? It's relaxing. Look here, I'm no puritan, but I'm no lush either!'

'I'm going to prescribe a sabbatical for you, a retreat. There's a place in Scotland that would be perfect. Doctor there is a chap called Rivers, William Rivers. The break will do you the world of good and you'll be able to come back to your duties refreshed and whole. I'll make the referral. Don't you worry, I can do all the paperwork. While you wait, you can take a bed here or return to your billet. Your choice.'

Things were moving a little too quickly for Wolseley. 'Wait. Scotland? What are you saying? What about, yes, what about the Mother Superior? Wait a minute, I have duties, work to do...'

'The ethical martyr. What do you say, Colin? Classic case?'

I nodded soberly, 'Classic case. Poor chap.' I daren't say more in case I burst the immaculate bubble of belief that Spindrift had blown into Wolseley's head. Or burst out laughing.

The Preacher continued in a gentle, understanding tone. 'Leave the Mother Superior to us, Ida. We'll deal with her and your colonel. He's a good man, he'll understand. Your mental health must come first. Neurasthenia is a tricky Johnny, ignore it and you pour lamp oil and coals onto the fire. Next thing you'll be hearing voices and seeing things that aren't there. Leave it to us, Ida. Let go. You've done enough as it is to bend your mind, just a little more might be too much and you'll break it altogether. You don't want that, surely?'

He paused and Wolseley slumped forward, collapsing around his empty glass like a boneless man. His head drooped. When he looked up there were tears glistening in his defeated eyes.

'I thought I could manage, you know? It was duty, you see, all of it. Every terrible moment of it. Every vile second. The colonel...' He wiped snot from his nose with a shaking hand. 'The colonel... He has... He has... Needs. You know? Who will help him if I'm not here? He can't, he can't...'

And he wept like a child.

I handed him the handkerchief I had waved at Susan. I was stunned and confused by his collapse. He was no longer a figure of fun but a tragic victim who deserved pity. The transformation was total. Spindrift moved to his side and wrapped a gentle arm around the man's shoulders. He spoke quietly.

'That's good, Ida, that's good. Bring it out for me, let it go.'

Wolseley flung his arms around the Preacher's neck and buried his face against the tall man's shoulder. He made odd, mewling noises. And then suddenly he lifted his face and kissed Spindrift full on the mouth. Spindrift remained completely still, his eyes open and steady.

Wolseley pulled away and smeared the back of his hand across his lips. He looked horrified, his eyes wide. 'I'm sorry, I'm, I'm sorry, I didn't mean to do that. I'm sorry.'

And he dropped his glass and leapt from his chair. All pretence at sophistication evaporated. His tailored uniform seemed to clutch at him like a noose and he writhed in its grip, panting and whimpering. His knees were bent and his hands balled into fists as if he wanted to lash out but couldn't find his target. He looked from one to the other of us and his mouth opened in a soundless scream, and then he clenched his teeth and groaned. Finally, he spoke.

'I'll be in my room at the château. Thank-you, both of you. I'll wait to hear from you. Thank-you, I have to go now.'

And he dashed from the room.

~30~

Spindrift touched a finger to his lips. He spoke through gritted teeth.

'If we do nothing else today we must get that poor devil away from the colonel. You saw that, Colin? He's been driven to breaking point. Monstrous! I'll not judge a man by his choices – and we can't choose where we find love, nobody can – but to take advantage of a man's nature like that? It's, it's wicked. The colonel must take his greatest pleasure from cruelty.'

My imagination was running riot, but I suspected that the worst I could envisage would prove just a pale reflection of the truth about Ida Wolseley's nightmare existence. And we had let him return to the colonel's château.

'What are we going to do?'

'Exactly as I promised, I'm going to get Wolseley out of that monster's clutches and have him sent to Craiglockhart War Hospital. William Rivers can talk him through his trauma if any man can. Wait for me here while I get the paperwork in order; and whatever you do, please, try not to think anyone else into a vacuum until I get back. You and I seriously need to talk.'

He strode from the mess with a fierce light in his eye. I stifled a yawn and hoped we were done with excitement for the day. Much more would probably see me needing my own chat with the good doctor Rivers. And then I smiled ruefully to myself. No. No, it wouldn't, I had to be honest with myself, what I needed most was a chat with Rowan. One to one.

Something was confusing me. The events of the last few days should have been terrifying; I should be sitting, twitching in the corner of a locked and darkened room, scared witless and jumping at the slightest sound. But I had taken everything in my stride, almost as if I had done nothing more than take a walk along the promenade on a balmy spring day.

My mouth was dry but so were the palms of my hands, and my heart, which should have been pounding, beat a steady, calm tattoo.

What had happened to me? I had experienced fear before, I could still remember the gut churning dread before we went over the top at Cambrai. When did I become so resolute? I couldn't think of myself as courageous, nor did I believe I was foolhardy enough to think myself suddenly invincible. I was as mortal as the next man, if I was still a man. What I had to discover is how much of what I was now had been part of the 'me' I had been before I met Rowan, or even the more innocent 'me' from before I had met Preacher Spindrift.

I thought back to that day when I woke up under canvas in a hospital cot, paralysed and afraid because I couldn't see the sky. The sky. Involuntarily I looked towards the room's largest window. And she was there, framed behind its glass. Beckoning. Rowan. Perhaps the day's adventures were not quite at an end.

She was even more enchanting in daylight than by firelight, and just as exotic. My heart leapt into my mouth and I felt all my waning energy surge back. I felt as if someone had thrown open the shutters in a darkened house and let the light come flooding in. I almost ran out of the farmhouse to where she waited for me – but when I reached the spot she was gone. I spun on my heel. She was looking back at me from over a hundred yards away, halfway across a fallow field. She continued her long-legged stride towards a copse of trees I had never noticed before. I ran after her. The trees had a lush greenness to them that seemed out of sorts with the time of year, and Rowan glowed as if she walked under a different, brighter sun.

She chuckled when I reached her side. 'Alone are you? Where's your fine dark shadow? I thought you two to be glued to each other's heels. Mind you, to see you without him makes you shine brighter yet. He has a stern, martial aspect that he shares with you when you stand at his side, but you shrug it off quickly enough. And are you well, master Cahoon? Has your mistress embraced you to her cold bosom yet?'

'My mistress? I don't...'

Her warm chuckle tightened something in my gut. She looked up.

'The sky, your natural element. Are you finding your feet up there amongst the clouds? I felt you do something not long since. It clathered across the ether like a hobnailed boot on a dance floor, so it did. 'Tis a powerful natural gift you have for making so much noise where such as I can hear it.'

I loved the sound of the word 'clathered', and I immediately knew what she meant. I had heard enough hobnailed boots just recently. We entered the shade of the trees and I felt momentarily dizzy. The copse seemed larger and denser from the inside than it looked from the outside. Filtered as it was through rich and glossy green leaves I could have sworn the sun was shining brighter and the day had taken on a fresh warmth. Something fizzed through my veins and I felt a surge of glorious happiness that made me feel light as air. I closed my eyes and surrendered to joy. I felt Rowan's hand tug at mine and I looked down at her. *Down?*

Her upturned face plucked at the strings of my heart and played music only angels could hear. Her plump lips were parted in a full smile that dimpled her flawless cheeks. God, she was beautiful. And about three feet below me. I hovered above her, light as a feather, only her firm grip was keeping me from floating away like a soap bubble.

She pulled me to her and we kissed, at first gently and then with mounting hunger. The next several minutes saw us fumbling with each other's clothes until at last we were flesh to flesh and there was nothing to impede our love play. She was everything I had ever wanted in a lover. We clung together like the survivors of a storm and for long minutes we were the only things that mattered while we explored each other and found pleasure I had never known was possible. All too soon I felt the pressure build within me until I could hold it no longer and I groaned in sweet release. She held me tight and sighed with satisfied contentment. She pulled away with a little moue of regret. She took my penis in her hand, bent down, and kissed it. Her action sent a surge of lust raging through me that couldn't be denied, no woman had ever done that to me before, even my wife had never touched me there. We coupled again in the middle of that emerald island of spring. Adam and Eve discovering each other in our own little paradise adrift in the grey winter of a French warscape. I was lost in the sheer joy of her, lost beyond the simpler pleasures available to the less subtle human body. What we were sharing was something vital, something profound. It was as much of the belly as the heart, and while my spirit soared in grace my flesh was firmly anchored between her thighs in our slippery, hot union. The journey from our first kiss to that place of heat and scattered senses could have taken us a million miles and a lifetime to travel and I would still have been happy. I never wanted it to end. And then something in me came alive. I felt it wrench itself free. It reared up and roared in triumph to finally be rid of its human trappings. Suddenly I could feel everything Rowan was feeling, the sliding power of smooth muscle against smooth muscle, hearts pounding in perfect unison. Her eyes jolted open in surprise. She could feel it too. She pressed her lips against mine, opened her mouth and her elixir flooded into me once more, sending coruscating sparks of fresh knowledge to my brain, while intense streams of pure bliss flooded to my extremities. All my extremities. I reacted on instinct, my strokes into her becoming longer and stronger. I felt her hands on my buttocks and I gripped the firm globes of her behind while we thrust at each other in a mindless rhythm. And then, finally, it ended.

The second climax had us both grunting in hot, sweet sympathy and when it peaked Rowan uttered an involuntary shriek that I echoed. Anyone hearing us would have thought we were being tortured to death, skewered on red hot wires. They would have been close to the truth. Every nerve in my body vibrated with sensual electricity and I quivered like a harp string. Afterwards we held each other close. Rowan panted, making small, surprised breathy sounds. I took a long while to catch my breath, all the while stroking her moist body and radiant, flushed face. Naked, sweaty and with her streaked mane of russet hair matted to her head, her body quivering like a new-born colt, she was sublime, magnificent. And then she uttered a deep sigh.

'Can't you hear him?'

'Who?'

'Satan. Your shadow. He's calling for you. We'd better go.'

We dressed and walked out together, out of the sun-drenched copse and into the chill winter evening.

~31~

Spindrift was back in the officers' mess, two pints of beer on the table in front of him, one by an empty chair. That one was for me. His forehead tightened for a moment when he saw Rowan by my side and then he grinned. He lifted both glasses.

'Shall we take these to my rooms? I believe we'll need a little more privacy. Rowan, my dear, you look radiant. Would you prefer beer or wine?'

She chose wine and Spindrift told her he had a fine vintage in his rooms. He looked keenly at both of us and nodded as if with approval, then led the way. I was still in a pleasantly bemused state and happy to go along with just about anything so long as Rowan was involved.

Once in his rooms Spindrift soon got a fire blazing and settled Rowan in a chair with a glass of red wine. I sat next to her with my beer. Without thinking we held hands. A mild electric current passed between us, enough to make a dead frog jump a full yard.

The fireplace seemed unusually bare that evening and it took me a while to realise what was missing.

'Doc, where's your dog? I haven't seen her for a while.'

'Yes, she's hunting. She'll be back.' He regarded Rowan and smiled. 'Has it happened? Has the transition happened?'

She nodded and her grin was shamelessly replete. 'He is awake to the spirit now, I have welcomed him and soothed him through transition.'

'As a brother?'

'No, Satan, not quite.' She coloured slightly. 'I am Earth and he is Air, we are not brother and sister. Perhaps we are much more than that. When Earth and Air conjoin, you get lightning. When it is quickened, storms and hurricanes might tremble the great tree of life to its very roots. It is a rare and powerful conjunction, perhaps one that would be welcomed by fools, and, perhaps, feared by the wise.' She cast me a long, lingering glance. 'But I don't think we need to fear this one.'

At that moment, something jolted hard between us and threw our hands apart. Rowan gasped in shock and gripped her palm as if she'd been burned. Spindrift was at her side in an instant. He examined the skin of her palm and then wordlessly strode out of the room. Rowan's face was pale and a slight sheen of sweat sprang onto her skin. Her eyes were wide with pain and something else, shock? Disappointment? Her beautiful mouth was twisted as if she was about to burst into tears and she protectively cradled her damaged hand against her breast. I reached out to her and she cowered away.

'No, Colin. Please, wait. We must wait.'

I drew back, confused, and hurt. What had just happened? Something had just slapped our hands apart with incredible violence. Less than an hour before we had enjoyed the most complete and intimate union possible between a man and a woman. It had been wonderful, the most intense experience of my life. The entire length of our bodies had been pressed together like the pages of a book and I had felt our hearts beat as if one. Two people could not have been closer without sharing the same skin. What had come between us since? What was that energy that had struck our hands apart so forcibly, almost like a small explosion? And why did I feel guilty? As if what had happened had somehow been deliberate on my part?

And then I remembered the roar of triumph that had bellowed in my chest, the sudden charge to my senses, as if something had woken within me and become fully alive for the first time. Had some physical change taken place as well? Had something in my body become active? Some strange kind of receptor? Had I since become a conduit or even a generator for some sort of static electrical charge that had just been released into the flesh of the woman I loved? What was I? A Van de Graaff generator? Misery and confusion had washed away my intense feelings of happiness. I felt as if I was poised over a dark and mysterious pit filled with unknown peril, and that I had no choice but to fall into the blackness and accept my fate.

Spindrift returned and knelt by Rowan's side. He took her hand and gently massaged something into her cupped palm. The crucifixes on his lapel caught the firelight and burned red like bright blood. Seeing him kneeling there I was reminded of his calling. He was a preacher, yes, but also a battle-hardened warrior for his God. I had been with him three times when he fought the enemy and won, sometimes against unthinkable odds. He had supernatural abilities and inhuman talents, I knew all that, yet he was also the most completely humane person I had ever met. He was a complex being, a fierce soldier and ministering angel, a servant of God and guardian for the innocent. The fact that he could fly took some getting used to, but then so could I.

Completely unbidden, a question popped into my mind and out of my mouth in the same instant. 'Doc, why do you take me with you when you fight the worm? Each time you've had to rescue me. Why take me with you when I just get in the way?'

He continued layering his balm onto Rowan's hand, his eyes creased in concentration. I wondered if he had heard me and made to repeat my question, when he turned and regarded me with shadowed eyes.

'That's a strange thing to ask at this precise moment. I would have thought you'd be more concerned about Rowan's wellbeing. She's been hurt. Aren't you curious about that? Or are you a man who takes his pleasure with a woman and then discards her when he's finished? If such is the case I've seriously misjudged you, Captain Cahoon?'

'You're right, I'm very sorry. Rowan, how's your hand?'

She ventured a weak smile. 'Not your fault, Colin. I should have been more careful. But after, after, this afternoon...' some colour returned to her ashen complexion. 'I felt we would be safe to touch. Foolish of me. I should have known.'

She took her hand from Spindrift's grip and held it up so I could see. My jaw dropped. A black, five-pointed star had been burned into her palm. Its edges looked perfect as if it had been drawn with a rule by a fanatically precise mathematician.

I sputtered, 'But, how's that possible? What is that?'

She studied her palm and bright tears sprang into her eyes. 'It's a warning, that's what it is. Look at your own hand. See what's there.'

I did as I was told and gaped liked a gaffed fish. On my palm was the mirror image of Rowan's star, but mine was silver. I rubbed at it, then held it up to show them.

'What's happening to us? What is this? I don't understand!'

For once Spindrift seemed as confused as me. He rocked back on his heels and looked from one to the other of us – as if I had a clue about what was going on. Rowan looked at me with a heartbroken expression on her glorious features. I wanted to hug her but was afraid of what might happen if I did. She reached out towards me and then drew her hand back, folding it into her lap. She looked down at her palm again and began to speak.

'There is a city called Scytaer Faehl. It is a place built by elementals, by us, and it exists between the worlds. It is the most beautiful place in creation, and it is our home. We can move between the worlds at will and rest where we please, or, at least, where we've been invited, but Scytaer Faehl is our nest and it is where we go to die. It's also where we're born.'

She paused and looked hard at me. 'Almost thirty years ago, a son was born to a prince of the city. It was a time of dispute. The son's birth would cement the prince's succession to the throne in place of his twin brother. An heir guarantees the crown, it is our way. We are a long-lived breed and birth is rare, very rare. A child is accepted as a good omen, a promise of great fortune. The news of the birth spread through the city and beyond like fire through tinder. Its father was proclaimed as heir to the throne and the accession Council ratified his succession. And then...'

She looked at Spindrift for a long moment and then at me.

'...and then the child vanished.'

~32~

Rowan continued, 'The prince's brother immediately lobbied for the Council's ratification to be withdrawn. Without an heir, he said, the question of succession had become moot, and for all intents and purposes his twin was once more childless.'

I looked at Spindrift and he at me. We both knew where this tale was headed. I felt strange. It was as if I had suddenly been inserted into the wrong story. In the space of a few days, less than a week, the roots of my old life had been ripped from the ground and then replanted, and a shrub I had once believed to be a common or garden weed was proving to be infinitely more exotic. Rowan was still talking, gazing, and rubbing at the blackened star on her hand. She made a sad figure in the shifting orange shadows cast by the firelight.

'This will fade, as will that mark on your hand, Colin. This,' she held up her hand again, 'this is the brand of an idiot, almost a criminal in our law. The mark of a woman who reached too far beyond her station.' She shook it, 'This is rejection, this is humiliation. This marks me for what I am, a lowly elemental burned because I dared to love one of my betters. Sex is fine, yes, no problem, that's just a matter of lust and shared flesh. We all know that kings may tarry where they wish, and sometimes where they're not wanted, but love? No, that's forbidden by everything we hold sacred.'

Her voice took on a bitter edge. 'I didn't know, I couldn't be sure, but I wondered.' Her amber eyes studied me and her mouth worked as if her next words had become too difficult to utter. 'You beautiful, golden man. Look at you there, glittering in your majesty. Those drab clothes you wear can't hide what you are; how could they? The son of the son of the King of the air. A prince of the winds. One of the four majesties made manifest and then stolen away and abandoned because of jealousy and ambition. We must thank the creator you weren't murdered out of hand; the abductors must have had some heart in them'

She stood up. 'I must return to Scytaer Faehl and announce the good news. After all these years, the lost prince is found, the heir is alive and well. These are tidings of great joy, ring the welkin with great gladness, for he is found.'

She held her hands out to either side and stood before me, 'You may kiss me, but you must not hold my hands. You may give me any gift you wish, but not love, that will get the pair of us into trouble.' She smiled with something approaching her accustomed impish charm. 'The woman burned because of her forbidden love of a prince, that sounds just grand don't you think? Well now, I'll have my own legend in the storybooks, so I will, and me portrait there on the cover. And we had a grand time while it lasted, didn't we? Didn't we just?'

I kissed her chastely, very aware that Spindrift was in the room. She kissed me back as if we were alone. Then she stepped away and made a curious little bobbing motion. 'Farewell, majesty. Expect visitors very soon.' She blew me a kiss, nodded at Spindrift, and was gone.

The Preacher poured us both a glass of his good red wine and bade me take a chair. He pulled the chair Rowan had been seated in closer to me and settled himself in it. He was haloed by firelight and his features were lost in inky shadows. We sipped in companiable silence for a few moments, and then he leaned forward and held out his hand. I took it and shook it right readily. He grinned his usual grin and studied the palm of his hand when I released it. I took another sip of my wine.

'It seems you can only burn creatures of your own breed after all. That's a relief.'

'Or perhaps I can only burn those who love me unwisely.'

'Unwisely? Well put, yes, well said.'

His dark eyes glittered in the shadows of his enigmatic face.

'And now, prince Colin of the city between the worlds, what do we do next?'

'What do you mean? We do what we set out to do. Nothing's changed. We've still got a job to do. An important job too. We must find and defeat the mother worm, eradicate it from the Earth, burn it with those crystals of yours. And I'll bet we find out what's been happening with the local children too. Something tells me those two things are closely connected, and that the convent is right at the heart of everything that's going on. We must go there tomorrow, and tomorrow morning too. We promised Wolseley we'd sort things out with the Reverend Mother and I keep my promises.'

The wineglass disappeared into Spindrift's shadows and emerged half empty.

He sighed, 'When we started this crusade I knew you to be a man from Texas. And what a man! Brave as Davy Crockett and ready to spit in a wildcat's eye. Now what are you, I wonder?'

'I'm Colin Cahoon, captain with the 11th Regiment of Engineers, part of the American Expeditionary Force and seconded to work with you, Captain Spindrift. And anyway, what are *you*? A man beyond time whose real name is Satan and whose home is out there somewhere beyond Mars. You've got some nerve asking me what I am. At least I was born here.'

'No, Colin, you weren't. Thieves dumped you here. You were born in that city between the worlds Rowan was telling us about, some place called Scytaer Faehl. I've never heard of it but you were born there. You're one of the fey and by the sound of it one of their royalty. You were stolen from your parents and abandoned out in the desert and you're damned lucky to be alive.'

'Well, that makes two of us, doesn't it? Two abandoned men. We belong together like peas in a pod, so don't think you're going to get rid of me anytime soon. I'm in, we're a team, so live with it.'

There came a knock at the door and we both jumped. Spindrift stood up and barked, 'Come in!'

The door opened just a crack and a tousled head in a small white cap poked round it. I recognised him as a corporal from the kitchens.

'Evening, captains,' he said nervously. 'Sorry to interrupt, sirs, but I was sent to inform you that dinner's ready when you are. And then I heard raised voices. Begging your pardon, sirs, but is everything all, you know, right? We wouldn't want to see you fine officers falling out over nothing when you seemed so friendly up until now. Is there anything I can do to help?'

Spindrift waved him away, 'We're fine thanks, corporal Lamb. More a heated discussion than a falling out. We'll be along in a few moments. Would you save some seats for us, please?'

'Right you are sir. It's pork and potatoes tonight, very nice.'

'Thank you, we're looking forward to it.'

The head disappeared and the door shut with a sharp click. Spindrift shook his head and grinned ruefully. 'If I had a dime for every plate of pork and potatoes...'

I chuckled, 'Yes, I know what you mean, but we haven't eaten anything since yesterday. They say hunger makes the finest sauce and I'm starving. This is going to be the best plate of pork and potatoes we've ever eaten.'

I stuck out my hand, 'I'm in, Satan Spindrift. We may be the oddest couple that ever sat down to dinner but you and I got a job to do and I don't see someone like corporal Lamb there stepping up to the plate if we walk away. We're in this together. We got a deal?'

'We do, we do. But I wonder what your father's going to say about it?'

'I can't get used to the idea that I've got a dad. You think he's going to want to get involved?'

'Wouldn't you if you'd just found out that your son had turned up after nearly thirty years?'

'You're right. Guess I would at that.'

'Then I suggest we grab a plate of victuals right now before he makes his entrance.' He opened the door, 'After you, fair prince.'

I snorted, bowed like a buffoon, and stepped through the door. We walked together to the refectory. I could smell the pork before we got there, and I was right, it was the best plate of food I'd ever eaten. I would have enjoyed a good night's sleep afterwards. But first we would meet my family.

~33~

I was on the verge of bidding Spindrift goodnight. We had returned to his rooms after a good dinner, finished two bottles of wine, and we had an appointment with sister Honoria the next morning. I was beginning to flag and my curiosity was waning as my tiredness peaked. I yawned and stood up, stretching my muscles.

'I don't think anything's going to happen tonight, Doc. I think I'll go to bed. See you for breakfast in the morning?'

He also rose to his feet. 'You're probably right. There's no point in sitting up all night. Yes, see you in the morning.'

I had turned to leave when what seemed to be an enormous gust of wind detonated against the side of the building directly behind me, followed by a second and then a third.

Spindrift said, 'You think someone's trying to get our attention?'

I nodded, 'You could very well be right.'

'Put the screen in front of the fire and let's pull the blackout curtain to one side. See what's out there.'

I did as I was told and then joined him by the window. He looked at me.

'You ready for this?'

'Why are we waiting?'

'Why indeed?'

He pulled the heavy curtain to one side. Three men stood out there in the darkness, shoulder to shoulder. Two were slender with light beards and long white-blonde hair. The centre man was taller and more massive with a fuller beard. It was dark and they were difficult to make out, but their clothes looked dated, almost medieval. They made a powerful impression even so.

Spindrift said quietly, 'You are welcome to enter here.'

A deep voice whispered back, 'No, thank-you. You are invited to join us. Are you willing?'

I shrugged and turned to my companion. 'What do I know? Your call.'

Spindrift raised an eyebrow at me, then replied, 'We are at your disposal.'

The deep voice responded, 'So be it.'

And Spindrift's room disappeared. There was a sensation of falling, but upwards and in a very long curve. It was nothing like my previous experiences of flying but very akin to the sensation of being flung away by a shell-burst. My eyes were open but there was nothing to see, neither darkness nor light. I was sure there was no air to breathe but it didn't matter because my lungs didn't seem to be working right. My whole body was numb and I felt as if I was being pressed into something both resilient and yielding at the same time. I squeezed my eyes tight shut. Then I heard a distinct 'pop' and I fell gasping to my knees. I blinked my eyes open again and waited a few beats before my vision cleared completely. I noticed two things. First, the three men were now sitting in odd but grand looking chairs, almost like thrones, which looked to have been constructed from branches, woven straw, bones, in fact everything found on a forest floor. Second, Spindrift was sprawled on the floor at my side. He was unconscious or worse. I reached out and gripped his wrist. There was no pulse. Without thinking I planted my mouth over his and attempted to breathe life back into him. Nothing. I began to pump at his chest, pressing down with both hands. He didn't even stir.

'Come on, breathe, damn you, breathe.'

I felt a firm hand on my shoulder and spun around. One of the two younger men was crouching by my side. His gentle eyes were exactly level with mine. He looked oddly familiar.

He spoke quietly, 'Don't worry, he's fine. We just deactivated him while we have a chat with you. He'll be fine.'

'What do you mean, deactivated? He's dead. What have you done to him?'

The older man spoke and I recognised his deep voice. He was the man who had invited us there.

'Dead, do you say? Nonsense! Satan is the timeless guardian of Earth. Strictly speaking he's never been alive, but he's certainly not dead. He's a wily old fox but an honest and a brave one. We know him well and we'd never hurt a hair on his head, God forbid. We just wanted a quiet word with you before we allow him to join the party. When he's awake, he has the knack of becoming the centre of attention, as I'm sure you've noticed. Leave him be and come over here. Don't worry, I promise you he's fine.'

I looked from my supine friend to the man at my side and then up at the two seated men. I stood up. The man at my side did the same and I realised he was the same height as me. He had an open, frank face that I would have trusted under different circumstances, but standing there with Spindrift splayed out and still on the floor I didn't know what to feel.

The man at my side smiled, 'We have long formal names, very tedious, but I am known to all as Pel-os. My brother over there is Pel-ani and this is our father, King Pel-ora.'

I found it difficult to take my eyes from Spindrift, but I glanced at each man as his name was mentioned. The King's eyes were steady and bright and his hawk's beak of a nose jutted proudly from a square, handsome face. The brothers must take after their mother, I thought. They were pretty rather than handsome. Pel-ani regarded me with bored disdain and evident distaste.

'My name's Cahoon,' I said, 'Colin Cahoon. I'm a captain with the US army in France. I want to know what you've done to my friend and what you intend to do with me.'

Pel-ani tutted like an old maid hearing a swearword in chapel. I decided I didn't like him much and the feeling seemed mutual. If he was going to prove the wicked uncle in this tale I wouldn't be at all surprised. I wondered if he practiced his sneer in the mirror or if it came naturally. Perhaps it was the result of a little of both.

Pel-os took my arm and led me to a chair that had the same bird's nest look as his own. I sat gingerly, but although it creaked a little it bore my weight with ease. Spindrift lay at our feet like a strange rug. I began to wonder when I was going to rouse from this odd fancy and see him awake once more. I wanted him to stand up and take control of the situation. I looked around the room and realised with jolt just how big it was. We five were on a raised dais which was the only part of the room illuminated by a clean, white light. I couldn't make out where it was coming from but it shone down on us and rendered the rest of the room into almost total darkness. A host of people stood in the shadows like an audience at a play, and we were evidently the main attraction. They were standing well back but I could tell every face was turned towards us. I hoped they were enjoying the show so far. My mouth ran dry, which wasn't surprising because water was pouring from my hands and a cold river trickled down my spine. I didn't think it was the result of stage fright.

'My dear, Cahoon. Please, don't be afraid for Satan.' Pel-ora boomed. 'Your concern does you credit, but he will be returned to you soon enough, I promise. We have brought you here to question your name and we must test your mettle. If you are who we think you are you will remain unharmed, if you are not... Well, there may be some discomfort.'

The way he said 'discomfort' made me feel queasy. I began to think of old-fashioned torture implements, I wondered what else might be hidden in the shadows. Were they going to stretch me on the rack until I told them whatever they wanted to hear? By the look on Pel-ani's face he would happily hear me scream. I wondered at his frank hatred. What had I ever done to him? As if in response to my thoughts Pel-ani looked around the room at the assembled host.

'Can we get on with it? These fine people must have much better things to do than loiter around here. I know I do.'

His voice was oddly high-pitched and had more than a hint of a whine to it. His eyes were the same blue as his brother's, but while Pel-os' eyes shone with warm intelligence like his father's, Pel-ani glared around him with an expression of angry and petulant sullenness. His expression would likely sour milk in a cow's udder.

His father growled, 'Peace! Cahoon must be given the choice. We don't threaten a man with pain without good reason.' He turned to me and smiled with strong white teeth. 'I think you know what we suspect. Little Rowan would have told you what she believed before she reported back to us. She has been forgiven for her trespass and the blot removed from her hand. She is here, somewhere.'

I looked around, but the crowd remained firmly back in the shadows, still, silent, and anonymous. I would have liked to see her again and was glad to hear the burn on her hand had been healed.

Pel-os leaned forward, 'There is a special kind of light, an intelligent light, that recognises manifestations of majesty. It is very pure and dangerous to common folk, which is why our audience stays back in the shadows. Its slightest touch might destroy their very fabric. The light is called the Conduit and it flows in us, and only in us, and those others like us, princes of the elements: air, earth, fire, and water. Say the word and it will test you, Cahoon.'

'Will you wake Spindrift afterwards?'

'If you wish.'

'Then do it.'

Pel-ani barked a command in a strange tongue. And my world instantly became a hell of screaming white light.

~34~

I believe something essential in me was scoured away under that relentless torrent of light. Something vital. My years as Colin Cahoon, orphan child, schoolboy, medical student, husband, and soldier had coated me in base layers of humanity that were firm grained and had become an integral part of my nature. I felt excruciating pain while it all melted from me and I was uncovered for the first time in my true form. It felt as if my tender flesh had been exposed to harsh acids, or something worse. I remembered one of the times when I was very small. I had dreamed about flying and the mothers thought I had wet the bed. They made me stand naked in a tin tub in the yard out the back of the big house. In front of the other kids they washed me all over with strong lye soap and my skin turned red and I felt scorched. I had tried to stop the tears but the humiliation was too great and they poured out of me like I was filled to the brim with hot salt water. I still cringe at the shame of that memory. The light on that dais was very like that. I buckled under its intense glare.

I couldn't see the bastard but I heard Pel-ani cackle and crow, 'See him, see him burn. I told you, told you! He is false as a paper promise and he will burn just as quickly.'

If this light was so intelligent, I wondered, why hadn't it burned the black heart clean out of that vindictive piece of shit? Then I heard a whispering voice answer me.

Pel-osen, only son of Pel-os and grandson of Pel-ora, scion of the line of majesty in the city of Scytaer Faehl, welcome home. As for Pel-ani's heart, how can I burn what is not there?

I answered, 'Are you the light?'

The Conduit, yes. I shine on you and in you, Prince Pel-osen. Your heart is strong and kind. You will make a great King when your time comes, but, please, be merciful towards Pel-ani. His heart is weak and tainted because he knows he stands in the shadows of those greater than he could ever be. His is the petty jealousy of a weak man confronted by the strong. His neck pains him because he is always looking up at his betters. Pity him, it will annoy him much more than your anger.

I heard another voice, 'He speaks with the light! He has proved his mettle! The Prince is returned.'

The Conduit chuckled, *I shall see you soon, child of Pel-os. The future calls you. Be well.*

And the light was gone.

My grandfather studied me. 'What is your name?'

Almost unbidden the answer came out of me with an air of complete confidence.

'My name is Pel-osen, and I have returned home.'

My father strode to my side and embraced me and my grandfather pounded our shoulders growling, 'Well met, very well met! Welcome, welcome!'

My uncle turned his face away. It was dark with anger. I pitied him. I had never had a family before and now here I was the 'scion of majesty' and at the centre of a loving crowd. I was dazed and off-balance.

That was when an astonishingly lovely woman stepped out of the crowd of onlookers and approached the dais. She was the perfect image of grace and blonde beauty. She stood silently and waited as if she needed an invitation to come closer.

I said to my father, 'Please, who is this lady?' But I was sure I knew the answer already.

My father smiled, 'Pel-osen, meet your dam. This is the gracious lady Ventari.' And he held out a hand to her. She smiled like a flower coming into bloom and rushed to kiss me. If she had been any other woman her intimate hug might have caused an embarrassing and instant physical response; she was a gorgeous creature with a face and figure that would easily keep a boy up at night. But she was my mother. My *mother*!

The crowd had begun cheering as if I was some great prize that had been awarded to all of them, and a crescendo of applause built to the point that even I could hear it, lost as I was in a fog of astonished happiness.

That was when my uncle made his move. My parents and grandfather made a tight group with me at their centre. We were, as my military training would have told me under different circumstances, a prime target.

I heard a high pitched, barked order, 'Take them! Take them all!'

Pel-ani leapt to one side away from the dais and drew a long thin knife from his sleeve. He pointed it at us and whined.

'None of you shall live. None of you.'

My grandfather emitted a great bellow of rage but the twenty or so hefty men who had detached themselves from the crowd and sprinted at us with drawn swords looked very competent and undaunted by his fury.

My father shouted, 'Pel-ani, no!', and my mother stood at my side with a sad and almost disappointed expression on her perfect face. She stood tall and regal, prepared to accept her fate as a true noblewoman should – and my heart broke. I had found her; must I now lose her and my own life so soon after meeting her? It seemed too wicked a fate. In just a few seconds we would be struck down and there was nothing I could do about it but put my bare hands against cold steel. I prepared to go down fighting. I would protect her with my own blood in the hope that, once they had me out of the way, she at least might be spared the worst. And then the magic happened.

A thick ribbon of fluid white mist streamed around us and encircled us, separating us from our would-be assassins. It looked flimsy as fog or steam and the attackers made to shoulder their way through it. They raised their weapons to strike, but were suddenly flung backwards like toys thrown away by an angry child. They clattered to the ground and lay there, reeling, dazed, and confused.

Pel-ani shrieked in disgust. 'Get up, get up, you carrion crows! Get up! Don't be afraid of a little smoke.'

He threw his dagger at me with an expression of pure hatred darkening his fine features. It flew swift, straight, and true like a shaft of light pointed towards my heart.

And it struck the mist and stuck there, quivering for the briefest moment as if its point had embedded itself in wood, and then it was pitched violently back at Pel-ani, spinning in mid-flight. He had to hurl himself to the floor to avoid becoming skewered on his own blade.

His men had regained their feet and were now standing in a group and regarding him with naked contempt. He was crouched on all fours and panting with fear, a string of drool hanging from his chin. His lips curled back from his snarling teeth and he spat his words at them.

'Are you children to be frightened of nothing? March to that dais and finish this now! Do it! Do it! There they are, there! Do it!'

The men looked at their screaming commander and then across to our stoic group of silent 'victims'. The contrast must have been evident, even to them, and they bowed their heads apologetically before approaching once more. This attack was much more cautious, but just as committed as the first.

A clear sweet voice rang out. 'Enough of this! Enough!'

A column of almost blinding white light blazed down onto the dais with physical force. It landed like a hammer blow and split the raised area into two. I grabbed at my mother to stop her from tumbling over. Her eyes were wide with surprised curiosity and shock, and her mouth set in a grim line. Father and grandfather stepped forward to shield us from the column of light. Mother and I clung together in their shadow.

The light increased as if it had somehow become more concentrated, if anything it looked whiter as if it had been purified. It condensed and took a cylindrical form which was quickly refined into a human shape. The world paused as if it had taken a deep breath and then the glowing figure threw out a last refulgent blast of light, and a lightly clothed woman stood tall before us. At first, she smiled at us, and then she turned to regard Pel-ani. Her expression hardened as if she was suddenly turned to stone. When she spoke, her words fell into the room's sudden silence like rocks cast into a deep pool.

~35~

'I told your nephew to pity you, Pel-ani, but you are not worth the time nor the effort. You are become a thing of shame and are no longer worthy of notice.'

My uncle screamed back at her, 'How dare you talk to me like that? What are you? Nothing but stale light falling through some dusty window. Your time is over, hag, and this is no affair of yours. Get out of here and let us deal with our own business in our own way.'

The woman gazed at him, and made a gesture with her foot as if she was wiping something from the bottom of it. Then she held her hand out towards Pel-ani, palm upwards, and she blew gently across it.

Something streamed from her to him. It enveloped him in a pall of clinging, spiralling smoke. It coiled closely around him and sat on his flesh for a moment like an aura of soft light, glowing greenly. And then it poured like liquid into him, sucked into his mouth and nostrils. It even seemed to seep into his eyes and ears. He clawed at his cheeks in horror, his mouth opened wide and he sank to his knees. He held out his hands as if seeking mercy.

The woman was intoning something musical and sinister. It sounded wonderful and dreadful at the same time. My grandfather cried out.

'Milady, must it be like this? Should we not show my son mercy?'

I heard two voices then. The woman continued her incantation as before and Pel-ani buckled under it as if scourged with whips, but I also heard that soft intimate voice that had spoken to me in the light. It spoke once more to me as if it had been projected directly into my thoughts, but it was not me to whom she addressed her words.

'Pel-ora, gentle heart. You plead for the son who would have seen his own family cut down without mercy? You plead for the creature who stole your grandson from his mother and abandoned him alone and helpless in the barren outlands of the world of men? You plead for a black-hearted whelp who dishonours his name and that of his sire? You would plead for this pathetic thing?'

'I would, noble lady, I must. Please, he is my son.'

'Had he one twentieth of your noble soul, gentle king, I would spare him all, and pray for his redemption. But listen to the thoughts that even now plague this sorry creature's lost and unholy mind.'

And we were treated to a hot spurt of the filthiest, most repellent bile imaginable. Pel-ani's heart was filled with poison and the bulk of his venom was directed towards me: for being born, for surviving the desert, and for returning to claim my inheritance thus wiping away his hopes of kingship. But he also saved plenty of hatred for my mother and father, and even his own father, the man who had favoured them for the throne.

Self-pity, ambition, and sick loathing erupted from his rotted soul like pus from a lanced boil. I was wrong to think that he might have spared my mother if I was dead. Along with my father and grandfather, she too would have died – eventually. After he had slaked the unnatural, envious lust he had nurtured for her ever since he first met her. The rage and madness that had been held under such a tight lid for nearly three decades spewed out of his seething brain and we heard everything. Everything.

For what he had planned to do to my mother, the mother I didn't even know I had until that very hour, I would have happily choked the life out of him with my bare hands. For what he had done to me when I was just a baby he deserved to be hanged or shot. But for his attack on his own father and his only brother, for that he should be burned. Burned like the Sha-aneer until the last drift of poisonous ash was blown to the winds and he was totally erased from existence, leaving behind nothing but a stark and sorry memory.

I realised my family were looking at me with understanding eyes and with a shock I understood that they had heard *my* thoughts as well as my uncle's. Grandfather nodded sadly and I heard his disembodied voice.

'So be it.'

My father's voice, *'Agreed.'*

My mother, *'I shall not say no. Please, make it so.'*

The Conduit nodded to us. She pointed at Pel-ani and spoke clearly. Her gentle voice had turned to iron and her face to stone.

'Pel-ani lack-love, Pel-ani child of spite and hate, Pel-ani the lonely soul. You have been judged and the sentence will be carried out immediately.'

He sneered, 'What Court is this? I see no judge. Who are my jury.' He indicated first us and then the watchers in the shadows. 'These, my family, are lambs for the slaughter and they, this crowd of milk bloods, are too weak and docile to defend the lambs when the wolves come for their blood. The strong must triumph and I shall! Who dares judge me and who dares carry out any sentence?'

The tall woman drew back her shoulders. She answered him with imperious gravity.

'That which I have given you I take back. I am the shepherd of this flock, and you, you puny half-thing, you are no wolf. An end to talking, I tire of you. It is time.'

Pel-ani climbed to his feet and gazed at her with mocking eyes. But then, when he opened his mouth to speak a cloud of fire billowed out. His hands blossomed red flame and he raised them before his incredulous face. Yellow sheets of fire zig-zagged along his body and his skin crazed with brilliant white light. There was a sound, a keening wail very like that of a small animal with its tail pinned in a trap. And then it was cut short. Pel-ani's eyes boiled out of his head to be replaced by jets of white hot fire. His body collapsed in on itself in a tumble of cindered bones. He continued to burn until he was little more than a drift of chalky ash which then began to spin and rise to a peak in the centre. It continued to climb until it was a fine pinnacle, a tall needle of floury white powder coiling ever upwards, and then, with a final shiver in the air, he was gone.

I exhaled hard and then took in a great lungful of acrid air. The room had a roasted, bitter tang to it.

'Wow,' I said. 'Sorry, but I'm new to this family business. Is it always like this?'

The Conduit looked at me. She smiled. I realised I could see right through her. It was as if, now her job was done, she had no further need for her corporeal form and could return to the ether.

'You will return to your family soon enough, prince Pel-osen, and it will be safe now the risk has been eliminated. Memories of such things can be a hard thing, but perhaps time will polish them smooth. But first you must complete the task that has been set for you. Another terrible beast must be destroyed before it can devour your once adopted people. The Sha-aneer in France must die or the Eden born will be wiped out to the last child. Satan Spindrift needs you, you are his Parsifal. Together you will triumph, of that I am sure; but without you France will be lost, and then the world will follow.'

By then she was little more than a woman-shaped glimmer on the air.

'Fare well, Pel-osen, fare well.'

And she too was gone.

~36~

Sound exploded in the room and swept over our little group on the broken dais like a storm. I ignored it. Even when the host of people surged forwards into the light and surrounded us I only had eyes for the lean, spread-eagled form of Spindrift on the floor. I looked askance at my family.

'Please, you promised to revive him.'

My father nodded. That was when it struck me hardest, I had a family. Father, mother, grandfather, it seemed so strange. Suddenly I was no longer a man alone in the world. I had family. And what a family. What an introduction to family life. I had already begun to accept that I wasn't strictly human; my time spent flying and my encounter with Rowan had firmly cemented that fact into my mind. But to combine a family reunion with an attempted military coup by my uncle and then to watch the man burned to ash in front of my eyes by an all-powerful woman made from light... It would take a while to digest the uncanny directions my life had taken since I woke up under that canvas roof and Spindrift had hoved into view.

My grandfather made a gesture and my friend rose to his feet as if he was attached to a hinge. There was no clambering or climbing upright, in fact there seemed little transition from horizontal to vertical. One moment he was sprawled out like a dead man and the next we were being treated to his familiar dark glare. His eyes became briefly unfocussed, and then settled on the people by my side.

'It seems I was deactivated for well over half an hour. I presume there was a good reason and that captain Cahoon was involved in some way, but I would like an explanation for such unusually inhospitable conduct. I have known many sprites over the years and such behaviour would be unthinkable to them. And, where are we? None of my senses recognise this place. Gravity's wrong, air density's wrong, even its composition seems unnatural.'

He turned his regard on me. 'You've changed, Colin. You look as if you've been rejuvenated from the inside out. It suits you well enough but I'm afraid you will stand out from any crowd looking like that.' His eyes narrowed as the truth struck home and his dark eyes scanned from me to my father and then my mother. He nodded as if listening to a silent voice. 'I see, yes, I understand. Please, would you be so good as to introduce me to your family?'

Even standing as we were in the midst of that crowd of strangers, it was an intimate moment. I did as I was bid after which my grandfather apologised for his rudeness, but then he explained that the deactivation had been for Spindrift's safety and comfort during my testing.

'It is your nature to protect, Satan, we understand that. But if you had attempted to protect Pel-osen from the light of The Conduit it might have done you harm. It is a subtle and a powerful force that would have found ways to remove you if you impeded it – we could not take that risk. Nor could we leave you behind when we brought Pel-osen here. You would have set out to find my grandson and rescue him from his abductors, and we know you as a formidable hunter once set in motion. Please understand that what we did was to protect you from certain danger, but it was also to protect ourselves from a powerful man whom we would rather have as a friend than an enemy.'

Pel-ani's twenty warriors had melted away as soon as their commander had been punished by the Conduit, but the remaining host seemed to number in their tens of hundreds and the hubbub of their chatter made it difficult to hear what was being said on the cracked dais. My grandfather quickly dismissed everyone from the room with a firm but casual thank-you, and a promise that all would be explained later. Within minutes we were alone and it was forcefully struck home once more that he was the king in this realm. My grandfather, the king.

He then led all of us out of the great chamber. I walked in a daze along enchanting walkways in which abstract shapes resolved themselves into noble looking and precise portraits of men and women who seemed to nod and smile as we passed and then dissolve into abstract line and colour once more. We crossed a delicate stone bridge that was open to a pearl coloured sky and spanned a raging waterfall. I gazed down at the torrent and was surprised to see naked, brown-skinned people sporting in the powerful stream. Some seemed to be swimming up it, and others had fishlike tails. I blinked, *mermaids*?

Pel-ora led us into a circular room at the centre of which was a large round table and more of those magpie-built, thronelike chairs. Massive arched windows allowed a view of a city that climbed up towards us as if we were at the apex of a mountain. It was a breathtakingly beautiful view. The collection of buildings was like nothing I had seen before, but they worked in exquisite harmony with each other and the surrounding landscape. It was a vision of lightness and strength, music made architecture, a poem of brick and stone. I felt something well up inside me and was surprised to find tears on my cheeks. *My people had created this fantastic place, my people.* I felt humbled and proud at the same time.

'Scytaer Faehl,' said my father. 'The city between worlds. It has grown over millennia to be what it is today, and after more millennia it will be what it is tomorrow. It is a fine jewel, created by masters and eternally changing. God, willing it will never be finished but always moving closer to absolute perfection. One day you will know it well, my son, but first we must talk of what happened today – and see how we may aid you in your quest to destroy the Sha-aneer.'

Spindrift was gazing at the city with an impassive smile. I wondered how he could accept its wonders so calmly. And then I remembered. Before he had been cast away on Earth his home had been called Heaven. This place must be little more than a pleasant diversion for a fallen angel. I wondered how he could stand to be away from such a place.

Grandfather requested that we join him at the table and we took our seats. Once we were comfortable he made a hand gesture and men and women flew through the windows carrying trays of food and drink. He thanked them and waited until they had departed before standing to pour us all a tall glass of what I soon discovered was a very fine wine. I drank gratefully. Pel-ora settled his eyes on me and beamed with pride.

'I never believed this day would come. I could never bring myself to hope you would be returned to us once more, but here you are and right welcome too.' He frowned and a shadow passed over his joy. 'I always suspected your uncle was involved in your abduction, but I prayed I was wrong. We all did. Well, enough of that. He has paid the price for his ambition, and perhaps we should be grateful that he at least lacked the belly for slaughtering a child. He could not bring himself to murder a baby...'

My father butted in, 'Please, do not try to find redemption for that evil bastard. You heard his thoughts, you heard what he planned for Ventari. And that was after his brutes had killed all of us. He thought he had left Pel-osen to die in the wasteland. That was not mercy that was cowardice, and his true nature was revealed to all of us today! I say we are well rid of him. Good riddance to bad rubbish and the city is a cleaner place without him. Best forgotten. So, what are we going to do about his cohort of thugs?'

Spindrift was looking at each speaker blankly and I realised he didn't have a clue what we were talking about. While the other two men made plans to track down Pel-ani's gang of assassins and to find out who else might have been involved in the plot to kill us, I outlined events that had taken place while my friend was out cold on the dais in the great hall. His mouth set in a grim line.

'Colin, sorry, Pel-osen, I can't ask you to help me with the worm. Too much has happened, it wouldn't be fair. You have your family now and your true home at last. You have all this and you are a prince of a royal line. I can't take the risk that something might go wrong.'

The sudden silence around us warned me that we had become the centre of attention once more. My father smiled grimly.

'We are sorry, Satan Spindrift, but the choice is not yours to make. Pel-osen must join you in your crusade against the worm called Sha-aneer, The Conduit has spoken and given your quest its blessing. It has said you must work together and that you will almost certainly succeed, and forgive me, Satan, but it also said you would fail if you made this attempt alone. The question is only how we might assist you in your fight against this terrible evil.'

Spindrift frowned. 'What is this Conduit and why must I listen to it? I am a creature of free will, my choices are my own. If I say Pel-osen can't help any longer then that's it! No sprite nor any genii of the light will gainsay me.'

Grandfather leaned forward, 'No, Satan, you're wrong. You must listen. Pel-ani didn't and he was burned to ashes and less than ashes. Don't make that same mistake. The Conduit is much more than your "genii of light" as you put it, much more. It is our channel to the word of God itself. It is the living light of the Creator and you must listen when it speaks. Its words are the words of God.'

~37~

We returned to Spindrift's quarters at almost exactly the same moment we had left, although hours had passed. I could understand why my new family had looked amused when I said we must get back or face being shot as deserters. Spindrift had finally and reluctantly accepted my aid but stubbornly refused any more from my family.

'If it's going to work it would be best with a small team, just the two of us. The Sha-aneer infected part of the German army, absorbed hundreds of men and became even more powerful. I dread to think what would happen if it could sink its teeth into an army of elementals like your good selves. It would devour you, it would breathe you into its foul lungs and drink your water cousins whole. It would warm itself at the fire sprites and grind the earth spirits to dust. Please, leave us alone to our appointed task. Lend us your prayers and when we are done I will return your son to you whole, God willing.'

My mother wept when I hugged her before leaving and my grandfather pounded my arm while repeating, 'Good man, proud of you, good man!'

My father pulled a circle of gold off his wrist and pushed it onto mine.

'When you are ready to come back,' he said, 'touch this with your fingers and say Scytaer Faehl. It will bring you home to us. May it be soon.'

I tried to shake his hand but he embraced me hard and kissed my cheek.

'See you soon, son,' he said, blinking away his tears. 'See you very soon.'

I experienced that long fall once more and I landed hard. My knees buckled and I staggered against the table. Spindrift barely bounced, he had stepped back into our world as if through a door.

My mind was buzzing like a firework and I wanted to talk about recent events but my friend had other ideas.

'No, not now. Let's get some rest and meet for breakfast in the morning. We've neither of us slept for two days and this day just got considerably longer thanks to you. Sleep now, talk in the morning, agreed?'

He was right. I knew he was right. I might be a prince of the elementals but he was the protector of Earth, and that made him the boss. We shook hands and I retired. I lay in bed and I thought about my family. The last thing I remember before sleep claimed me was a vision of my mother's beautiful face, and she was smiling at me.

A sharp knock at my door roused me from my slumbers. I had forgotten to replace the blackout curtain before climbing into bed and the cool grey light of pre-dawn bathed me where I lay. The staccato knock was repeated and I heard a plaintive voice shouting 'Sir, I've got your coffee! Sir, the Preacher's waiting for you and sends his compliments. Sir, I've got your coffee.'

Within ten minutes the foul coffee had been dumped out of my window and I was striding out to where Spindrift stood with our mounts.

'Morning, Colin. Sleep well?'

'Like a babe, how about you?'

'Like a top. You missed a good breakfast too, bacon with toasted bread dipped in the hot fat.'

'It's always bacon and bread dipped in the fat.'

'Must have been hungry, tasted real special. You ready to confront Mother Superior in her den?'

'Rather. Time to keep a few promises. I wonder how Wolseley's doing?'

'I'm told he's locked himself in his room. He has his transport papers and will be away later this afternoon. The colonel's fretting around like an old cock denied its hens.'

'Serves the old bugger right.'

'Precisely, couldn't put it better.'

'How d'you know all this? About Wolseley and the colonel? Someone been in touch?'

'Little bird told me.'

That was when I became aware of the fluid elegance of his dog in motion. It was prowling around us before regaining its position at his heel. As usual it was taking notice of everything in its vicinity. As always it seemed to be taking keener than usual notice of me.

'Little bird told you? Or was it a big black hound?'

'Colin, what are you suggesting? Come on, let's away. Sister Honoria Pietas won't wait another day.'

As was our wont we didn't talk about anything much until we were out of the hospital grounds and well on the road to Natres. Spindrift's dog blazed the trail, continuously looking back to make sure his master was still following. I was struck once more by both the intensity of its gaze and its lack of common doggy attributes. Other hounds might let their tongues loll from their mouths while they ran, barked, wagged their tails or frolicked with pleasure just to be out on the road for a jaunt. Other hounds might flick their ears around and grin their lop-sided hounds' grin, but not Spindrift's.

That sleek, black shadow of a dog was beautiful all right, a grand sight, but I swear it had the same absolute concentration of purpose as a sniper. I'd heard tell about old time Red Indian warriors who could walk right into a white man's camp and kill their targets without being seen, and without making a sound. They were said to be like ghosts in the night, ghosts with razor sharp blades and a fierce thirst for white men's blood. I don't know if all that's true, but I believe it might be. I've seen Red Indians at the wild west shows and they seemed quiet, dignified fellows to me. At least a lot quieter and more dignified than the yahoo hicks in Stetsons they rode with. Unlike the rowdies, the red men had a way about them, I guess it was a compressed kind of energy. They looked capable of getting the job done without any fuss and without even breaking a sweat. Spindrift's dog reminded me of those red men, and the fact is so did its master. I was in good company if we found ourselves in a tight spot. I hoped I could hold up my end in the fight.

And then I started thinking about the last couple of days and the things people had said, and my question popped out like a Jack from its box. Surprised even me.

'Doc, you know lots of strange things, would you know anything about a fellow called Parsifal?'

'Parsifal? Why? That's an odd question, Colin. Sorry, please excuse me, should I be calling you Pel-osen when we're alone?'

'Whatever fits, I could live with "hey you" if it suits you best, and I've been Colin Cahoon all my live long days so I'll need some time to adjust. Whichever comes to hand first is right dandy with me.'

'Then between us it shall be Colin, at least until you come fully into your new estate. And please allow me to congratulate you on discovering your roots and heritage. Perhaps that's two good causes for celebration and another late night, and right soon. But, Parsifal? Why do you ask?'

'The Conduit said I was your Parsifal. Those were her exact words. I don't know, the name rings bells but... I figured you might know what she meant.'

He frowned a little and we rode together in silence while he chewed that one over. He made as if to speak a few times and then thought better of whatever he was about to say. At last he grinned.

'I'm going to have to mull over her description of you for a while. It sounds subtle, sophisticated, and although I think I might understand her meaning I might just as easily be wrong. In legend Parsifal was the pure knight who found the holy grail for king Arthur. He was described as a pure and holy fool by some, a saintly innocent by others, but it was he who had survived his quest when so many others failed and died. He was the only knight able to bring the grail to the court of Camelot and cure both Arthur and Avalon of its ills. Is she saying I'm Arthur? Is she calling you an innocent fool or a saintly man? I wonder. I fail to see how either of us fill those boots. Maybe she sees us as friends on a worthwhile quest, men able to depend on each other. I would be happy enough with that, what about you?'

'Arthur was just a legend, wasn't he?'

'An elemental prince asking a fallen angel if someone was just a legend – that's one for the record books. Arthur was a nickname for a powerful Walesa king who stood up to the Saxons back in the day. It means "The Bear". He was a big man with a beard and he ruled the tribes of Gwynedd. Had a loose attitude towards other people's property. The Irish still have legends about the pig thief Arthur. Most legends have their roots in fact somewhere. Maybe one of his warriors *was* called something like Parsifal, a fool and a pure man might be handy enough in a fight if he's foolish enough to face terrible odds.'

I grinned back, 'I'm damn fool enough to fight with you, even though I have a very good idea of what we're about to do. I should be hightailing it to anywhere else on this planet rather than face that Worm again.'

I sobered and spoke firmly. I strongly believed everything I was saying.

'But that monster must be overcome, it has to be. It's a greater threat to everything I've come to know and love than the Boche will ever be. They're just war hungry fools who die when you shoot them. Even if they win mankind will survive and peace will return one day, God willing. But the worm, that thing's just plain evil. I don't know what it's got to do with missing children and that convent, but my gut tells me that everything is tied together with a nice neat bow – and our friend Morel is bang in the middle of it. What do you say?'

'I say let's go cut the ribbon and see what falls out!'

~38~

There was time for a cup of good tea with Michael Worsnip before making our ascent to the Sisters of the Weeping Heart. Helen made a point of joining us and laughed a lot in a girlish fashion that drew an arch grin from Spindrift. He looked knowingly from her to me. Even Worsnip asked if she was 'sitting on a feather'?

'Lovely to see you in such a fine humour, my dear,' he said. 'Good company obviously brings out the beauty in you, or perhaps it's the good tea?'

She giggled pinkly and smiled at him, 'I don't know what you mean, Michael, really I don't.'

Spindrift asked if there was any word about the missing children, or any more gossip about Morel or the nuns. Michael shrugged but Helen leaned forward in a confidential manner.

'Well, yes, actually. Funny you should ask. Captain Morel has been in a dreadful high state for the last few days, practically dribbling over any woman who came near him. You could smell the rut on him from yards away. But yesterday he was like the fat cat who got the cream, strutting around fingering that stupid moustache of his. What day is it today? Tuesday, yes? Right then, on Sunday little Aceline Durand asked her parents if she could stay and play with her friends after church. They said yes, but told her she must be home for dinner in a few hours. They waited at table but she didn't turn up. Her father stormed out to tell her off for being late, but she was nowhere to be found. When questioned, her friends explained that they hadn't seen her for ages, except for a few minutes when she'd joined them for a game. They had been playing some sort of tag in the churchyard and Aceline got excited. She fell over a gravestone, tripped you see, and the other children said she came down quite hard. They said she cut her knee rather badly and then she limped off home, crying. Poor girl, she's only seven. Nobody went home with her because they were enjoying their game too much, and anyway, they said, her house was just a few hundred yards away, just down the road and around a corner. How could she get lost?'

Helen shifted in her seat and leaned further forward, speaking conspiratorially. 'Aceline's parents went straight to the gendarmerie and asked to speak with captain Morel, but they were told he was away on official business. Official business my sweet Fanny Adams, he'd been away with some woman while children were getting stolen from right under his men's noses. One of his lieutenants took over and organised a search of the local area, but no joy. Of course, Morel was back by Monday morning, wiping the cream from his whiskers. And you've seen the size of those stupid whiskers. He was told what had happened to the girl and what his men had done and he washed his hands of the whole affair. Said his men had done everything they could and without more information they would be wasting their time in pursuing the matter any further. He said they would be playing a pointless game of "blind-man's buff". I ask you, what use is he? The man's a filthy cad of the highest order, and the poor Durand's are distraught. Monsieur Durand has been wandering the streets looking for his little girl, knocking on doors and asking all sorts of questions, while poor Madame has taken to her bed with a sedative. Somebody must have taken little Aceline. Why? And who would do such a thing?'

Spindrift sat more alertly on his seat, he cast a rapid, covert glance at me. I could tell he was wondering if I was making the same connections he was. In my mind's eye, I was seeing Morel up in that high room with Sister Matilde. Was that his reward for stealing children? Was his lust such that he would abduct a child in exchange for a night of passion with a pretty nun? I felt anger begin to boil in my blood. If Morel had been in front of me at that moment I would have shown him what it feels like to face a firing squad of one; and my gun would be loaded.

I felt a gentle hand on my knee. Helen was studying me with concern written plain across her face.

'Colin, are you, all right? You look furious. What is it?'

I shook my head, 'I was thinking of that poor family and that little girl gone missing, that's all. Morel's a poor sample of manhood that's for sure, but I wish there was something we could do to help. Fair boils my beets, Helen. I feel so damn useless!'

I must have been a little het up when I said this, and maybe a touch too loud. She jumped and gasped at my outburst, drawing her hand away and touching her lips with her fingers. She flushed crimson to the roots of her hair and her eyes glittered.

Spindrift cut into the pregnant moment with a word. 'Colin.'

I turned to face him. He smiled, 'Colin, we have a date with a lady. We promised Wolseley, remember?'

I breathed slow and nodded. 'You're right. We must be on our way. Helen, Michael, thanks for the tea and the news. As doc says, we have a date and we can't be late.'

Helen muttered under her breath, 'Lucky, lucky lady.'

We had plenty of time for a parley while we rode through the fine, icy mist that coated everything with a bright soaking dew in seconds. I felt it start dripping down the back of my neck but it couldn't cool my anger.

I reined in and said, 'You thinking the same as me about Morel?'

'That he gets to spend time with Matilde in exchange for stolen children?'

I nodded, 'Could a man be viler? The bastard is stealing kids just so he can tup a nun. Is there anything left? Is there a single blasphemy left to him? How many people are involved in this, this *monstrosity*. How long has it been going on? How many children has his lust cost the poor parents here? He makes me feel sick.' I looked back towards the town, it was lost in the mist. 'Let me go back and ask him a few questions, let's see how long he lasts when he can't breathe. Let's see what he says when I carry him a mile into the air and threaten to drop him on his wicked fat head unless he talks?'

Spindrift regarded me with bleak eyes. 'I want to do the same. I want to take the slimy filth by his throat and choke the truth out of him, but not yet. Let's make him our next port of call, but let's get some proof first. Then we'll hang the despicable bastard in the town square and we'll make sure the grieving parents get front row seats. Agreed.'

I hissed agreement, but my fingers twitched, aching to teach Morel that he wasn't going to get away with his vile trade for a minute longer.

'What kind of slut is Sister Matilde to allow this to happen?'

'Ah, yes, Colin, what indeed? We need to find out. We don't have the full picture yet, do we? We're only looking at the skin of the onion. It's time to start peeling away the layers to see what's underneath. And you know something?'

'Yes?'

'I think we're going to find a worm coiled up in its heart.'

~39~

Sister Bridget met us at the gate. She had done nothing to temper her poor humour and the gaze she raked over us was scathing.

'Got lost yesterday, did you? Mother Superior isn't used to being let down like that. You had better have a good excuse or she'll skin you both alive and salt you for Christmas. Not that there's much meat on either of you.'

We had both dismounted. Spindrift chose to ignore the woman's jibes.

'Is your Mother Superior free to see us?'

The same whey-faced girl as before had appeared at Bridget's side and she took our horses in hand, leading them away and hopefully taking them out of the weather. The mist was thickening and seemed filled with tiny but stinging shards of ice. I shielded my eyes and squinted at the squat nun.

She snarled, 'Better late than never.'

I bit back a retort, but Spindrift filled the silence.

'I'm sure such a fine Christian woman as Sister Honoria will understand that sometimes the war stands in the way of common niceties. Man proposes, but the Kaiser disposes.'

Something in his ice-cold regard silenced the fat, sullen shrew, and she stumped away. We followed behind just close enough to hear her continuous muttering. It was a relief to enter the convent and escape the weather. It was no warmer but at least the onslaught of ice had ceased. It was dark in the hallway but I could still see the slight robed figure standing on the stairway. It was Matilde, of that I was sure.

The fetid stink of corruption seemed stronger that morning, and it grew worse as we approached Honoria's offices. I looked around to see where it might have emanated from. This time we were not being distracted by a pretty nun's bright chatter. This time we had the taciturn Bridget, and she was certainly *not* a distraction. Spindrift tapped my arm and nodded further down the corridor. I saw it, an opening leading to a dark stairway. I could almost feel the air curdle with evil around that dark mouth. Who would welcome such a thing into their house? And a house of God at that? I raised my fingers to touch my tunic above the crucifix I always wore and I asked for God's protection while under that terrible, haunted roof.

Bridget knocked perfunctorily and opened the Mother Superior's door. She ushered us inside, reserving an especially snide grimace for Spindrift.

Could she not see that he was a brother in the Lord, a Preacher? He said something quietly to her that I didn't catch, but her porcine eyes widened and her flabby jowls quivered in shock. She scurried away without another word.

The black, mantis-like form of the Mother Superior was already on her feet. She had her hands clasped firmly together at her waist and her head tilted to one side. It was a distinctly insect-like pose and her chilly smile did nothing to warm me towards her. Somehow and for some reason she was involved in everything evil that was happening in Natres. She was the spider at the heart of a sticky and very complex web. Matilde might have become a willing whore for Morel, but this midnight creature was the whore mistress – and I wanted to know why. I made as if to take a step towards her, but Preacher Spindrift held my elbow and shook his head slightly.

'I think I should talk with the Reverend Mother first, Colin.'

I took a step back and left the field clear for my friend. He bowed slightly to the old insect and opened his mouth to speak, but she beat him to it.

'Gentlemen, I'm so pleased you could spare me some of your valuable time today. I missed you yesterday and our little buffet of sweetmeats had to be thrown to the pigs. The dishes do not like to be kept waiting, they spoil so quickly.' She indicated a table that held an array of covered plates. 'These, however, are at the very peak of perfection. I shall pour you some sweet water and invite you to help yourselves. I'm told the food in the allied trenches leaves much to be desired, you'll not find that to be the case here.'

Spindrift started, 'Mother Superior, we have much to discuss...'

She held up her hand, 'Young minds are in such a hurry to arrive at their destination. Once you've tucked a few more years under your belt you'll soon realise the importance of appreciating the journey itself, it is over all too soon.'

She began lifting covers from plates and warm aromas filled the room.

'These little bites are so much better when still hot, please help yourselves.'

Spindrift opened his mouth again and like a snake striking the woman popped a piece of food into it. It became obvious she would not be gainsaid, we would have to sample the convent's fare while we talked. We sat at the table and placed snow-white napkins on our laps. She poured ice cold water. There was no cutlery so we took up the delicate savoury fancies with our fingers. I was immediately starving. The food was miraculous. The flavours were so good I became dizzy with them, I soon discovered I had almost become drunk on their savoury richness.

Spindrift took the opportunity to ask if the inmates of the convent had been able to tell her anything about the missing children, if she had discovered anything since our last visit. She seemed to find this amusing.

'We are an enclosed order, captain. We sponsor goodness by example not by gossip. The local people appreciate that we are praying for them and our prayers are more likely to be answered than, for example...' She took a pointed squint at the crucifixes on Spindrift's lapels, 'For example a military chaplain who squats in the mud and filth of the trenches. The Lord prefers not to get his ears dirty I can assure you.' She smiled at me. 'A good appetite is the sign of good health. How I wish I could join you at table, but I'm afraid, in my case, the flesh is weak. But, please, enjoy the fruit of our labours.'

Spindrift put down his plate and dabbed at his mouth. He said, 'What can you tell us about captain Morel of the gendarmerie?'

She drew back in surprise. 'Why, what could I possibly know about the man?'

'We believe he has much to do with the convent and the sisters, perhaps more than is... shall we say... quite proper. And his lieutenant, Albert Fournier, he said I should speak with you, and to mention his name.'

She leaned forward. 'Are you accusing us of something, captain? I must warn you to be very careful what you say, very careful indeed. This is a holy order, not a dormitory for fallen women... And what should I know of this Albert Fournier? It is just a name to me. But, enough, come, let us enjoy good food and fine company.' She flashed her yellowing teeth. 'Let us be friends. Tell me, have you visited the theatre recently? I so loved to attend a good play before I was called to the narrow path. What's the latest? Have you seen anything by that divine moralist Émile Augier? I believe he's dead now but what a great talent...'

The Reverend Mother continued to twitter brightly while we ate, but I wasn't listening. For all I knew she could have been imitating birdsong. All I heard was something like 'Caw, caw, caw, caw...' She looked like an old crow sure enough. I drank some of the water and tried a fishy pastry. It was a small thing that packed a powerful punch. The flavour swept through me like a wave of pleasure. I think I moaned with delight and my head wobbled on my neck. I began to laugh.

I found a pinched, narrow face close to mine. Its mouth creased in a thin, bitter smile and small, black eyes glittered with malicious glee. Her voice had lost none of its light, amused lilt.

'You want to know where the children are?' She said. 'I think we can help you there. Yes, we can help you meet them. I'm sure they'd love to get together with you, love to. They so like to meet new friends.'

And suddenly she had three heads. One was hers, narrow, spare, and archly evil, another looked pig-like, angry and smug, Sister Bridget, and the last was pretty in a cold, hungry way, Matilde. I wondered what it would be like to make Matilde sweat the way Morel had, make her close her eyes and pound, pound, pound her lovely body up and down, up, and down, like a sexy horse on a carousel. I smiled at the thought and tried to gain my feet. That was when captain Morel's head filled my view. He pushed me down, hard. And my world dropped away into darkness.

~40~

My wits spiralled down into the abyss like a wanton spark, falling deep into the shadows. I saw the sullen orange glow of fast approaching fires and I crashed into the black, molten stone of a pit in Hell. The rock burned me, I felt my back crisping where it touched. I screamed. And then hissing demons wrenched at me, fighting with each other to see which would be the first to torment my poor beleaguered soul. I begged for mercy and called upon my God to rescue me from my sore affliction. Then they all took a firm hold and pulled. They tore me apart. I saw my heart burst free from my quartered torso and fly away on a thick torrent of blood. It was still beating.

And then everything became darkness. The demons began eating me. I could feel their pointed fangs tear into me, and although that stygian gloom had rendered me almost completely blind I could plainly hear them crunching and slurping at my bones. I heard the wet smack of their leathery lips and the sticky sound of my raw flesh being ripped away in greedy mouthfuls. I wept in shame for I had been judged and I was now one of the damned.

And then I wondered where my head was resting so I could listen while all this gourmandising was taking place. Shouldn't it be over there in the mouth of a monster? Through the darkness, I could just barely make out glimpses of long strips of my glowing, golden flesh being sucked into hungry jaws. And then a shadow fell across my vision and my head was gripped in scaly, taloned hands. I felt burning breath blistering my eyes. I had no wind in my lungs, no lungs to hold it, so I couldn't scream when needle-like teeth crunched down and pierced my skull. I felt them stab into my poor brain. The agony was exquisite. I felt the creature's rough tongue against my cheek while it chewed, and there followed a hot, rough, lapping sensation. I wondered if it was sucking my skull like a boiled sweet. My spirit quailed in terror. How much longer could the torment last?

And I awoke.

Spindrift's dog was licking at my face and making short, urgent, huffing sounds. When it realised my eyes were open it stopped what it was doing, looked up, and issued an eerie whine.

'Hello, girl,' I said. 'Good to see you.' And I buried my fingers in her glossy pelt. She nuzzled at me and I realised she was trying to get me to sit up.

'Okay, girl, I get it. Get off my lazy back and get back in the game. Right you are. See, I'm moving, okay?'

I had just finished levering myself into a sitting position when an unstoppable surge of vomit burst from my mouth. I quickly angled myself sideways away from the dog and the hot, stinking grey stream sluiced several dozen yards down the sheer cliff face inches from my side, to land smoking on some pine trees. I vomited until my belly ached, until my ass was puckering with the sheer force of it. I vomited until my sight faded and tears stung my eyes. I was just a channel for partly digested food and drink. I didn't think I'd eaten that much in a year. I must have been vomiting for a whole party of gluttons.

And then at last it was over, replaced by a succession of dry heaves and choking noises. I wish I could have said I felt better for it, but I didn't. I envied those quiet corpses mouldering under their blankets of green algae in the shell craters of No Man's Land. At least they were at peace and didn't have a bellyful of boiling acid.

I wiped at my mouth with a quivering hand and felt my body shudder like a fever victim's, but I wasn't burning up. No, sir. I was cold and damp and in pain. My guts were churning like a wash paddle in a bucket of linens, and my joints creaked and screamed in agony. I swear it hurt a lot less back when I'd been blown up on the battlefield.

And then I felt a strong, warm, dry palm cup the back of my neck and a familiar voice said, 'Drink this. You'll feel better.' Spindrift poured his liquid balm between my lips and I swallowed eagerly. I soon felt my strength begin to rally and something of my old self returned to the bruised shell my carcase had become.

Spindrift smiled, 'It's good you've been sick. Your body was purging itself; it has a very strong survival instinct, be grateful for it. You've been badly poisoned with what they call a "Micky Finn", and a powerful dose at that. Everything you ate and drank in the Reverend Mother's room must have been doped with chloral hydrate. You were already being knocked senseless by the drug when Morel took his poke at you. That cowardly hound would never have tried that stunt if you'd been fully conscious.'

His dog growled at that and he apologised. 'Sorry, I didn't mean you.'

That was one smart canine.

I shook my head and something creaked dangerously in my neck. I moved gingerly after that. Nothing felt broken but you could never be too sure.

I gritted my teeth and mumbled, 'What happened? Where *are* we?'

Spindrift sat on a handy log and spread the skirts of his long coat wide to the sides. He drank some of his own elixir, the only time I ever saw him do that, and he leaned forward, his forearms on his knees. He grinned, and that half-moon of white teeth shone in his dark jaw.

'I'm afraid Mother Superior will be feeling the cold until she gets one of those big windows of hers boarded up. It got broke during our hasty departure. Properly smashed it to smithereens, as Rowan would say. Some of your bruises might have come from then. Yes, they probably did. You were out with the birds and looser than a drunk man, more like an old rag-made, mop Jenny doll. I did my level best to protect you, but I was in a powerful hurry. I'm sure you'll understand and find it in your heart to forgive me if I gave you a few knocks on our way out that window.'

'Forgive you for what? Saving my life again? Why were those bastards trying to kill me anyway? And why didn't it work on you?'

'I guess I'm just a tough nut to crack, Colin. Your kin knew how to turn me off, I don't know how, but even they couldn't poison or drug me. Let's just say I'm made of more resilient stuff. And I can promise you something else too, they sure weren't planning to kill you, and that's a fact. They wanted you dead to the world, but they needed you alive.'

My face must have showed my confusion, he shook his head.

'No, my friend. The Worm has no use for dead meat. Remember what I told you, it devours the body *and* the soul. I guess a dead man has no flavour. You were going to be handed to it alive, and awake, the same way those poor children must have been for God knows how many years. It has been a wicked trade, a wicked trade.'

'Why would nuns do such a thing? And how did you get us away from there?'

'I'll answer the "how" before I approach the "why". I can only surmise the "why", although I'm certain I'm correct in what I believe. "How" was easier than spit. The womenfolk couldn't wait to lay hands on such a fine looking, golden haired fellah like yourself. You've seen how you affect the ladies? Don't be modest, you're like catnip to them, and nuns are women for all their trappings. Now I'm not saying they were planning anything indecent, other than feeding the pair of us to that vile worm, but they were right happy to lay their hands on you. I saw it in their faces, they got hot and greedy. Morel saw it too, he could see something of it in Matilde's eyes. He got jealous and that's why he took a poke at you. He's a coward and a bully, that man. When this is done, he will pay for his sins. He will pay the full price and then some.'

Spindrift clenched his big fists and gritted his teeth. If Morel had been with us he would not have survived. He would have been pounded into the ground by the Preacher's bare hands. Of that I am sure.

Then Spindrift smiled sheepishly and shook his head. 'Listen to me talk, are those the words of a doctor and a chaplain? Shame on me. I guess I get riled same as the next man. But this isn't getting the story told. How I got us out of there? To begin with I faked it. I slumped down with my head on my chest and my arms limp by my sides and I faked it. Kept my eyes open like slits and looked for my chance. Morel came into the room behind Bridget and Matilde, and they crowded around you like starving hogs around a pail of slops. Morel took his poke and the women turned on him to push him away. That was my chance. I grabbed you and I ran for the nearest window. We hit it like a cannon shell and shot straight through. I was planning on landing on the grass and running for it with you in my arms, I'd seen Morel had a gun and we needed to move fast, but I quickly realised that wasn't going to work.'

'Why not?'

'Because I came out of that window right bang over a hundred-foot drop, that's why. You know the convent is built on a hill? Well that window was right over a steep scarp. Ha, no never mind, it was better for me that way. I dropped clean out of sight before I flew just below tree top level and came here. The convent's just about a mile over yonder. I guess they'll think us dead and won't bother to search for bodies. We're safe enough for now, and we can rest up awhile before we go back.'

'What? Back? Why are we going back? Why don't we go get a troop of men and storm the place?'

'No, Colin, we can't do that. A whole regiment would be no good; an army would be worse. You saw what the worm did to the Germans and they're brave men, whatever else you think of them. We would just be feeding the beast a mighty and right welcome banquet, and that's no good. It would swallow the lot of them and double in size. The whole of France would be next. No, it must be us, my friend. I'm sorry, but it's got to be just us, we two, and no-one else.'

I sighed, and suddenly felt a whole lot sicker. But I knew he was right, it had to be us and no-one else.

~41~

Spindrift glanced at the sky. 'We've got a few hours before nightfall. How are you feeling now?'

'Better, thanks. My stomach has calmed down some and my joints don't feel broken anymore. I tell you I feel more than a little riled by the way we've been treated by the so-called Sisters of the Weeping Heart. I reckon we need to complain to a higher authority. I'll be glad to grab a little payback on those maniacs. And why would anyone want to work with the worm? It makes no sense. They can't hope to gain from it, surely?'

'Morel's doing it so he can spend time with Matilde, that much is obvious. She's got his cock on a chain that he never wants to break. She looks sweet enough but the way she acted today proves she's as hard-nosed as Honoria. She knows how to make a man come to heel. And then there's Bridget. She's a piece of work okay, but I think she's an old bird hound who just does as she's told. I can't fault her loyalty but I wouldn't want to rely on her brains. But they're just the bit players in this game, someone else is the puppet master. Yes, it's the Reverend Mother who fascinates me. She's the key to what's going on here, I'm sure of it, and I'm willing to bet she's doing it for what she thinks are all the right reasons.'

'But, what? How?'

'I think she genuinely believes she's protecting the town and the surrounding area. She believes that if she can keep the worm satisfied with a child here and there it will stay in its hole and leave everyone else alone, including her precious Sisters of the Weeping Heart. Sacrificial lambs, Colin. The *Bible* is full of allusions to the lamb that offers up its blood to save others. Even the Galilean is described as the lamb who died to save us all. Those stolen children are lambs to the slaughter, and my bet is that this has been going on for a very long time. What was it Wolseley said? Ah, yes, I remember, he said, "Children have always disappeared around here, and that's a fact." But the numbers have noticeably increased recently. Why? It's evidently nothing to do with the British being here, that much is patent nonsense. I think Morel's lust for the lovely Matilde is making him foolish and he's started grabbing kids every chance he gets. That would explain the increase. Matilde thinks she's got herself a pet hound by the pizzle, but she's wrong. She's let the hungry fox loose in the hen house and that critter won't stop until he's taken every chicken he can find. Then what? Women? The elderly? People are already starting to take notice and they'll become increasingly wary, and then one day he'll make a mistake and he'll be caught. People won't worry about a judge and jury for the man who's been stealing their kids. When they catch him our little turkey cock and his lady are going to swing from the highest tree – if we don't get to them first. The fox and his vixen have gone too far and done too much to be allowed to escape, they're going to pay.'

I grunted assent, I'd willingly hang the bastard Morel myself, and string Matilde up right by his side. I would kick the stool out from under their feet and watch their last dance together. I'd take great delight in punishing him for his vile lust, that the rope would excite the manhood that damned him and her womanhood would be engorged. I could feel myself grinning at the thought. And then a curious stream of electricity crawled up my spine and into my hair. All sense of tiredness and pain was swept away.

'Would you say no to a kiss for luck from a lowly earth spirit?'

The voice was close-by. We looked around and at first the place seemed deserted, then we watched as Rowan unwound herself from the trunk of a tree at the edge of the clearing. One minute she wasn't there and the next every delectable inch of her was standing before us.

She held her hands up. 'Don't go burning me mind. I'm not being presumptuous and expecting your love, Pel-osen, just your friendship. I'd hope we're proper friends at least.'

'More than just friends, I hope.'

'No, don't say that. You really don't understand, do you? Your head's all muddled-up with human ideas about liberty, equality, and choice, but that's not true for us. You'll have to learn how to think and see like a sprite. I'm an elemental like you and I have my talents same as you, but I'm not from the same line of majesty as you are. You burned me because of who and what you are – and because of what I am. You couldn't help it. One day you'll understand.'

Her beautiful face creased in misery. 'I'm too coarse a creature to dare love you and expect you to love me in return, the Conduit knows that, but I can support and care for you as I would any warrior about to go into battle. May I kiss you for luck without my hair catching fire?'

'I don't know, shall we try?'

She tentatively pressed her full lips against mine, a brief pressure and then away. Her breath seemed unsteady.

She murmured, 'Again?'

I nodded. This time she kissed passionately, the way we had in the glade, and I felt her elixir flood into my mouth. I swallowed gratefully and the familiar cool glow burned right into my extremities. I would happily have flown with her back to that spring glade of her's right then, and done everything I remembered from the last time, perhaps more, but I was very aware of Spindrift just a few yards away. And we had a job to do. Reluctantly I opened my eyes and gently pushed her away. Her eyelids fluttered and she licked her full lips. Her cheeks held a fine rosy glow. There was nothing coarse about her, nothing at all. She smiled, and regarded me with impish glee.

'Tell me again why something so fine could be against nature?'

I shook my head, 'I'm not the man to ask, but thank-you. That was a proper hero's send-off.'

She touched my cheek with her nose. 'Wait until you see my returning hero's welcome.'

And she was gone.

Spindrift was talking with his dog and making a studied point of looking the other way. I wiped my mouth and it tingled. Once he realised Rowan was away he looked over at me and shrugged.

'You two make a damn fine couple. I don't see what sprite nature could hold against you being together. I'd be proud to hold the good book and offer the rings so you could get married legally and make it binding. If ever a man and a woman looked set to walk the same long path it's you and Rowan.'

'They'd probably call it a burning passion, problem is she really gets burned. I don't want to hurt her, but I don't want to lose her either. It's a conundrum and no mistake.'

'Well I'm no man to mess with nature, but I'd say there has to be a way. Anyhow best we take that pot off the stove for the time being. We've got other victuals need frying and they must come first. I'm reliably informed that there's no way into any caves under this hill other than through the convent and down those stairs. We've got to get in there and deal with the beast, you okay with that?'

'Let someone try to stop me.'

He grinned his reassuring half-moon grin.

'I'd like to see that, I surely would.'

He studied the pearl grey sky. The rain had ceased but the clouds looked heavy with water. We were in for a drenching before the day was out. Spindrift ruffled the hair on his dog's neck. He spoke to it.

'Stay hidden, I'll call you when we're through. But first, can I borrow one of your eyes for a few minutes to get a look at the lie of the land, best lend an ear too.'

The dog looked resentful, but it lay down in the grass obediently. I gaped with astonishment when the flesh and muscle around one of its eyes peeled back and exposed the naked ball in its socket, which popped clean out and hovered for a second over the dog's head. Then one of its ears unwound from the skull and mounted itself under the macabre, floating orb. It looked like a peculiar plant, or a strange fruit.

Spindrift sat cross-legged next to his prone animal, he nodded to me and said, 'Excuse me for a minute, please, Colin. I want to see what we're facing.'

He shut his eyes. Instantly the eyeball sped away towards the convent – and the lair of the worm.

~42~

I was soon proved right about the rain. A few minutes after that strange little device flew away it first started to drizzle and then began to pour. I hastened to rouse Spindrift to his feet and walk him back under the relative shelter of the treeline where some tight knit evergreens offered protection. He remained silent and his eyes remained closed the whole time. He was like a sleepwalker. Once he was comfortably re-seated I fetched the dog. It lay as if in a drugged sleep so I decided to carry it to the dry. God, it was heavy. Damn near pulled my arms from their sockets. That animal weighed as much as a grown man, perhaps more. It made a grateful, huffing sound when I placed it on a bed of brown pine needles next to its master, but its remining eye remained closed. Whatever they were doing required all their concentration, I left them to it.

With both my companions otherwise engaged I stood sentinel and quietly watched the sky turn from shadowed murk to darkness. The air seemed to thicken but there was no breath of a breeze. The rain threatened to become a deluge and pounded on the dense foliage of the blue pine over our heads, otherwise there was silence. Even the birds must have been sheltering from the downpour. It was strangely wonderful to stand on the edge of that vertical lake as if surrounded by a dense, watery cocoon. I would not have been surprised to see a fish swimming towards me, and I tasted the water in the air and breathed its cool sweetness. I had never felt more strong and vital than at that moment. I experienced a true sense of awe. The air filled me and made me strong. Sister Honoria had poisoned me and I had survived. Spindrift had told me that we two together were stronger than a whole army. And Rowan had shared her tincture with me once more, that and a promise. It had been a glorious day. Glorious.

I knew that later we had a mission to complete and that we might be going to our deaths. I knew that what we faced was the parent worm, the great Sha-aneer. This would be an immense battle. It was the huge and powerful creature that had seeded the area with every threat we had overcome so far. In truth, I couldn't countenance what that might mean. I had seen its offspring burn a man, destroy a tunnel, and explode like a volcano on the German frontlines. The sheer force of its child's death throes had been enough to fling several tons of British tank around like a child's toy, and this next enemy was the parent. The mother. I couldn't visualise it, couldn't fathom what that might mean in real terms, but I felt tranquil standing in my dark silver cocoon of pounding fresh water.

Spindrift knew what we were facing and he was calm enough. At least he seemed so. He was an enigmatic character and it was obvious there was much more to him than I had learned so far, much more. Him and his fabulous dog. But just recently I had learned there was much more to me too. A whole world more. I hoped I got the chance to discover just how that would mean. I was no longer the abandoned foundling raised by harsh 'mothers' in a raw, white, weather boarded house with a red tile roof and a packed earth backyard. I was no longer the naked kid scrubbed with lye soap in front of other kids. I had been found. I was a son. I had family.

I gazed into the rain and thought of the fabulous Scytaer Faehl, and wondered when I would finally make it back to my new home. Would it ever feel like my proper home? The way my cosy little place back in Dallas was home? I had once had a bigger house with a wife and a future but all that had vanished like morning mist. I thought of Rowan cursing Rachel with fertility and wishing my ex-wife a continuously baby-filled belly. I thought of her misery, a wet nurse suckling an endless parade of mewling nappy-fillers until her pork futures husband decided his best future lay elsewhere. I truly hoped it wouldn't happen – but I must admit the thought put a wicked smile on my face.

Spindrift jolted beside me and I wondered what he was seeing. The dog made running motions and whined. I fretted because there was nothing I could do to help, and I turned away. The pounding timpani of the deluge intensified until it was a deafening drumroll of pure sound. I began to doubt we would be able to carry out our mission in the face of such a storm. We would be battered flat before we reached the convent. The clouds were hurling down a solid sheet of water and I marvelled at the sheer power of it. I felt the energy of the storm gather and clench, and something in me responded. I held my hand out into the curtain of water and *pushed*. A sheet of soundless lightning flowed across the sky and a stupendous report of thunder followed. I howled. *Did I do that?*

Then something started to take shape in the rain. The drops began to curve away from an invisible mass as if they were falling onto and around something I couldn't quite make out in the gathering gloom. And then the shapes solidified into masses of golden light, condensed, and took the forms of men. Pel-ora and Pel-os, my grandfather and father. We gazed at each other for long moments, and then in unison they raised their right hands in salute. I returned the gesture. The rain fell on them like a river but not a drop dampened their clothes. Pel-ora glanced up at the sodden clouds, looked at his son, and nodded. They both did something complex with their hands and the fat droplets began to spiral around them. They concluded their performance with a powerful outward thrust of their arms. A bubble of light exploded away from them, expanding into the night. As it passed over my head the rain ceased. When it touched the clouds, they parted and dissipated. The promise of a dangerous journey beginning with miserably sodden clothes was broken. They grinned at me wolfishly and then disappeared as completely as the rain. What had been a sullen day had become a brilliant, shining night. Yes, I had a lot to learn.

'*That* is a very useful trick.' I jumped at the unexpected voice. Spindrift stood by my side. 'I was worried we might drown on our way to the worm, but this is just dandy. Are you going to learn how to do that?'

'Be handy I guess.'

The eyeball gadget flew out of the night and separated into its component parts. They reattached themselves to the dog's sleek head. The ear looked a little ragged but was otherwise unharmed. The dog shuddered and climbed warily to its feet. Spindrift made a big fuss of it, but it regarded him mournfully.

'Thank-you, old friend. You've done us a great service. At least we know what we're dealing with and where to find it. Now we must wait until Vespers and the sisters are busy in prayer, then we go in for real. You stay out of the way, old friend. Wait for my message, understood?'

It made a keening noise.

'Yes, it will be dangerous, but listen, we know how dangerous it is, don't we? *It* however, has no idea how dangerous we are. We'll be fine, I promise you. Fine. Now, make yourself scarce. Go on, and stay safe.'

The dog melted into the trees, but before it had vanished completely it turned and gazed back at us. It howled gently, a tender sound a wolf might make to its cubs. And then Spindrift and I were alone once more.

~43~

'We fly.' Spindrift said.

'I wondered.'

'We have to get over the wall so flight is the easiest option. We need to find our horses too.'

'I forgot about them.'

'Military horseflesh, those are precious beasts. We need to get them back.'

I took a deep, calming breath. He looked at me steadily.

'When we get there, you can wait with the horses. I can join you when the job's done, you don't have to go in.'

I sighed, 'Came this far, be a shame not to see it through. Anyway, I'm curious to see the beast. Must be a big bastard.'

He thrust his hand out towards me and I shook it. I felt that same galvanising surge of wellbeing I had felt before. I grinned.

'That's a fine gift of yours, that pick-me-up charm. Thank-you, I won't ask how you do it but I appreciate it.'

His half-moon smile glowed in the shadows.

'It would make for very boring conversation and we've got an appointment to keep. Ready?'

'Shee-it, yes. Let's go.'

He rose into the air as if on wires, smooth and steady. I hit the sky as if I'd been fired from a bow and was already hovering over the dark bulk of the convent when he joined me several seconds later. He came close enough to speak quietly.

'If there's trouble you get out of there. Do it just like that, I'll be right behind you. Don't wait for me, you hear?'

I saluted, 'Sir, yes sir!'

'I mean it, Colin. Now, where are those horses.'

The rain soaked convent grounds were deserted, so we circled them in the air until we found the neat little stables at the rear. Our horses were there along with a donkey and a pretty pony that made a great show of wanting to know us better as soon as we entered. Spindrift rubbed its nose, then turned to me.

'Let's lead our mounts outside, I need some clear space to do what I must do next.'

He led his horse out of its stall. It was still saddled, as was mine, which was evidence of poor care by the sisters. He headed out into the open. Mystified I followed with my mount. He walked to a broad, grassy area and bade me bring my horse to him. Curiosity burned questions on my tongue, but he put his finger to his lips and I had to swallow my questions. He arranged our mounts so they were side-by-side, and then he stood between them. My horse tried to turn its head and nuzzle him, she was a sweet natured creature. He ignored her and stood poker straight, then held his arms out like a crucified man. He tucked his hands firmly under the horses' saddles, grabbing the girth straps and making sure he had a solid grip. I felt what happened next like a twist in my groin or a tug in my guts. I can't say which, but something *pulled* at me.

And Spindrift rose into the air with both those horses rigid either side of him. I saw they were rolling their eyes with fear, but they didn't twitch so much as a muscle during their terrifying experience. The bizarre trio floated silently towards the west, I guessed they were heading for the trail leading down to the town. I muttered, 'Well there's a sight you don't see too often,' and found myself a place in the shadows where I could await his return unseen. It didn't take long before a barely perceptible dark form moved gently through the night sky and settled down beside me under my tree. How he saw me in the shadows I don't know. How he did anything I don't know. How can a man hoist two full grown mares into the air and fly off with them? Better not to ask. Call it magic.

He gave me a thumbs-up and whispered, 'They're secure and will be waiting for us when we need them. Let's go see about a worm.'

I nodded and went to follow him. And then it hit me. My mouth was suddenly dry. I could feel the tremble start in my legs and rise into my body. My feet didn't know how to move and my heart pounded loudly in my ears. My knees weakened. I was struggling to breathe. Spindrift had moved away a few paces before he realised I wasn't with him. He hesitated and glanced back at me quizzically. A look of realisation dawned across his face. He knew. He smiled, nodded, and then held out his palm towards me. He was telling me everything was okay, it was fine, he understood. He could see I was funking it. I'd been right with him until that moment, but at the time when he really needed me, the end-game, the final conflict, I had funked it. I didn't have the belly for it. And he was telling me that was *fine*? I would rather die.

I regained control of my feet and I ran. I caught up with him before he had reached the door at the side of the house. This was the door that led into the long corridor which contained Honoria's office and the arch that opened onto the downward stairwell. The stairwell from which the breath of the worm seeped into the rest of the house. The stairwell we would descend while the sisters were at prayer. It was six o'clock. It was time.

Spindrift squeezed my shoulder. He put his lips close to my ear. 'The men fighting in the trenches believe they are fighting a great war, a war to end all wars. Maybe they are, yes, maybe they are. But if we lose today all that bloodshed will have been for nothing. Everything men have ever fought for will be lost. Prince Pel-osen, will you join me today? Will you join a fallen angel to help destroy a monster and preserve the souls of all mankind?'

At that moment, I would have willingly followed him into Hell. And who knew, perhaps that was where he was taking me. I had no voice with which to reply, my throat was too tight, so I just reached out for the door handle and turned it.

The corridor was long and most of it was in darkness. Fat tallow candles cast rare pools of light, and I could smell the nose twisting stink of burning glycerine. It was nauseating, but it couldn't mask the sullen stench coming up from that stairwell.

It took me a moment to get my bearings, we were at the other end of the corridor from the way we had come before, but eventually I could make out the time blackened virgin on her ledge. That was by the Reverend Mother's office. The arch to the stairwell was a black shape in the shadows between two candles. Spindrift touched my elbow and strode confidently forward. He knew the way. Of course, he had been here before thanks to seeing through his dog's eye.

We crept towards the arch, I was barely daring to breath and was worried in case the pounding of my heart might give us both away. We reached the top of the stairwell and hesitated. Barely any light leeched down into its depths. Spindrift looked at me and touched a finger to the cheek under his right eye. I understood, we would have his ghost light to aid us. He took a step down onto the stairs.

'I knew you weren't dead.'

The sneering voice broke the silence. It was directly behind us. We turned.

Morel stood in in the doorway of Honoria's office. The hard, black muzzle of a pistol was pointed straight at us. When he next spoke, there was little trace of his French accent. His words were precise and harsh.

'I want to shoot you so badly I have a hard-on thinking about it. I'll use that on Matilde after Vespers. She is a great fuck you know. And all I need do is bring her a few little children. She uses them, she gives them to Mother Honoria. I'm sure you two will be just as useful, but don't think I won't shoot you if I must. I promise you I will. Just give me an excuse. Please, mon amis, give me an excuse.'

His moustache moved, his mouth was smiling but his eyes were not. They shone with madness.

'Non? Well then, carefully now, drop your weapons. VITE!'

~44~

Spindrift had been right about Morel and it didn't surprise me one tiny jot. He had endured a lot of years on Earth in which to develop his insight into mankind's ways and witness their behaviour. I doubted Morel was the worst he'd seen, but I reasoned that any man who would exchange children for sex without caring what happened to them afterwards must be a tough act to beat. I noticed my friend was slowly reaching for his weapon with just his fingertips. He didn't want to give Morel the slightest excuse to pull his trigger. I followed suit, but while my hand moved prudently my mind acted quickly.

I thought about Wolseley's unfair attack on us back at the hospital. And a little girl with a gashed knee limping home with tears streaming down her face. I thought of numberless stolen children, abducted so this corrupt and filthy man could have his way with a nun in the back room of a convent. I pictured small innocent faces and imagined their fear when they were confronted by Sister Honoria and the monstrous worm. I let my anger build until it became hot and I let him see it writ plain on my face. He gazed at me and the moustache sneered. And that was all I needed. That pulled the trigger for *my* weapon.

Moments later a look of puzzled alarm spread across Morel's face. His eyes bulged and he grabbed at his throat with his free hand. His gun wavered. His head began to rock. He dropped his gun with a loud clatter and used both hands to push his moustache away from his yawning mouth. His jaws were open and his tongue protruded. He was turning blue. I think his panic was accelerating the process of suffocation but I hoped he wouldn't die too quickly. I wanted the vile bastard to suffer. And, on behalf of all the children of the world I wanted to watch him suffer.

He slumped to the floor, the only sound the rattling drumbeat of his boot heels on the wooden floor. He thrashed like a beached fish, coiling into a tight knot, and then throwing himself towards us. His thick tongue and his face were black by then and his eyes red as raw blood. At last his struggles became feeble and his arms flopped to his sides. He stopped moving except for his neck which made odd contracting motions for a few more seconds, and then he was still. The people of Natres had been robbed of their hanging, but they could be happy that their number one criminal, the man who had had stolen their children, had been brought to justice.

'What have you done? My God, what have you done?'

The Reverend Mother, Sister Honoria Pietas, stood a few yards away with a look of abject horror on her gaunt face. The candlelight gave her a ghoulish, grey pallor and her skin was stretched taut across the thin bones of her skull. She was so close to death that all I needed do was reach out...

Spindrift spoke coldly. 'Mother Superior, you and your sisters must leave here tonight. You must get as far from here as you can or your lives will be forfeit, I can promise you that much. The worm dies tonight, or we do. If we succeed your convent will be destroyed along with everything and everyone remaining in it. If we fail you're all finished anyway, along with us. We're your only hope for a future. Do you understand? Do you?'

He spat these last words at her with a look of disgust on his face.

'Do you?'

The woman seemed to collapse in on herself. She bent at the waist and made a harsh keening sound followed by a guttural choking noise. I thought she was going to faint and almost stepped to her aid, but Spindrift held out his arm to check me. Honoria raised her head to us and I saw the sly look in her eyes. I realised she was laughing at us.

'Kill it, will you? Kill it? How? You pathetic, stupid little man. We have been feeding it for years. We have, and those who served before us. For thousands of years, longer, we have lived in peace with the Sha-aneer. We sisters and the priestesses who came before us, we serve it. We are its handmaidens. What's the loss of an occasional child in exchange for the lives of the many? What do children matter? The filthy scum breed like pigs, they don't miss one or two of their brats a year. Plenty more where they came from, plenty. And you think *you* can kill it? You don't even know what you're facing, you ignorant, foolish little soldiers. You have no idea. It is a god, an ancient and powerful god, and it will smite you down and devour you. Guns won't hurt it, knives won't pierce it, nothing can kill it. Go on then, go to your deaths. Stupid, stupid little men. Or take your last chance and leave here while you still can. Your choice is a simple one.'

She wiped spittle from her lips with the back of her right hand and sniggered, showing her flat, yellow, clenched teeth. She looked down. Morel's body lay twisted at her feet. She tapped its head hard with the point of her shoe.

'Typical man. He got greedy. Immoral Morel. All he wanted was to pay for his next time alone with Sister Matilde. Greedy and careless. Too many children taken too quickly. And once they were here we had to deal with them, didn't we? Of course, we did. We couldn't let the little piglets run home to daddy, could we? No, of course not. I told him to slow down, I warned him, told him to be careful. But he wouldn't listen; he couldn't. Lust had made him deaf. He had to scratch his pathetic itch. And you know something? Every time he scratched it the itch got worse. Men like him are pathetic.' She rocked her hips in an obscene way. 'Bumpety, bumpety, bumpety...' And then she imitated the actions of a man jacking-off with her right hand and I looked away in disgust. The woman was mad. She wiped spittle from her chin as if it were semen and flicked a dismissive arm at us.

'Go on, leave or die. I don't care.' She toed Morel again, harder. 'I'll get rid of this shit so you needn't worry about the gendarmes. He had become too much of a risk anyway. Filthy, stupid whoreson. Kept his little brains in his trousers. Perhaps they got overheated. Eh? Eh?' She made the horrible and haunting choking sound again, laughing at her own joke.

Spindrift closed his eyes and opened his mouth wide. For a moment, I thought he was going to scream at the harridan. And then a great sound filled the corridor. It roared and bellowed and it took me some seconds to realise it was his voice but amplified until it sounded like a giant thundering from a cave. I involuntarily curled in on myself with my hands pressed hard against my ears, but it didn't help. My nose began to bleed.

'SISTERS OF THE WEEPING HEART. THIS IS FATHER SPINDRIFT. LISTEN TO ME. YOU MUST LEAVE HERE, YOU MUST LEAVE NOW, STRAIGHT AWAY. YOU ARE IN TERRIBLE DANGER. IF YOU REMAIN HERE YOU WILL DIE! I REPEAT, YOU MUST LEAVE HERE OR YOU WILL DIE. GO NOW!'

Sister Honoria reeled away in shock, her eyes bloodshot and her mouth open as wide as Spindrift's. Then she launched herself at him, fingers extended like claws towards his face. I gathered my anger into a tight knot and *pushed*. She was thrown away down the corridor, screeching in horror and her robes binding around her flailing limbs. She fetched up against a wall and pressed herself into it, whimpering and scratching at the plaster as if trying to dig her way through it. Her red eyes were burning hot in her white, contorted face. And then she started laughing, high pitched and maniacal.

Sister Bridget came clattering down the stairs. She saw her Reverend Mother crouched like a lunatic on the floor and dashed to help her up. She cast us a look of utter loathing before enclosing Honoria in her tender arms. She made soothing, twittering sounds and rocked the old woman as if she was a distraught child. Behind her a stream of nuns hurried away through the big front door and vanished into the darkness.

Spindrift touched my shoulder, 'Come, Colin. We can do no more for them. Let's go.'

To the sound of Honoria's crazed and hacking laughter he turned and stepped through the archway and down onto the stairs. The stink of the worm filled my mouth. I wiped blood from my upper lip and followed close behind.

~45~

We descended into total darkness. A darkness so dense it pressed against my eyeballs like hard, blunt fingers. After what seemed several minutes the stairs reached a flat floor that felt and sounded like cement. There was a musty, damp flow of air blowing into our faces and I moved forward with very tentative steps, feeling my way a foot at a time with my hands stretched out before me. After just a couple of yards Spindrift took my elbow and held me still for a few breathless moments. I was happy to stop. I hated my helpless blindness and my eyes ached to see something, anything, of my surroundings.

'Be patient just a while, Colin. Just a while longer.'

With a sense of relief, I realised sight was returning to me. Ghost light seeped into the darkness. Slowly I saw the intense blackness transformed to a formless grey, and then silver light picked out the details of the tunnel before us. I saw how, if we had gone just a few more feet, we would have blundered into crates and heavy, metal rimmed chests. If we had tried to blindly pick our way forward we would have tripped over them and ended up sprawled on the floor. The obstacles had been arranged in a staggered fashion and looked as if they had been deliberately placed to catch the unwary.

Spindrift muttered, 'Really nasty mind at work here. Look, can you see there?'

He pointed. I saw tight coils of German barbed wire arranged precisely where someone might have fallen to their hands and knees when they had tripped over the objects cluttered in their path. The razor-sharp blades would have ripped them to ribbons.

I whispered back, 'So much for the Sisters of the Weeping Heart.'

'Imagine what this would have looked like to a terrified child by flashlight.'

'It doesn't look much better to me.'

'I know what you mean. Be careful, my friend. Stick close to me.'

I did as I was told. We carefully picked our way through the wicked clutter, careful not to tread on anything that might injure us or send us headlong into the wire. When I took a moment to glance around me I was surprised to notice that several framed oil paintings had been hung on the walls down there, what was the point of that? They were difficult to make out but they all seemed to be portraits of women. I wondered if these were the handmaids of the worm.

We must have gone at least two hundred yards before we reached a stout gate constructed from wrought iron poles topped with spikes. It was locked. Spindrift reached up to an ornate key hung high on a hook above our heads.

'I saw this during my flight earlier, let's see if it fits.'

It did. The gate swung open smoothly and soundlessly on well-oiled hinges. Spindrift fetched a small crate from the tunnel behind us and used it to securely prop the gate open.

'We might need to leave in a hurry,' he explained. 'And we won't want to waste time fiddling with this. I think we're getting close now. I believe they would push the children through the gate and then lock it behind them before returning the key to its hook. The key would be too high for the children to reach. I suppose the children were told they would be able to get out if they went on in that direction, or perhaps they followed this path out of desperation. Colin, I honestly believe they would have been left alone down here in the dark. The last thing they would have seen was the flashlight receding back the way they'd come, the circle of light getting smaller and smaller until it vanished altogether. And then they were left alone and afraid, blind in the pitch blackness. It's inhuman. When we finish here, Colin, I want to find that bitch Honoria and make her pay. I want her to realise what she's done and I want her to suffer for it. The worm is a nightmare creature but it has its own peculiar moral values and it attacks its enemies for a reason. It thinks we stole its home world and it wants it back, and we must defend ourselves against it. That's why we're at war with it. But for women to do this to children is unnatural. How could they walk away and leave a child alone like that? I don't understand, I can't...'

His face was bleak and cold in the ghost light. He had been reliving the victims' last moments, when they realised the horror of their fate and abject terror would grip them. Would they stand here screaming for help until the worm took them? Or would they stumble blindly on, searching for a way out until they met their deaths? It was a terrible thought. What would be their motive for moving on? Why were there no little skeletons huddled here in the dust?

And then I heard it. With a start, I realised that the silence down there was faintly punctuated by the distant sound of running water. It seemed to be coming from somewhere further along the tunnel ahead of us.

'Thirst,' I said. 'No matter how scared they were, after a while the kids would get thirsty, and then they would have to go looking for water. I bet that's it. Can you hear that?'

'Yes, well done, Colin. That must be it. Now we must do the same. Or would you rather wait here while I go on alone?'

'I'll come along, the view around here leaves plenty to be desired.'

'Of course, you can't see your sky. I'm sorry, please, go back, wait for me in the grounds.'

'Well, I don't know. If my company's boring you so much, well, maybe I should leave you here and go kick the worm's butt on my lonesome. I don't need to see the sky to know it's there, my friend, any more than I need to see the air to breathe it.' I squinted down the tunnel. 'I guess it's time to go deal with mommy. We can worry about the nuns afterwards.'

'Or they can worry about us. Just be careful, Colin, okay?'

'Careful? That's my middle name.'

'Nothing would surprise me.'

The floor and walls of the tunnel no longer consisted of man-made cement and plaster but roughly hewn living stone. It seemed to have been hacked from an existing fissure, widened to make a practical, man-sized path. We had to duck to avoid low knobs and ledges that would have given us a severe head injury if we had hit them at anything like normal walking pace. Spindrift bent down and picked up a semi-circular, shaped stone. He held it up to me.

'This is a flint axe-head, and over there, see, a broken antler. I was wondering how old this tunnel might be. Well, it looks like it was dug out thousands of years ago, maybe even earlier than that. Much earlier. And perhaps the worm has been accepting human sacrifices for all that time. This is a story told by a madman, Colin, let's hope we can finish it and end the slaughter.'

'Amen to that.'

The sound of running water grew louder, but the tunnel itself gave no indication that it was ending. We could no longer see where we had come from and there was no clue where we were going. We were just two little spots of awareness lost deep in the belly of the world. The sky and the rain, the clean wind and green forests, the stars, and the sun, they were all lost to us. All we had was the weight of stone overhead and the never-ending length of rocky gut that led us to God only knew what.

The stench of the worm gusted into our faces on a scant breath of moving air. I stumbled and gagged with the strength of it. Spindrift held out a steadying hand. We turned a corner, and I almost stepped out into empty blackness. We had reached the end of the tunnel – and it was a sheer drop.

The waterfall was somewhere off to our right. I could hear it splashing merrily down into the abyss, but I couldn't hear the water landing. Nor could I see into the cave, the far wall was too far away and lost in darkness, even to my ghost sight. The floor was just a pit of featureless gloom. I was blind as a baby mouse but my nose worked just fine. The stink of the worm was like a physical blow. It was here, it was in this place. The children would have reached this last stretch of tunnel and fallen to their deaths, helpless to stop themselves. And the worm squatted down there like an open mouth, eager to receive them, body, and soul. Anger burned through me like a furnace, I *had* to see. I stepped out into the void.

~46~

Was it courage that sent me out over the abyss? I don't believe so. Nor was it the image of endless generations of children falling to their terrible fate in the clutches of the great worm. I was thinking of nurse Helen and the baby she had delivered when first we met her, of her happiness at the successful birth. I didn't want that new life ending here after too brief a journey. I didn't want that child's future happiness dashed away in a moment of blind terror. The bastard Morel was gone but no doubt Matilde could lure a replacement. Albert Fournier perhaps. He dreamt of being her brother, what crime might he not commit to be her lover? Get rid of the worm and the insidious reason for her whoring would be gone. It would be over.

Something smashed into me from the side and swept me across the mouth of the abyss at tremendous speed. I hit the far wall like a sack of grain and all the breath was driven from my body. I was wedged behind a stalactite or some other stony outcropping and I realised it was Spindrift who was pressing me down behind its shelter.

I gasped, 'What are you doing?'

'Stay down, you've told it we're here.'

'I what?'

A storm of hail or pebbles or *something* cracked against the rock around us. I flinched down further into my cover and Spindrift held his long coat out like a shield. Another shower of missiles erupted around us.

Spindrift said, 'The worm has a projectile weapon, it can fire hundreds of quills, they're like venomous spines. They pierce and incapacitate its prey until it can reach it with its tentacles and fetch it into its body. It would have knocked you out of the air and waited with open arms until you landed in its mouth, and its whole body is a mouth. It would have been over for you already, I had to grab you. You okay?'

'Winded, bruised, but I'm still here thanks to you.'

He pressed his metal cylinder into my hands and unscrewed the top.

'Take another drink. I need you to be able to see to shoot with me. We won't get two chances at this. Go on, drink. Finish it.'

I drained the cool elixir in a single gulp, doubting that such a small draught might help improve my sight. In fact, it did the opposite, for a long moment a pall of darkness stole away what little sight I had. I fought a surging wave of panic. What little hope I had of getting out of that terrible place depended on me being able to see, however poor my vision might have been it must be better than total blindness.

'I can't see anything now.'

'Be patient. Wait a moment.'

I started when a thick, unctuous voice rumbled from all around us. It was as if the cavern itself had found a tongue. The sound was huge, slow, and sly.

Satan, you have come to us at last. We have been waiting for you, yes, we have. Waiting for your visit. For long, long years. And here you are at last What little toy do you bring with you? We can't smell blood, shit or delicious man meat on that one. Is it a breath of fresh air? It smells of clouds and rain. Shall we breath deep of it? Shall we taste it in our noses. Shall it join the host forever, or be tasted and gone like a little puff of wind? Hmm? What is it? Shall we play awhile with your little toy before we take it? Shall we?

The ghost light brightened and my confidence grew with my returning sight. It was good to see Spindrift's resolute face once more.

His eyes were steady and calm. He looked hard at me. 'You can see now?' I nodded. 'Good. I need you to help me shoot my crystals out of the air. Once they begin to burn our job here is done and we must fly before they touch the beast. Shield your eyes or you'll be blinded for a few seconds – and we won't have a few seconds to spare. Nod if you understand me and fetch your pistol from its holster.'

I nodded and drew my gun. I thumbed the safety off. Spindrift tugged out his own weapon and then reached deep inside his coat. He pulled out fistfuls of those glowing crystal balls. While he was doing so another cascade of spines peppered the wall around our shelter. The worm was still talking and seemed to be getting louder. I wondered if it could climb up to our eyrie. I was very aware that our plans would be ended by just a single touch of the foul creature. We would die and it would live. Worse, we would become part of its body. I wondered how much of my mind would remain. Would I know what I had become? Nurse Helen's smile burned clear before my mind's eye and I thought again of that newborn child. We couldn't let that happen, we couldn't let the worm win.

Spindrift hurled his crystals into the heart of the abyss and we opened fire. I don't know which of us did the deed but three of those suckers flared like the sun in June. I covered my eyes for a moment but even through my fingers I saw them fall into the pit like blazing meteors.

Spindrift shouted, 'Come on, now. We go, now.'

And we threw ourselves across the void. I could see the tunnel mouth clearly in the glare of the burning phosphorous and hurled myself at it with all my strength. Spindrift flew below me. Even so, thanks to the flaring crystals I could see around him and down into the bottom of the pit. With mounting horror, I saw the huge, greyish pink mass of flesh that boiled and heaved there. It was a lake of shapeless meat, and it was truly immense. It filled the bottom of the abyss with its seething bulk, and it sent a spiralling, rearing mass of tentacles stretching up to snatch us from the air. Spindrift's glaring crystals seemed to shrink to nothing against the body of the behemoth. They vanished into its impossible bulk and their light was quenched. Thanks to my enhanced ghost vision I saw the elephantine monster take a firmer grip of the crevasse walls and rear up towards us. With sick certainty, I realised the truth; we had failed. The crystals hadn't hurt it and the worm was coming up after us.

I can't describe the terrible noise in that nightmare place. The worm was shrieking and bellowing the name *Satan* with manifest hatred; and the walls of the pit had begun to shatter and crumble under the sheer force of its furious attempt to climb up out of its nest and snatch us down before we could escape. I wasn't going to wait for it. We would live to fight another day. It was then that I realised why Spindrift was flying below me. He was acting as a human shield. A veritable rain of spines cascaded up towards us and ricocheted off the walls and ceiling of the great cavern. That I remained untouched was a miracle, but how Spindrift kept going was a pure mystery. He must have been skewered hundreds of times, if not thousands. And then the belly of the beast began to burn. Fire raged through it like burning tar. White hot fissures split its hide, and then it exploded. A plume of white fire surged up towards us. I put everything I had into increasing my speed but the heat crisped my skin and I felt my hair singe. The air around me seemed riven by the inferno. It bucked and buckled like a mad serpent, and I was sent veering off course by waves of superheated wind. My lungs were emptied of anything breathable and my throat was scorched and tender. I could do no more. My strength was sapped away and my vision dimmed. I seemed to be falling rather than flying. Below me the writhing beast heaved and splashed like a sea of white hot lava in an erupting caldera. Great gobbets of molten flesh were flung towards me and I tumbled helplessly around in a storm of heat and fractured air. And then I saw it just to one side and above me. The tunnel. I was rapidly dropping away from it. I reached for my last ounce of strength and threw myself upwards. If this failed I knew I had nothing left. I was finished.

Even above the bedlam in that place I heard myself scream with effort, but suddenly I was racing along a calm haven away from the relentless buffeting. I had made it. Before I burned like a human torch I had rocketed into the tunnel and reached temporary shelter. There was no time to lollygag near that erupting furnace, so I flew back down the tunnel until I reached the open gate. I hovered there, waiting for Spindrift. I thought I saw a flashlight coming towards me and then with horror realised my friend was just barely outpacing a ball of white hot flame. He furiously gestured that I should keep going so I kicked away and within moments I was racing up the stairs to the convent, my flight like that of an arrow. When I reached the corridor I narrowly passed over the heads of three harpies clustered there. I scattered Honoria, Bridget and Matilde like skittles and powered my way through the open front door. I was outside. I felt the air cool against my skin. At last, I could pause and turn to look behind me. And there was Spindrift. With the fire at his heels he had those three terrible women grasped firmly in his powerful grip. He was carrying them the way he had our horses.

~47~

The three witches hung limply in his grasp. I flew to his side and kept pace with him. I indicated the women. My voice was weak and scratchy but I made myself heard.

'Why did you save them?'

'It's not for me to choose. These women are monsters but they're also Eden born. Whatever they've done I couldn't desert them, no matter how foul they are. It's not for me to judge.'

'Then I will. Let me deal with them.'

'No time. The worm's burning down there and the pressure's building like boiling stew in a kettle. You saw what happened back at the German lines? This is bigger, much bigger, and it goes down much further. I don't know how much of Natres is going to survive, if any, and I have no idea how long we've got, but we need to get people as far away from here as possible.'

He directed me to where he had left our horses and I landed carefully so as not to alarm them. He had explained he would fly the women to the edge of town and wait for me there.

'Hurry,' he said with urgency in his voice. 'Fast as you can. Hurry'

I couldn't appreciate his concern. Surely the worm was buried deep below the rocky mantle of the hillside, and to use his analogy, that was one heavy lid to hold down a kettle of stew. Part of me believed we were home free and he was being overcautious. But I did as I was told. The horses were tugging furiously at their bindings when I reached them, and I had to spend precious moments calming them before I could untie their reins from the stout tree Spindrift had chosen for a hitching post. They snorted, stamped their hooves and their eyes rolled in fear. They wanted to get away from there and needed no urging to the gallop. I wondered what they could sense that I couldn't. The trip down the path seemed peaceful and other than the pounding of hooves it was quiet. Spindrift met me as he had promised, but he was alone. He climbed into his saddle. I took my first good look at him. His uniform was a ruin and his long coat was gone, but he looked physically untouched. He regarded me with an arch expression.

'I'm sure your eyebrows will grow back in time, and you have a fine skull. Baldness suits you well.'

I ran my hand over my head and discovered that my mop of thick hair had been cropped short by the heat.

'It'll grow soon enough. What happened to the worm's spines? I thought you'd be peppered with them.'

'You're right. At least, my coat was. I left it to the flames.'

There were some suspect rips in his jacket, but I felt it best not to mention them. Instead I said, 'What happened to the witches?'

'I let them go. Funny you should call them witches. They suspect we're some sort of black wizards. Bridget told me we should be burned at the stake.'

'After what they did? That's some iron clad nerve they've got. If anyone needed burning...'

A ripple passed through the ground and our horses danced sideways in alarm. Spindrift cast a wary eye up towards the convent.

'The pot's boiling and the lid's about to blow. Come on, we're wasting time.'

We cantered into the town square and found it crowded with people. In the centre of them stood our three nuns. They were yelling as if the town was on fire. Then we hoved into view on our horses and that put the icing on the cake. Honoria stopped shouting and pointed at us. I don't know what spectacle we presented in our burned and battered state but she looked stark crazy.

'See them,' she shrieked. 'See them! They are devils in league with Satan. They are demons in the shape of men. They fly like bats and the ground trembles where they walk. They will eat your children and make your bellies barren. Your cattle will perish in the fields and your crops shrivel away to dust. See them. Burn them! Burn them!'

Matilde and Bridget were shouting agreement. 'True, true, it's all true. Burn them, burn them!'

One of the men closer to us said, 'Look's like someone's already tried. Are you all right, messieurs?'

Spindrift thanked him and said we were fine, if a little singed. He asked what was happening to bring so many people together so late in the day.

The man pointed towards the nuns. 'They did. They came into town shouting alarms about murder, fire, rape, you name it. Blamed it all on two American devils, I suppose they mean you, begging your pardon.'

I spoke in an aside to Spindrift, 'And you made a point of saving them?' And then a realisation struck home. 'Hang on, I'm understanding them perfectly. When did I learn French? Did you do this?'

'No, not me. I think Rowan did. Did you think the people of Scytaer Faehl spoke American? Nothing like it. You were talking the old language there like a native. Something in your mind must have changed. You must have learned how to translate languages automatically. A neat trick. Matilde and Honoria were speaking to you in French the whole time, so was Morel when we met him in the convent. I thought you knew.'

I shrugged. The ground trembled again. This time it lasted several seconds and was accompanied by an ominous grinding sound. Spindrift climbed out of his saddle and handed the reins to me. He approached the crowd holding out his hands towards them.

'Please, listen to me. It's very important that you hear what I must tell you. Please, you must listen. We have very little time.' He indicated his clothes and pointed at me. 'You can see how badly we are scorched. It is because we have just escaped from destroying a German secret weapon called the Dragon's Breath. We have damaged it beyond repair, but I'm afraid it has become very unstable. The Germans built its storage tanks under that hill, right under your convent.'

There were cries of 'Boche bastards' and 'murderers' from the townsfolk.

Spindrift continued, 'The weapon has a two-fold purpose. It is an incredibly powerful flamethrower, but it also emits a mind altering hallucinogenic drug in the form of a gas. Some of that gas has been accidently released in the convent...' he held an open palm out towards the witches, 'and you can see the terrible effect it has had on our good Sisters of the Weeping Heart. Tragic.'

Honoria screeched like an owl, but now people just regarded her with sympathetic pity. I heard a rumble of 'poor old girl' and one voice that quietly opined, 'Serves the stuck-up bitches right, I say.'

Spindrift raised both arms, 'The gas is dreadful but it's the fuel for the giant flamethrower that we must prepare for. The tanks contain enough fuel to wipe out the allied lines for the entire Pas de Calais. If it all goes up at once, and we think it will, it might destroy Natres and everyone in it. You must get everyone away from here. Call on your neighbours, go from house to house. Make sure you help the young and the elderly.'

His message was reinforced by a stronger quake that threw some of his audience to their knees. There was genuine fear at large in the town square.

The nuns were forgotten in the face of a German superweapon about to explode. I had to hand it to Spindrift, he'd packaged it with care and handed it to them tied up with a beautiful bow. I almost believed him myself, and heck, I had *seen* him flying like a bat. And he'd seen me. Something on the hillside sent a ball of flame into the sky like a giant signal flare. There came a high-pitched squeal of escaping pressure. The people in the square scattered and I heard shouting from all around. The nuns had vanished in the melee. The ground jolted hard and tiles fell from roofs. Spindrift leapt into his saddle.

'We've got to warn Worsnip.'

~48~

The doctor and nurse Helen were standing in the open at the door of his offices with Susan, the pretty FANY driver. Her ambulance was parked at the side of the street, facing back towards the road out of town. They were looking around at all the commotion and their faces held expressions of deep concern.

Spindrift and I dismounted. I held the reins in a firm hand while he spoke. The horses were becoming very skittish and would have run for it if we had let them.

'Michael, ladies, have you got any customers today?'

Worsnip shook his head. 'No, we thought we were going to have a quiet night of it. Susan tells us it's been a peaceful day. She tells me the men have been drilling for hours, poor devils. I think they'd rather be fighting. What's all the rumpus? And what's happened to you two? You look like you've been in the wars.'

He didn't realise the irony of his observation.

Spindrift repeated his tall tale about the Dragon's Breath superweapon.

'We've crippled it but the thing's on fire and might blow at any time, you've got to get out of here. We're going to ride out of range until things blow over, then we're coming back to see if there's any casualties. There's sure to be some people who don't believe what they've been told and stay put.'

'Well said, that sounds like a good plan. I've heard of this Dragon's Breath thing. Thought it was squaddies' scuttlebutt but it sounds bloody lethal. You blokes should get a medal for this...'

'Yes, yes, Michael, but come on, get out of here will you.'

An explosion of spurting flame and a sound like a thunderclap punctuated his words. Worsnip ducked as a large red roof tile just missed his shoulder.

'Bloody hell. Right, come on, Susan, fire up the bus and get us out of this, there's a good girl.'

He cranked the starting handle of the jalopy while Susan did things behind the wheel. The engine burst into life and the vehicle was soon bouncing down the road with its three occupants huddled together in the cabin.

We climbed back into our saddles. Spindrift cast a grim eye over the town.

'What will be left after the apocalypse? It survived the worm and was surviving the war, but will it survive us?'

'Thanks to us they can rebuild, and their children will be safe at last.'

'Thank God for that, at least. Let's get clear.'

We let our mounts have their heads and they galloped after the ambulance with their heads down and their ears flat to their skulls. We were making good speed away from the town and I allowed myself a touch of hopeful confidence. We had made it, we were free. And that was when the world became pandemonium around us.

The lid had finally been blasted off the stew pot and it had released Hell.

The nightmare started with a high-pitched scream that built to a deafening ululation. It was as if the world was shrieking in torment and the sound of its agony launched an unbearable assault on my senses. It was too much for my horse which reared up on its hind legs in blind terror. The steed had been more than spooked. I had considered myself to be a fair horseman, but that was too much for me. I never was a rodeo man, and I was flung clean out of my saddle, landing like a sack of meal. The wind was knocked out of me. I added even more bruises to the collection. I realised I was going to be tender as a babe for days afterwards, if I survived that long. Which looked doubtful.

A brain numbing eruption shattered the top of the hill. The convent and its grounds must have been blown to fragments while molten rock and boulders were spewed hundreds of feet into the air by an expanding globe of white-hot magma. I realised that tiny, silhouetted black sticks which looked at first like splinters must have been whole trees torn from the earth and sent spinning into the air. Shock waves had me staggering like a drunken panhandler. Debris began to rain around me and I ran in increasingly panicked circles, desperately seeking shelter. I knew I was well within the blast radius and I considered flying up out of danger, but the air was filled with smoking missiles. It was more dangerous up there than it was on the ground. My only hope was to get under cover and fast.

And then the ground started to tear apart, yawn open and belch foul air and sulphurous fire. Whole fields split wide like opening mouths. They spat flame and strings of burning liquid. Arcs of fire boiled overhead and I cringed down, trying to make myself the smallest possible target while boulders as big as houses crashed and rolled around me. There was no sign of Spindrift and I was glad for that. I hoped that he at least had escaped the inferno. The ground under me began to pitch and roll like a ship in a storm. The heat was merciless. Hedgerows exploded into flame at the side of the road and the earth buckled and tossed like a wild thing trying to pitch me to my knees. Something punched me hard in the shoulder and I felt bones crack. The air was too hot to breathe comfortably, and explosions were happening so fast they were impossible to distinguish one from the other, sounding like a rolling cloud of thunder. I think I was screaming in pain and terror, but my voice had been lost in mayhem. It was as if I had found myself trapped in the very heart of an erupting volcano and all avenues of escape had been closed to me. I was going to die there, crushed, and burned to a cinder. Lost without hope once more.

And then from the bedlam grew another sound, and this was the worst of all. The heat had dragged cold air and water into its conflagration and swallowed it whole. The cold air coming in met superheated air streaming out and they began to rotate around each other. As I watched a huge twister of flame slowly spiralled up from the crest of the hill. It looked like the burning finger of God – and then it began to move. That monster roared while it rolled down the hill, and it roared even louder when it found the road. The sound was like the grinding of an immense corn mill, big enough to render all of France to powder. My belly turned to water when I realised the twister was rolling straight towards me. There seemed to be no escape. The sky was on fire as were the fields either side of me. Sheets of flame boiled across the road leading to the hospital and now the great twister was growling its way towards me from where the town used to be. I was trapped. The heat increased and my sight started turning red. I wondered if the blood had begun boiling in my eyeballs. Flecks of burning debris stung my skin, sending intense shocks of pain along my nerves like burning needles. I turned away from the twister and started to run along that bucking and trembling road. Better to die doing something, anything, rather than just sit down and admit defeat without hope. I knew I was kidding myself, but I guess I'd never learned how to give in without a fight.

Then the ground lifted before me like a rising drawbridge. It tilted me helplessly onto my back and then curved over above me as if it was going to crash down onto my body and flatten me. I tried to scuttle away but met another barrier of earth that had risen like a low wall behind me. The noise was hardly bearable.

The road slammed down onto the barrier and grassy verges on either side swung up to make the walls of a box. I found myself trapped in the darkness of an earthen coffin. I started to desperately claw at the walls of my prison, panting in confusion and despair, when a sweet, familiar voice whispered in my ear.

'Would you rather be safe with me in this shelter or back out there in the inferno?'

'Rowan?'

'You have a bad habit of putting yourself in harm's way my lovely prince, but you've really excelled yourself this time. This little box will keep us safe for at most a few seconds, but it will soon bake like clay, and after that we're trapped in an oven and ripe for the roasting. Shall we go elsewhere?'

As soon as she said it I became aware of heat piling on heat and the pressure of that heat was thickening the air in the box to an impossible degree. Every breath was blazing agony.

'How can we get out?'

'Well, I can go anytime, but I suggest you touch your father's gift, and do it right quickly at that.'

My father's gift? The amulet! I had forgotten. Just as the turf shelter-cum-oven began to fracture under the onslaught of the firestorm I touched the fingers of my right hand to the metal band on my left wrist. Just as I shouted 'Scytaer Faehl' I saw the lid of the box split open and I looked directly up into the eye of a murderous tornado of flame, and then it was gone. I felt again that strange sense of falling upwards in a long arc, and then the moment of intense pressure as if I was being pressed bodily through fine leather. I shut my eyes – and opened them again in the city between the worlds.

~49~

The peace was deafening and I collapsed into it. I was lying on a bed of soft, moist grass. Its scent made my head sing with pleasure. My glorious saviour was kneeling close by my side, silver light haloing her beautiful head. She was bending over me, groaning quietly with sympathy for my wounds, and running cool fingers over my blistered scalp. She traced the line of my lips with a tender finger, and then kissed me gently, almost cautiously. I tasted her cool infusion on my tongue, and then again, and again. When she withdrew, her eyes looked pained and exhausted. A chalky pallor whitened her perfect features. I wondered how much it cost her to provide me with her blessed balm. Did it somehow drain her a little each time she leant me her strength? I wanted to know. Could I do something similar for her? Could I revive her? There was so much I needed to find out. So much I didn't know about who I was, I wasn't even sure about *what* I was.

I heard running feet coming towards us and after the excitement of the last few hours my pulse began to pound. I had learned to expect new threats to pounce on me from every quarter. I was exhausted and hurt badly, but I would fight to the last drop of my strength to protect Rowan from harm. I would have died to defend her, if only I could get off my back and onto my feet. I needn't have worried. It was my parents hurrying to my side. My mother gazed down at me and her aspect changed instantly from an initial look of joy to one of deep shock. My father gasped in horror and turned away, his hand over his eyes. I wondered how bad I looked. If I appeared remotely the way I felt it would be very bad indeed. Rowan regarded me with conflicting emotions chasing themselves across her features, but I could clearly see her underlying reaction was one of care for me. She would never look away.

My father was barking orders and soon some people came with a stretcher made from some strange kind of elastic wicker stretched between two ornate poles. I was lifted carefully onto this contraption and then hurried away at a mindful but urgent pace. I held my hand out to Rowan, but she tearfully shook her head.

'No, my love, no, we can't.'

I clenched my hand into a fist and fought back my own tears. There was so much I wanted to say but I couldn't find the words. I held my breath and gritted my teeth. It was both foolish and frustrating. After all I'd been through, no, after everything *we'd* been through, after all she'd done for me, we couldn't even hold hands. The slightest, most innocent act of love was forbidden to us. It seemed so deeply unfair. I wanted to rail against the sheer stupidity of that ancient culture. It was a culture that had seen me become a son once more after the empty years I had grown to maturity without a real family, but then it insisted on dictating how I should feel and who I should feel it for. I felt myself to be a cuckoo in the Scytaer Faehl nest and wondered what I needed do to overturn such an insanely rigid status quo.

It was too much; my body was too battered to support the strength of my anger. My blood boiled with a rage hotter than the inferno that had almost claimed me, but consciousness was slipping away. Darkness closed over me like a thick layer of blackout material. I fought to stay awake, fought like a titan, but despite everything I was feeling, despite the biting cloud of conflicting thoughts worrying at my mind, I found myself sinking deeper into the still, quiet waters of unconsciousness.

I found myself travelling in a strange land of moving shadows. At first the shadows seemed infinite and lightless. I couldn't tell if I was dreaming or if I was wide awake and fully aware yet my vision had been blinded by trauma. I remembered my sight turning red in the heat of the firestorm. Had my sight been burned away along with my hair and skin? Was I bald, burned and blind? What kind of pathetic creature had I become? I envisaged myself as a helpless, wormlike thing, scorched pink, skinless, eyeless, and feeble. Then I realised I was none of those things. I had also somehow become completely detached from my body. My consciousness seemed to be floating in a black pool without sensation. There was no pain, and I felt neither heat nor cold. There was no sense of movement, no direction, no up nor down. There was nothing. Nothing? It was then that I realised I must finally be dead. I must have succumbed to my injuries. The race was done. I had reached the mortal finish line early, as so many young men had done before me in that stupid war, and as so many more would after me. Age and ambition were no more my lot. It was over. I hoped Rowan would be all right without me, and my mother. We had had barely any time to get to know each other. It seemed such a shame. Father seemed strong, he would offer a good shoulder for both to cry on. They say time heals all wounds, but does it? I wondered which idiot had said that first? It seemed trite and stupid. And then I thought about Spindrift, my good friend Satan Spindrift. I prayed he had escaped the fiery furnace that had swept me to my grave. He was a good creature, Preacher

Spindrift, a fine man for all his alien ways and surprises. I hoped he had survived. What would he make of my disappearance? He would believe me totally consumed by the fire.

So, then, I wondered, is this it? Floating like an anchorless bubble of thought in a sea of nothingness? If this was to be my lot for the rest of eternity, I'd have plenty of time to marshal my thoughts and ponder some of the great mysteries. Is there a God? I had hoped my death might answer that question. I had hoped to meet my maker and stand before Him to be judged, but even if He had been seated in majesty before me I wouldn't have been able to stand. At present I lacked feet. In fact, I lacked everything in the limb department. I seemed to be just thought, thought afloat like a bubble in the midnight sea.

And then a tiny speck of light whirled into the darkness. It was so tiny, but it held all my attention. I lay a huge weight of importance onto my seeing that mote. Suddenly my existence had regained dimensions. Once more there was direction and I could see. If I had eyes I must have a head, if a head a neck, a body, hands, and feet. I was a man floating in darkness, but I shared it with a mote of light. It was cheerful and bright, a wonderful thing to see.

I noticed that the bead of light seemed to be growing, or at least coming closer. And it was coming straight towards me, straight at my face. All the time it approached it remained in front of me. It never disappeared behind me and I never had to turn my head to keep it in view. Now it was the size of a pearl, and then a porthole, and then an arched window, and then the mouth of a tunnel rushing pell-mell towards me. I burst out of the darkness and into a place of light and air. There was too much light, it was too brilliant. It struck me blind for frustratingly agonising moments. I waited on all fours for the world to make sense once more. I realised my heart was pounding and my pulse was beating an accelerated tattoo behind my eyes. I opened them, coughed, dragged air into my parched lungs and forced myself to my feet. At last I stood tall. The woman I knew as the Conduit stood before me and smiled. There was pity and love in her eyes, and more than a hint of pride.

'You have proved yourself, Pel-osen. Well done, son of Pel-os, strong branch of the line of majesty. The ancient worm of the deep earth, Sha-aneer, is finally cleansed from this land. What would you ask from me as reward?'

'Reward?' I asked. 'I don't understand?'

'A hero can ask me for a boon. A reward. What would you like?'

'What kind of reward?'

'Only you can know. It will become obvious. Take a good long moment to examine your heart. Take however long you need to think. Time is not an issue here.' And she smiled again, a gesture of heart breaking beauty.

And I knew. I had no doubt.

'Rowan. I want Rowan.'

'But, you can have Rowan whenever you choose. She is yours for the taking.'

I was thrown for a second. What was she saying, our love was forbidden? And then I realised, and I shook my head.

'No, I don't want a handmaid or a sex slave, no matter how willing. I want her to be my wife, I want her as an equal partner. Someone who can hold my hand, as well as share my bed. Do you understand? I want Rowan to be my wife.'

The Conduit seemed to ponder my words at length. It was almost as if I had said something in a foreign tongue and she was having difficulty translating its true meaning. She regarded me coolly.

'Are you willing to be cut from the line of majesty to accept your bride?'

'Whatever it takes, lady. I can't face a future of treating Rowan like a concubine. I love her, and I believe, no, I know, she loves me. Whatever I must do just point me at it. If I must sign in blood open my veins. Make me her equal. I'd be proud to stand by her side.'

The Conduit walked up to me and embraced me. She kissed my mouth and opened my lips with hers. I could do nothing to stop her. What flowed from her into me was profoundly different from anything I'd ever taken from Rowan. I can't really describe the sensation other than to say it was as if a swarm of electric bees had flown into my bones, and even that doesn't come close.

I heard her say 'It is done' and darkness descended once more.

~50~

His great dog a silent shadow at its side, Spindrift's horse picked its way carefully across the broken metal of the ruined road. His shoulders were hunched and his eyes downcast. He made a dark portrait of despond. It wrung the sinews of my heart just to see him. I let him draw close before I stepped out from under the shadow of a tree and called his name. He looked up at me in shock and uttered an incoherent sound. He leapt from his horse and took a few, stork-like steps towards me. His muscular face was a theatre of conflicting emotions while his mind worked hard to come to terms with what was in front of his eyes. He took a few more cautious steps, a couple more, and then it was as if he had been fired from a gun. He leapt at me and threw his arms around me. He lifted me bodily from the ground and hugged me until I had to protest that I couldn't breathe and could feel my ribs cracking again. Only then did he release me, but he kept patting my arms as if to reassure himself I was real. His dog licked at my hand, its tail wagging like a black banner in a hurricane.

'I thought you were lost,' Spindrift said at last. 'Your horse went past me like a crazed thing. Poor creature's mane was on fire and it was screaming. I immediately turned to come back to get you, but the road was gone. Everything was ablaze. It was impossible to find a path through the flames and the heat was like a furnace. There was even a kind of burning tornado, it was devouring everything in its path. Colin, there was no sign of you. You must believe me. I stayed until I had no choice but to succumb to the heat or retreat to safety. I reasoned that if I survived I could come back and look for you. The fire around the hill burned for nearly two days, but I'm sure you know that. This is the first day I've even managed to get this far. And now look at you, you're here. I can't believe you're here... How did you survive?'

I told him my story. How Rowan had saved me and how I had used my father's gift to take me to Scytaer Faehl at the very last moment. Another second would have been too long. And then I gave him details about my recovery.

'It's been months for me,' I explained, 'but time in the city passes without registering here. I was in a poor state and it took a lot of time and some skilled medicine, some of which didn't come out of a bottle, but now I'm good, very good. Even got my eyebrows back, and my eyelashes.'

He scrutinised me with his black gaze. He touched the skin along my cheekbones and examined my hands, then he looked at the scorched ruin that had once been my uniform and boots.

'You'd think any man wearing that sorry outfit must have been cooked alive, but you look great, possibly even better than before. Your hair's a bit shorter, which the Regimental Sergeant Major would approve of, but the rest of you looks untouched by your ordeal. That's some powerful medicine they have in the city, powerful. I'm glad to see it.'

I shrugged and grinned, happy to see him approve.

'Hey,' I said. 'While I was waiting for you I've been looking around to see if there are any people in there.'

I indicated the slate grey ruins of Natres almost half a mile away. Even at that distance it was evident that some of the buildings had been razed to the ground while others looked almost untouched, as is the way with fire and war.

'I can't speak for anyone taken by the fire, they're likely just ash, but there are some bodies in there. Not too many, thank God. It looks like most of the townspeople got away and that's likely to be thanks to your Dragon's Breath speech that night. That was a piece of pure inspiration, still makes me smile to think of it. Oh, and I must tell you, I found three corpses huddled together in a cellar under that bar Michael Worsnip liked. Sister Honoria, Matilde, and Bridget. Looks like they died from smoke inhalation. There's not so much as a scorch mark on any of them. They just looked peaceful, as if they'd fallen asleep. In a way, you know, I'm glad. Their judgement has been placed in the hands of a higher court. The hangman has been saved from doing his job on three women, nuns at that, and there'll be no need to explain what really happened to those poor kids in that convent. There's going to be enough to do without giving the town the responsibility of dealing with the crimes committed by those terrible women. Were any of the other nuns involved? Who knows. They've gone, and their story has gone with them. Let's leave the dead children at peace and move on. It's the living who will need your care now, doc, yours, Worsnip's and nurse Helen's. But for the immediate future, Natres will need builders and craftsmen more than it needs doctors, and it will need just five graves dug. I'm afraid the other two are for an old couple who must have slept through everything. I found them together, they died resting peacefully in their bed. And that's all, I've made a thorough search. You might want to organise some armed guards to protect the place from looters. There's some valuable property been left behind and the wrong types will be tempted soon enough.'

'Thanks, Colin. What about Morel's body?'

'Gone completely, along with the convent and everything in it. If anyone wants to remember the good captain, they can grow a bigger moustache in his honour. Personally, I think it's a name the world can afford to forget. Worsnip should be happy though, the sacred spring still flows and it'll be open to everyone now. Fresh tea and toast will be back on the menu.' We laughed, and then I regarded my friend with a shy smile.

'I guess you know I won't be coming back to the war.'

'I wondered.'

'Have you reported?'

'Yes. You're officially listed as "missing, believed killed in action". Everyone buys the Dragon's Breath story. You've become quite the military hero. There's talk of a posthumous medal. Susan and Helen are both still burning quite a torch for you, you'd probably be a lot safer remaining as a missing person.'

We chuckled easily together. Damn I was going to miss him.

I said, 'Spindrift, I need to ask a favour of you.' I felt myself blushing. 'See, it's just... Well, you once promised you would do something for me. Well, I should say, you once promised you would do something for Rowan and me, or at least it sounded like a promise. And... I wondered if that promise still stands.'

He looked at me curiously. 'Of course, anything I can do for such good friends will be a pleasure, a real pleasure. What are we saying?'

Then the penny dropped.

'Wait, wait just a moment. Are you and she...? Are you...? You? But by all... That's just wonderful. Wonderful!' He laughed with affection. 'Just you tell me where and when and I'll stand before you with the good book all right, stand right proud. But how? I thought there was a problem? You know, the whole incompatibility issue and the burnt star on her hand. How did you resolve that?'

I looked around. No-one was in sight but that couldn't last. I didn't want Spindrift to be saddled with explaining how he had been spotted chatting with his friend who he had listed as 'missing, believed killed in action'. I would switch from hero to deserter in an instant, and he would be labelled my accomplice. We would both end up in front of a firing squad.

I said, 'Let me come to your quarters tonight, after dinner. I don't like the fact that we're out in the open here. Someone might see us. Will that be okay?'

'Yes, of course. You'll be very welcome. Make it later than nine, please. Dinner might take a little longer today. You see, today's Christmas day.'

'Is it? Well,' I thrust out my hand, 'I wish you the compliments of the season, doc. Merry Christmas.'

He shook my hand with a firm, dry grip. 'And to you, Colin, right heartily and I wish you many more to come. Merry Christmas.' He smiled. 'I do believe that meeting you and finding you alive is the greatest gift anyone could have given me this day. Thank you, it has become a very merry Christmas indeed.'

I believe I was grinning like a damn fool when I stepped away.

'I'll see you this evening,' I said, and he faded from my sight.

It would take too long to explain how time works between the city of Scytaer Faehl and the mortal world. It would require an understanding of dimensional pathways and how to make choices in temporal spin. Let us say that I had learned how to open a door back to my city, and that I could choose where and when to visit the world of men, but, like every sprite, I could only enter a private place to which I had been invited. When I rejoined Spindrift that evening, I was wearing my more accustomed garb as an air sprite, a loose silver robe, woven pants, and soft, laced boots. I should never have reason to wear my old uniform ever again. There was talk of having it preserved as a keepsake, a memento of the destroyed worm. And I was holding Rowan's hand. We appeared in Spindrift's living room to find him seated comfortably before his fireplace, his dog stretched out before the blazing logs, and a bottle of wine nested with some glasses on his table. He was in civilian dress, looking relaxed in an open-collared, linen shirt and a pair of dark grey trousers. He leapt to his feet and shook my hand once more, then accepted a warm embrace from my fiancée. His words of congratulations were hushed. It was late and he didn't want anyone to hear him apparently talking to himself in his rooms. He poured wine and we toasted each other before he invited us to sit. He complimented Rowan on the way she looked, and I heartily agreed. She had been beautiful before, but now she positively glowed with inner radiance. She was a fine jewel amongst women, an ornament to her sex. I hated being away from her. Whenever she was out of my sight, my day seemed starved of light and colour.

Spindrift couldn't contain his curiosity a moment longer. 'It's wonderful to see you so happy together, truly wonderful. But please, you promised to explain, how is this possible? You told me the laws of elemental nature forbade you to be like this. Why are you not burning?'

Rowan released my hand and held hers palm outwards so he could see. Impressed on her palm was a five-pointed silver star. I held up mine so he could see its mirror image. She glanced across at me and egged me on with a smile. I leaned forward and quietly explained about my most recent encounter with the Conduit. I told him about her 'reward', and that I had been willing to accept her cutting me from the line of majesty in exchange for Rowan's hand in marriage. My love was worth more to me than succession to one of the four thrones of Scytaer Faehl.

'It was a test,' I said. 'She wanted to test the depth of my love. I would have cut off my right hand if that's what it took. After she said, "It is done" I went back into a deep sleep while my body repaired itself. I was unconscious for days.'

Rowan frowned, 'Over a week. And he was burning with a fever.'

I agreed, 'Yes, so I was told, but when I finally came around, Rowan was sitting by my bed dabbing at my head with a cool cloth. When she saw that my eyes were open she took my hands in hers and she kissed me...'

'You see, Satan, the Conduit had visited me in Pel-osen's sick room after she had spoken with him. She told me about his bargain, that he had said he would surrender his right to the throne in exchange for my hand in marriage. Oh, my heart nearly burst with joy when I heard that. And then she asked me if I would accept him as a lowly elemental instead of a prince. Of course, I would. I told her I would work my fingers to the bone in the fields to put food on his table. I loved the man not the chair he was sitting on. And then I told her that I couldn't allow him to make such a bargain. I told her I would go away in the hope that he would forget me and meet someone else. Then she embraced me and she kissed me. The sensation was like nothing I'd ever felt before. She seemed to touch right down to the very core of my being, even my bones buzzed...'

I muttered, 'Electric bees.'

She agreed, 'Yes, that's it, electric bees, just like that. Then the room got brighter and everything became clearer. I could see Pel-osen on the bed begin to glow, as if his spirit was reaching out me. Then the Conduit said, "The throne of air must not lose such nobility of spirit. Rowan of earth, you are now Rowan Pel-oren, bridge between land and sky, and a princess of the line of majesty. I bless your union, and pray the fruit of your union will be beautiful." And then she gave me a little bow of her head, me! I burst into tears on the spot, and by the time I wiped my eyes she had gone.'

Rowan shook her head in wonder. I leaned over and kissed her lovely hands.

'So then, Preacher Spindrift,' I said. 'The Creator says it's okay, so, how about you? When will you give us your blessing?'

End: Scytaer Faehl

The wedding was the event of the year. The ceremony took place on the broken dais in the great audience chamber of the sky palace, and thousands attended. Princess Rowan Pel-oren shone like a russet star in a dress that fitted like a second skin and was the colour of autumn in New England. Prince Pel-osen wore complex silver robes over a short, toga-like affair and long pants. Spindrift looked almost regal in finely-tailored black vestments and a brilliant scarlet stole at his neck. The service was almost completely traditional except the bride, groom, and priest all hovered in mid-air. At the very moment that Spindrift intoned, 'I now pronounce you man and wife,' a column of blinding light enveloped all three and the massed witnesses had to scamper away and cover their eyes. If there had been any doubt about Rowan's right to be by her husband's side, that light burned it away. By surviving the corrosive light, she had been proven to be a new daughter of the elemental line of majesty, and the common people curtseyed or fell to one knee when the light fell away and the newlyweds reappeared in all their glory. Only four groups of men and women stood tall and raised their right hands to their chests in silent salute, the royalty of Scytaer Faehl recognised their own.

Afterwards there was music, feasting, and fawning flattery. When he had had enough of being lionised by strangers, Pel-osen sought out Satan Spindrift, whom he eventually found alone on a stone balcony, gazing across the remarkable cityscape. Pel-osen handed over one of the two glasses of potent red wine he taken from a tray carried by one of the slender, white apes acting as waiters. It had nodded and smiled broadly when he thanked it, demonstrating its powerful, cream coloured canines. Pel-osen wondered how long it would take for him to get used to his new home.

He smiled, 'Cheers.'

'Cheers.'

The two friends touched glasses.

'Will you be going back to the war?'

Spindrift shook his head ruefully, 'Perhaps just for one more day. Long enough to collect my things. And then I shall have to be on my way once more. The war in Flanders will end one day, and men trying to kill each other this year will probably start trying to sell cheese and wine to each other instead. What a waste of lives and effort it will be. But the Sha-aneer is the true enemy. I must take the battle to it whenever I hear the call, and I have heard it on the midnight breeze once more.'

'And what will you do when the worm is finally defeated?'

'Do? I shall have a damn good glass of wine, something like this would be perfect.' He took a swallow. 'And then I shall travel. I shall look for somewhere like this,' he raised his glass to the city spread out below them. 'And maybe I shall settle down. I might become a painter and stay somewhere just long enough that the locals don't realise that I'm not getting any older. Develop a few grey hairs, you know?'

'You will always be welcome here, I hope you know that.'

From an inner pocket Pel-osen took out a flat piece of carefully carved metal. He handed it to Spindrift. 'Hold this and call my name. Pel-osen or Colin it doesn't matter, either will work. Call me and I will come. If you need help in fighting the worm or want to spend some time in Scytaer Faehl, just call me. This is your home whenever you want it. It might not be heaven but it comes close, what do you say?'

Spindrift studied the piece of metal and said nothing for a long time. When he looked up his eyes glistened with emotion.

'Colin, thank-you. It's been a long time since I could call any place home. This means more than I could possibly say. Thank-you.'

Careful not to spill their wine they hugged, then they touched glasses.

Spindrift said, 'A toast, death to the worm.'

'Death to the worm.'

They looked around for somewhere to place their empty glasses and one of the white apes suddenly appeared at their side with a tray. They put their drained glasses down and accepted fresh ones. The ape rewarded their thanks with a toothy smile and loped back into the throng. Watching its departing back Pel-osen suddenly remembered the question he had been intending to ask.

'Doc, on a different subject, how's Wolseley doing?'

'Wolseley, he's doing fine. Scotland and doctor Rivers are doing him the world of good. Rivers has recommended that he doesn't come back to Flanders, said he has a genius for administrative duties and would serve his country better from an office in Washington DC. He'll do well, I'm sure.'

'That's great. More's the pity Colonel Peacefarthing will soon find another victim for his nasty little pleasures, and you won't be there to help.'

'Put your mind to rest there, Colin. The colonel died earlier this week.'

'Died? How? Did you...?'

'Me? No, of course not, what are you saying? No, he was killed by a fish.'

Pel-osen laughed, 'Did it eat him?'

'No, he ate it. You saw what he was like with food. Wolseley used to make sure the colonel's meals could be eaten in great mouthfuls, like coal being thrown into a fireplace. His replacement wasn't so careful. The colonel choked on a fishbone the size of a darning needle. Took a while for him to die, but it seems nobody knew how to help him – or they didn't want to. New fellow threw out all the silk and the slippers on his first day. Guys there are much happier now, or so I'm told.'

The friends pondered the colonel's sad demise for a few seconds, and then Pel-oren asked. 'So, right, good. And so, you're off worm hunting again. Where will this new call take you?'

Spindrift's eyes tightened. 'China,' he said. 'And an ancient city called Lijiang.'

~*~

Satan Spindrift will return in GODS' Warrior

Author's note

The Battle of Cambrai mentioned at the beginning of this story took place pretty much as has been reported here. It was the first great tank battle in history, and at first inflicted a crushing defeat on German troops. And then the tide turned. By the Battle's close two weeks later the many thousands of troops killed, injured, or captured was about equal on each side and the German military command called it a draw.

However, while the German's never saw the value of tanks, the allies saw their immense potential. They continued developing both the technology and tactical arts, and by the start of the second great Battle of Cambrai, in late September of the following year, tanks would help win a major allied victory and prove to the German command that the Great War was unwinnable. The end of that conflict was soon at hand. The Armistice came into force on the eleventh hour of the eleventh day during the eleventh month of 1918. The 1914-1918 conflict was called both the *Great War*, and the *War to end all Wars*. However, just over twenty years later, Germany would march into Poland, and the world would be at war once more.

The closing days of the Battle of Cambrai in 1917 was also the first time that troops of the American Expeditionary Forces would officially face Germans in combat, albeit engineers in a supporting capacity and again as reported here.

Dr W H R Rivers is famous for his pioneering treatment of men such as Siegfried Sassoon and Wilfred Owen for shell shock. His work at the Craiglockhart War Hospital, also known as 'Dottyville', was famously detailed in Pat Barker's Man Booker nominated *Regeneration* trilogy.

The town of Natres, the convent and the Sisters of the Weeping Heart are all fictional, as was Spindrift's hospital. In fact, nearly everything in GODS' Fool is fictional apart for some of the towns mentioned as being around Cambrai.

Special thanks must go to that fine American author, Colin P Cahoon, creator of *The man with the black box*. He allowed me the use of his name without first finding out what kind of odd adventure I was launching his namesake into. I hope he enjoys the result.

I must also thank my good friend, an excellent translator and media specialist, Catherine Domanski of Positive Communications. She helped make Captain Morel's French credible and proved great fun to work with during our literary collaboration. She will always be my go-to expert for the French language.

Other GBP Science-Fiction
www.gbpublishing.co.uk

The ordinary series Christopher Ritchie
SILVER WINNER
2015 Indiefab Book Awards Horror
Dante: "Fusing horror and new age religion, this winner repels as much as it fascinates with death, destruction and nuggets of ironic black humour."

Slave Skin Derek E Pearson
Release July 2017

GODS' Enemy Derek E Pearson
FINALIST
2016 Indies Book Awards Fantasy
Read2Write: "Texas 1883, a terrifying story that fuses sci-fi with history and theology. Pearson is in electrifying form"

Soul's Asylum trilogy Derek E Pearson
FINALIST
2016 Indies Book Awards Science Fiction
The Sun ☆☆☆☆:
"a weird, vivid and creepy book, not for the faint hearted. But its originality and top writing make for a great read."

Body Holiday trilogy Derek E Pearson
Surrey Life:
"Pearson's galactic-sized imagination delivers, with veiled gallows humour, a compelling image of a chic, high-tech society infused with a toxic strain that feeds on extreme violence."